Hayes and Hayes

by Kimia Wood

Copyright © 2016 Kimia Wood

To my own precious little brother.
And to Mom, because she's awesome.

With special thanks to Anna Klenke and
Becca Smith, beta-readers,
Amanda Pearson, proofreader,
Rev. J. David Wood, editor,
and the Grant County Sheriff's Department!

This is a work of fiction. No reflection should be made on the officers and agents of any real-life law enforcement organization. These organizations have been used in the story, but we have the utmost respect for the hardworking officers serving in these positions.

If you like this book, please consider reviewing it online, such as on Goodreads.com. Your reviews are what help other readers find worthy books! Thanks!

Table of Contents

1. "Clumsy" 1
2. "Diamonds on the Soles of Her Shoes" 9
3. "Occupy" 18
4. "Grave Robber" 23
5. "Angel of Light" 34
6. "Sitting in My Kitchen" 40
7. "Speak Life" 45
8. "Country Church" 49
9. "What If I Stumble" 57
10. "Lonely Boy" 61
11. "Do Everything" 66
12. "Somewhere Out There" 74
13. "It's A Personal Thing" 80
14. "Flood" 84
15. "Lose My Soul" 90
16. "Curses" 95
17. "Just Between You and Me" 103
18. "Gumboots" 111
19. "What Have We Become?" 117
20. "What Is the Measure of Your Success?" 123
21. "Talk About Life" 130
22. "Sock Heaven" 136
23. "Run to the End of the Highway" 141
24. "Words" 149

25. "Charm is Deceitful" 153
26. "Day By Day" 160
27. "Gone" 164
28. "Fall Apart" 170
29. "You Are More" 179
30. "Let the Rain Fall Down" 190
31. "The Finish Line" 199
32. "Me Without You" 206
33. "Take Me To Your Leader" 217
34. "Killing My Old Man" 227
35. "I Can Be Friends With You" 230
36. "Whatcha Gonna Do When Your Number's Up?" 236
37. "Love Liberty Disco" 245
Author Bio 254

1. "CLUMSY"

The key stuck in the lock. Again. Derek jiggled it back and forth, chewing his lip. After an eight-hour shift of staring down teenage mall-roamers, the last thing he needed was one more little thing. To make matters worse, he hadn't used his private investigator license in six months. *You can be whatever you want* hadn't come true for him yet.

Finally, the lock yielded with a disconcerting snap, and the door lurched open. Derek suppressed an exasperated grunt and yanked his key out of the door. One day the landlord would find him climbing in the window of his own apartment.

"Hi!" a voice called brightly.

Derek smiled in spite of himself. His brother always had a smile for him, and always managed to get him to smile back.

"Hi, Robbie," he answered, slamming the door.

"What's up?"

"Nothing!" Derek dropped his briefcase on the floor and started unbuttoning his uniform shirt. "I'm ten hours older than I was when I left, but that's it!"

Robbie glanced over his shoulder from where he sat at the computer. "You stop to see Mr. Hudson after work?"

"Yeah..." Derek grabbed a Diet Coke from the fridge, and thumped back into the living room. "But he didn't have anything he wanted to tell me about."

Hudson, Hudson, & Mann had provided the bulk of Derek's cases for the past year and a half...mostly probate, and mostly very boring. Hunting down long-lost heirs wasn't the complex job it used to be.

"Something's bound to break soon," Robbie continued, tapping on the keyboard.

"Like the kitchen sink..." Derek groaned. He cracked his soda can open and took a large slurp. "That'd be the kiss-of-death to the security deposit for sure."

"Why so morose?"

"Eh..."

Derek looked up. Rob had swung his wheelchair around to face him. He hadn't complained recently, but Derek could tell his back had been bothering him again. He probably needed more therapy and different drugs and other things Derek couldn't buy him. Derek didn't need to vent his frustration at his own ineptitude on him; that wasn't fair.

He heaved a deep sigh. "I'm okay. Enough about me. Have you had supper?"

"No. I was waiting for you. I was going to make Ramen, but we're all out of pans, so I started the dishwasher instead."

"Alright." Derek put his can down and walked into the kitchen. For several moments, he stared blankly at the shelves.

"What if we have mac & cheese instead?" he asked, glancing over the peninsula.

"We had that last night!" protested Robbie, looking up.

"Well, that's about what there is. And the dishwasher won't be done for a while. I'll go shopping tomorrow."

"Okay."

He ripped the cover off a package and shoved it into the microwave. Around and around it went, while the microwave hummed mechanically. Just like his life. Around and around, and always the same place in the end. Rob's disability allowance helped with the rent, but not much more than that.

Derek squeezed his eyes shut and ran his fingers through his hair. He'd heard rumors that the mall was going to downsize. He knew the first one to go would be him, not the guy who'd been there ten years, nor the manager's elderly brother who spent his shifts sitting in front of the Cinnabon. Was it too late to follow Dad into finances?

The microwave beeped. Derek blinked slowly and opened the door. Robbie didn't need to worry about it. He'd probably grow up to be a famous, brilliant mathematician or computer programer or something cool... If his older brother's bad luck didn't shoot him down before he'd had a chance.

As he walked into the other room, the TV crackled to life. Probably dating back to when color was a big thing, it took a while to warm up.

"MacGyver reruns on at seven, in case you're interested," Robbie commented, rolling to the coffee table and dropping the remote onto it. "I figured you'd want to watch the news, at least."

"I guess..." Derek handed Robbie his bowl and slumped into the couch again.

"Seriously...what's wrong with you tonight?" Rob exclaimed. "It's not like you've never had no cases before! Something's bound to break!"

"I know... It's okay."

Derek muted the TV while they prayed over their meal. It was a simple thing, but it always made Derek think of their parents, who had taught them that. Sometimes the thought was a comfort, sometimes it just made his guilt dig deeper into him.

He looked up at Robbie, curled up in the wheelchair, picking the macaronis out of the cheese and popping them into his mouth. He'd probably have been a tall, strapping, athletic type if he'd had the chance. Robbie had gotten the short end of everything.

"Hmm...They're showing a clip of that Tough-on-Crime Citizens' Initiative summit you went to," Robbie commented.

Derek looked up. Sure enough, the extensively made-up, exquisitely blonde anchor was in the middle of an artificially excited report of the mayor's "stirring" speech on the issue. "Stirring" in the sense that the audience did a lot of stirring in their seats for the duration of his spiel.

"Huh..." Derek grunted. "I wonder if any of the five hundred business cards I handed out that night are ever going to do anything for me."

Robbie shrugged. "Like you said, it's all about getting your name out there, right?"

"Yeah. You're right." Robbie was right. Derek didn't have anything to complain about. They got by...and if anyone was going to gripe about dreams prematurely shattered, it was Rob. But he didn't. It was good for Derek to have him around...especially since that was all he had.

The telephone rang. Derek leaped up and grabbed the handset off the end table. "Hello?"

"Mr. Hayes? The investigator?"

Derek's pulse skipped a beat. "Oh, yes! Yes, ma'am."

The woman on the other end cleared her throat. "My name is Cindy Lane. I'm calling because — I must admit, I've never contacted a private investigator before, but I have something that... needs looking into."

"Yes, ma'am. Go on."

"It's about my husband."

"Husband?"

"Yes...he's dead."

"Oh. Oh, I'm sorry." Probably not the thing to say, but it was the best he could think of.

"You might have heard about it; he's the DEA special agent they found..."

Something clicked in Derek's mind. *Cindy Lane...Brian Lane...*a slew of news reports almost two months before about a Drug Enforcement Administration agent found in his own car, dead of a meth overdose. Tragic, superlative, and tragically ironic, officers still investigating, and look! cute dog with cute kid owner doing something. And the news cycle had rolled on.

"I remember hearing about that, yes," Derek said. *What could you say to this?* "You'd think something…like that…would get more air time."

"I don't mind if the investigative journalists, so called, give it a rest. The way they dramatize things…"

"I know what you mean…"

Mrs. Lane let out a chuckle – a small, desperate chuckle. "Well, they didn't give the whole truth. I mean, he didn't take those drugs himself. I mean, Brian wouldn't…"

Her voice caught, and she paused a moment. Derek waited, leaning against an end table and glancing at Robbie.

"I'm sorry. Brian wouldn't do that. I knew him; I was his wife, for goodness' sake. I know it sounds silly like that–"

"No. You've got every right to be mad at people misrepresenting your husband."

A sniff sounded over the line. "I'm sorry. I'm not a hysterical person, really. You see, the police think the thing's resolved. I'm sure they did their best, but I guess they've got a million cases on their hands – and the couple people I talked to thought it was pretty straight-forward, which I don't understand, since I know Brian would never do something like that."

"I see."

"I don't mean to sound like that; I'm sure the detectives did their best — but they must have missed something. Anyway, I was talking to some of the people at the DEA office, agents and administrators and such, and you were recommended as a reliable investigator who might be able to spend more time on this."

"Thanks." Recommendations were good, but if the police had closed the case, what more could Derek find out? There were some good officers on the force — on the other hand, if she thought he could help, he wasn't going to turn this down. And who knew – he understood about juggling cases, and maybe the detectives had missed something.

"So do you think you'd be able to help with this? I'm sure you're busy, but I can't just let this rest. My husband wouldn't have committed suicide – and I'm not sure where else to go with this."

"Absolutely. Would you be more comfortable discussing this in person?"

"Would you be willing to consider this case?"

Consider it? Derek flexed his fingers. He'd take drug overdoses over serving papers any day. "Absolutely. What time would work best for you?"

"Anytime after eleven tomorrow should be fine, or some time next week –"

"Tomorrow would be great –"

"I realize your time is valuable –"

"Where would you be most comfortable? There are a number of places –"

"I didn't see a location on your card."

Oh, yes. About that. "I don't exactly have an office…but there are lots of good, sort-of third-party places…"

"The Moose Cafe?"

"Perfect."

"Are you sure it isn't too short notice – ?"

"Of course not. I'll see you at – eleven?"

"Unless…"

"Eleven would be great."

"Excellent. I'll see you then."

"I'll be there."

Derek clicked down the receiver. He drew a long breath and puffed it back out.

Robbie stopped twirling the remote and grinned. "A case…"

"It's the wife of that DEA agent who was on the news that one night–"

"Huh?"

"It was a while ago; he was found dead of a meth overdose."

"Oh?"

"Yeah…He had a hypodermic and meth in his car, and was parked in that abandoned parking lot." Derek flopped back onto the couch and grinned. "Talk about interesting!"

"So what's she want?"

Derek grinned, grabbing the remote. "She insists he didn't do it — that it wasn't a self-inflicted injection."

"Murder?! That should get you a few days' pay at least."

"At least it isn't *intestate*…" Derek laughed, and wrapped his mouth around a large spoonful of macaroni.

"And you were just griping about all those business cards you handed out," exclaimed Robbie, gesturing at the TV. "Maybe the lady got your name there!"

"Could be…huh. Well, maybe it wasn't a total waste of brain cells to listen to all those speeches."

"That's not nice." Robbie sucked on his spoon. "Are we going to watch MacGyver?"

"Sure." Derek grinned. "Hey…Maybe we'll stream some Columbo, too."

"So you can brush up on your technique?"

"Yeah…my cigar-smoking technique," Derek laughed, bopping Robbie's nose and grabbing his dish to carry into the kitchen.

2. "Diamonds on the Soles of Her Shoes"

Derek swung his glance around the small coffee shop and sipped his cocoa. If he were a *real* private detective, he'd have an office people could come to, with a secretary and everything. Relax. He was going to have a case; not a deliver-some-papers case, an interesting case.

He glanced at his watch and bit his lip. At least he wasn't keeping Mrs. Lane waiting. Tapping his fingers on the tabletop, he drew a deep breath. It would be all right. Someone had recommended him. That was good; it meant he was getting his name out there and people were respecting him. He was a responsible professional. Strangers could trust him. Things were looking up.

The cafe's clock must be fast. He glanced down at his watch again. Just about exactly eleven. At least it was his day off… he had all day. It would be all right.

When he looked up again, a woman was stepping through the door of the coffee-shop. She looked around vaguely, and smiled when she noticed him standing up to meet her.

"Mr. Hayes?" she asked, walking forward and holding out a hand. It was a pretty safe assumption on her part; the only other customers were an elderly couple in the corner.

"Mrs. Lane?" he answered. What fantastic grey eyes she had.

"I hope I haven't kept you waiting," she murmured, unslinging her purse. It was about as un-flashy as denim comes.

Derek smiled. "Not at all," he answered out loud. "I'm sure your time is just as valuable as mine." Probably more so, but she didn't need to know about his recent hard luck.

"Thank you." She smiled again, gently. "I work in the OR at St. James, so I'm not scheduled weekends. This worked out perfectly."

"This must be a very hard time for you." What else could you say to someone so young who'd lost so much?

She nodded. "Thank you. If you don't mind waiting just a little bit longer…" She took a step toward the counter.

"Whatever will help you relax and think."

"Thanks."

As she walked up to the counter, Derek realized that her height wasn't due to heels; hers were the flat and sturdy type, the kind you couldn't turn your ankle in.

Mrs. Lane slid into the seat opposite him and set something on the table that smelled like oranges and spices.

Derek offered a few more pleasantries while she stirred her cup and tried a sip. Finally, she sighed.

"I'm not sure exactly where to begin, so I'll probably stammer a lot."

"Take your time and start at the beginning."

She smiled. "Well…it's hard to know exactly where that is. Brian and I have been married for about five years. Five years this August, actually. August 23." She sighed. "We were very happy, and I know because we're Christians, and so we had this ideology of sticking to it. Naturally, we had the arguments that all married people have, but we were committed to each other because…because of our commitment to God."

She looked up and fixed him with those liquid eyes of hers. He drew a deep breath and nodded to show his understanding.

"I *know* he was always faithful and always loving and all that, not because I hired someone to watch him but because I know…knew…his character. Who he was inside. I trusted him – we trusted each other – and that's where our happiness came from. We were so dedicated to the same things."

"That's a wonderful thing, especially nowadays," Derek commented in a hushed tone. "That's what my parents had. Jesus in the middle."

She nodded, squeezing her eyes shut. "Exactly," she answered. "Exactly."

That was one of the reasons he'd tried to stay away from divorce cases; a bunch of selfish people making their own lives miserable and wanting him to prove the other person was worse… The burglary division was way more fun: punish "bad" people, protect "good" people.

After a moment, Mrs. Lane drew a breath, shifted in her seat, and sipped the tea again. "Now, my husband – Brian – was a DEA special agent. He'd worked hard to get that, and he very much believed that he was doing important work to protect people and improve society. Now, I don't know everything he was working on… He liked to keep it a secret, to keep me safe, I guess. Also, he wasn't allowed to talk about some of the undercover work he was doing. And he did do undercover work, a bit, as a part of this meth sting his team was developing in the area. And then, about – a year or so ago, I guess, something started bothering him. He would spend hours in his office with his computer, and not want me to see. I trusted him, I knew he wasn't doing anything illicit – just dangerous, potentially."

She smoothed back a lock of dark hair and tucked it behind her ear. It unhooked almost immediately, but she ignored it.

"He called it his 'private project', and it seemed to worry him a lot. Sometimes he'd sit at dinner and just talk, vent, about things, like he'd never done before. Things at work, that were stressing him or bothering him."

"Did those things have anything to do with his project?" asked Derek, pulling a piece off his muffin.

"I guess probably, but I never asked him outright. I respected his desire to keep me – 'innocent', I guess… It was part of our mutual trust."

She shifted again and swished the tea in her cup around and around, staring down at it. "I should probably tell you now that this is more than the police know... They were just asking about the night it – it happened, not about our... Well, they did ask about our relationship, but they weren't interested in the nitty-gritty of it, just 'statements'."

"The Report." Derek grinned. "The Report must be filled, and the Report must be satisfied in and of itself. The Report must go on."

"Exactly." She chuckled this time. "You understand."

"Yeah. The one thing I don't miss about the force."

She looked up at him again. "Oh? You were on the police force?"

Talk about putting your foot in your mouth, man!

"Uh...yeah. Several years ago," Derek admitted. After a pause, he added, "I quit." It wouldn't do to have her think he'd been kicked off the force. And he wasn't – not literally.

"So, do you like being on your own?" she asked, digging a chap-stick out of her purse.

"Well, you know...It's nice not to have anyone hanging over you all the time, to be your own boss. And there's a lot less paperwork." *There's also a lot less actual work.* "But I didn't mean to derail you. The police were only interested in their reports."

"Right. The self-sufficient reports. That's one of the reasons, I guess, why I wanted to talk to someone like you, Mr. Hayes. I kind of hoped you'd have the time to – really listen to me babble."

"Oh, I don't think you're babbling," Derek countered. "There's pertinent details in the strangest of places sometimes."

"Thank you." She sighed and sipped her chai. "Well – The night it happened... I think you said you remembered the case from the news coverage?"

"As much as the news gives out. Just give me any details you can think of, so we don't miss anything important."

Mrs. Lane cleared her throat. "Brian came home from work, and we had supper. He was – not exactly nervous, but on edge. I think he said something about things being on the verge of breaking, one way or another, or something like that. He told me he had a meeting… I assumed he meant for work or involved with work or something like that. I know he was going to meet someone — just not who or why – or where or how." She shook her head slowly.

"That's what I'm for," Derek murmured gently. "What did he do next?"

She rubbed her forehead and straightened in her chair. "It was about quarter-to-eight. He strapped his gun under his jacket – his own gun, not the department's, he had his own gun – and just… kissed me and left. I remember I was putting supper away, and washing dishes. Lasagna. He used to love my lasagna." Her voice caught. She looked down at her cup. "He turned me around to kiss me good-bye. He said not to worry if he was late, but that…that…"

Derek suddenly realized that he didn't have any Kleenex in his pockets. Mrs. Lane picked up a napkin from the table and sighed.

"It's like he knew it was dangerous," she continued. "I could see he was worried. Or excited. Something like that. And he took the time…" She sniffed and drew a shaky breath. "He always took the time to show he loved me. He took the time to say good-bye."

"At least you have that moment," Derek murmured, an image of his parents flicking through his mind. "I mean, you didn't know it was good-bye, but at least…you didn't end on a fight, or anything like that. You know it was a…a good relationship, right up 'til the end. No regrets."

She nodded without looking up. "Thanks," she murmured.

He drew a deep breath. Mrs. Lane had obviously loved her husband. If Brian Lane had known that, he'd be a fool to kill himself. Yet somehow, he'd ended up shot full of meth, and the police hadn't found any reason to keep the case open. Why?

Better get back to the point. "When did you hear?" he asked.

"When they recovered the body, they – the police, that is – called me. I guess they'd identified him by his driver's license. It was almost midnight, but I was sitting up for him. Sort-of. I'd already changed, but I was just reading. I thought it might be him when the phone rang. But it wasn't. It was the police."

She closed her eyes and drew another breath. "They asked me to go to the morgue and identify him. My mom drove in from Lafayette — I'd never have made it through the night, otherwise."

She dropped her face into her hands.

"Do you want me to get you something? Water, or anything?" Derek exclaimed, putting his hand out.

She swallowed hard. "I'm okay," she insisted finally, straightening and rubbing her face. "I don't know what came over me — I'm so sorry; I'm not usually hysterical like this."

"That wasn't hysterical," Derek assured her. "Seriously, you've got a good excuse. Take your time."

"Thank you." She sighed and set the napkins to one side. "Thank you, Mr. Hayes."

"Derek."

She cocked one eyebrow, but smiled. "Derek. I really appreciate you taking the time to just sit and listen to me for an hour." She slid her cup aside and straightened. "I suppose I'd better finish. From what the police tell me, he was sitting in his car, all alone, with a bag of meth under the seat and an empty syringe."

Derek nodded encouragingly.

"Now," she continued, gesturing with her finger. "I know for a fact that there wasn't a ziplock of *anything* there a week before, because we drove to church together in his car, and I think I even drove his car earlier that week since he was taking mine in to get an oil change. I'd definitely notice something under the driver's seat because he's taller than I am and I have to shift the seat every time I use his car." She smiled momentarily, but her eyebrows stayed stern.

"I know he wouldn't have given himself those drugs, no matter what the circumstances. He didn't have a drug problem, I should know, I'm his wife! And I've already told you about our relationship. He'd been asked to sub a Sunday school class at church. I can't see how – " She shook her head. "I shouldn't say that. I'm sure the police did their best. But anyone who knew him at all would know this isn't like him. I have no idea who would want him dead, but it wasn't him, I can promise you that."

If Brian had loved his wife anywhere close to how Mrs. Lane loved him, this was murder, hands down. Derek met her serious gaze. She'd bugged police officers and Drug Enforcement Administration officials for over a month, and now she'd called Derek to solve her husband's death. If he didn't help her, she'd find someone who would. Every husband could wish for such dedication.

Derek nodded. If there was an answer to this, he was going to find it for her, whatever the police thought. Even if it wasn't an answer she wanted to hear, she deserved to have all the facts brought to light.

"You make good sense, ma'am. Do you have contact info for some of his coworkers or teammates in the DEA?" he asked. "Maybe some of them would know something."

"Uh…yes. Here, I wrote some things down." She dug in her bag. "Someone else you might try is Brian's boss in the DEA. Alright, not his direct boss, but one of the directors of operations in Indiana. He actually gave me your name; he said that the circumstantial evidence was too strong for the case to get much traction in the police force, or the DEA. Which doesn't make sense to me, he's their man and I would think they'd want to know why he died, but...anyway. He suggested that I get a private investigator if I really wanted to, you know, dig up the truth."

"Truth is what I'm interested in," Derek answered, glancing over the sheet and filing the information in his memory. "So...who did you say this director is?"

"Mr. Gerald Stillman, who's like the Assistant Special Agent in Charge of the whole district. I'm actually very flattered that he talked with me about it."

Derek grinned to himself. It had been right before the mayor's infamous speech during the Tough-on-Crime Summit. One of those "you both reach for the onion dressing and stand for several awkward moments apologizing to each other" moments. Mr. Stillman, the Supervisory Agent in Charge of the district office in Indianapolis, had not stood holding the business card, ready to pitch it as soon as the young ignoramus turned his back; he'd shoved it absently into his suit-jacket pocket, where it could be forgotten, put through the laundry several times, and thrown out once it was illegible. Or pulled out along with a receipt for McClure's several days later – and handed to Mrs. Lane. Talk about coincidences.

"I'll see what I come up with," Derek told Mrs. Lane as they both stood up.

"You'll take the case, then?" she asked.

Derek smiled as competently as he could. "It'd be a pleasure. The case doesn't sit right with me, either, and I'd like to find out the truth. I'll let you know if I turn something up."

"I'd appreciate that. How much are we talking about here?"

Derek cleared his throat. He needed this case; almost as much for his own sanity as for the dead man's sake. Mrs. Lane was the type to have done her homework. Make a bid too low, and she'd think he was desperate; too high, and she might shop around. Best shoot for the national average. "A common hourly rate is about fifty dollars. I'll keep a log for you, if you like."

"Sounds good enough," she answered, raising her eyebrows slightly. "Oh!" She dug for another piece of paper. "I called from my home phone yesterday, but you might want to reach me on my cell phone, too. Here's the number."

"Sounds good. By the way, I'd like to check out the autopsy. Would you mind filing to view the report?"

"Sure, no problem. Thanks again." She smiled as they shook hands.

"Thank you."

Derek watched her walk out and picked up his trash. So he was officially investigating a death under mysterious circumstances. It was the closest he'd gotten to real crime in months, and he hoped it turned out to be something meaningful.

He pulled out his phone. He wanted a copy of the police report, and he knew who could get him one.

3. "Occupy"

"Hank."

The stocky officer looked up and grinned. "What's up, Rick?" Hank nudged a chair with his foot. "It's good to see you."

"You, too." As Derek joined him at the desk, the policeman bent over his reports again.

"I have a case," Derek began.

"You sound as though that was a big thing."

Derek dropped his head. "Take it easy on me, Hank. I moonlight as a security guard at the mall."

"Sorry, buddy. What's your case?"

"Brian Lane's wife. The DEA agent. Ringing bells?"

"That's right. I think I've seen her around, talking to Murphy about it. That's the one who apparently committed suicide…?"

"Right. By taking meth. You remember it?"

"I'm in burglary, bro. I don't do unnatural deaths."

Derek smiled. "Excuses, whatever. Anyway, Mrs. Lane doesn't think the authorities went far enough."

"Go on."

Derek drew a deep breath and scratched his head. "She thinks he didn't do it himself, and apparently someone at the DEA told her the case wouldn't get much traction."

Hank shrugged. "Murphy handled it. They kept it open for a couple extra weeks, trying to dig up witnesses."

Derek nodded, and sighed. "That's what I've been afraid of. But you never know – maybe he missed something."

Hank grinned. "Don't let him hear you say that. He still hasn't forgiven you for leaving, you know."

Derek shrugged. At the time, he hadn't had many other options – or so it'd felt.

Hank waved his hands. "Whatever. What do you need?"

Derek smiled. "I applied to see the police report. The clerk downstairs told me to come up here."

"Oh, yes. We had to ask the chief about that; not many people ask for that kind of police report."

Derek grimaced. If they'd mentioned the name "Hayes" to the chief, his request was dead in the water.

"Oh, relax." Hank grinned. "Richter moved out of state a year ago. Our new chief is a guy named Freeman. He's pretty all right."

"No kidding?"

"Yup. Besides, I really think even Richter would have given you another chance after all this time."

"Maybe," Derek mumbled, shrugging. His final meeting with the old chief had been pretty clear. *'You'll never be a police detective under me.'* Maybe Hank was right, and he should have stayed at it, even though he couldn't know that police Chief Richter was going to leave eventually.

"Funny thing about the Lane case," Hank continued, shuffling papers and pulling a folder out of a drawer. "I saw the photos. He had some kind of, I don't know, burns on his face. Like solvent burns."

"Yeah?" Derek took the folder and flipped it open.

"Yeah. It reminded me of a kidnapping case we had about, oh, a year and a half ago maybe."

"Chloroform can cause burns like that, can't it? If the contact is long enough?"

"Maybe. Or maybe meth could. Never been in vice."

Derek pursed his lips. He turned over the sheet, running his eyes over the words.

"On the left cheek and on top of the nose?" he murmured.

"Right. Do you know, can meth cause chemical burns?"

"Maybe during the production process..." Derek mumbled, flipping the sheet again. "But he wasn't huffing."

"No, probably not. He had a plain injection site."

Derek shook his head, going over the page once more, making sure to pay attention to all the words.

After a pause, he straightened. "So Murphy's still a detective, huh?"

"Yeah. There's been some talk that he's heading for a promotion soon, but I haven't heard anything definite."

"I see you're not doing too badly, yourself," Derek continued, pointing at Hank's sergeant badge.

Hank laughed. "Yeah, you hang around long enough, and these things happen to you. I tell you, you should have stuck it out."

Derek shrugged and looked away.

"You know, I just thought of another weird thing about the Lane case," Hank exclaimed. "Miller and Jenkins were the first guys on the scene. Miller thinks he smelled cigarette smoke in Lane's car, but there weren't any ashes in the ash tray."

"Miller? The youngish guy who loved to watch Monk?"

"Yup. Jenkins doesn't think he smelled anything, though. It's not exactly something you could bring to trial."

"Well, Mrs. Lane doesn't smoke." Derek ran his fingers through his hair. "I dunno. I had her apply to view the autopsy report. We'll see."

"You know, I'm glad you can do this. Murphy did what he could, but he's been pretty swamped. And it seems like that lady deserves better."

"Thanks."

"Well, take care, Derek," Hank said, rising and putting out his hand.

"You, too," Derek answered, shaking his hand and laying the folder back on the desk.

"It's good to see you again. Good luck."

"Thanks. I'll let you know what I come up with."

* * * *

Derek scanned the empty lot. Cracked cement, weeds, and broken glass were the only things nearby. Boarded up buildings towered on either side, and across the back straggled a broken-down chain-link fence.

Strolling along the fence, Derek eyed a rusty light-pole. This was where Brian Lane's car had been, according to the crime scene photos. Parked close to the pole, with the lights out and the hood stone-cold.

Derek scratched his head and leaned against the post. Glancing up, he could see that the light-bulbs had been smashed. From the lack of glass on the ground, it'd been a while. Why park under a dead light-pole in an abandoned parking lot?

Three youths strolled down the middle of the street. They glanced in Derek's direction, but avoided eye-contact as they sauntered past, tugging to keep their pants up. A pretty seedy neighborhood to be hanging around at 8:30. Lane must have been meeting someone. But who?

The police report said that two regular patrollers had spotted the car about 11 and investigated. According to Miller (Jenkins was off-duty today), he and his partner often hit that area of their route about that time. If Lane knew that, why choose a spot where he could be pretty certain of being found within two-and-a-half hours? Meth highs, from injection at least, tended to last at least four hours. Was he planning to leave before the patrol arrived? Was he planning to be found? Then again, was it reasonable to think that he would know when Miller and Jenkins would be making their rounds?

    Derek shook his head. It didn't make sense. Who was Lane meeting? And why?

4."Grave Robber"

The clerk adjusted her glasses and nodded.

"Yes, this seems to be in order." She laid the forms down and rose. "Come with me, please."

Cindy Lane drew a deep breath and glanced at Derek. He nodded encouragingly, and they followed the clerk down a hall. Opening a door, the latter ushered them into an office.

"You can't take the records out of this room, and you can't make any copies of them," she droned, laying a folder on the desk. "Just leave them here and come out when you're done."

"Thank you," Derek answered as she closed the door after her.

"Fort Knox," he muttered, pulling up a chair.

"Trust me, everything is like this," Mrs. Lane responded, sitting down and flipping open the folder.

Thank you, HIPAA. Well, lawyers had to make their living too, right? Right…? Derek smiled to himself and bent over the pages.

"Looks like he was in pretty good health," he muttered.

"He was." Cindy Lane shook her head. "I just don't understand. See this blood-work result?"

"Wait…" Derek picked up one of the sheets. "Cause of death was asphyxia?"

"Asphyxia?" Mrs. Lane glanced over. "The amphetamines are stimulants. He should have died from a stroke, or a heart attack, or something else related to the heightened blood pressure."

Derek nodded. He'd done an internet search the night before. "Well, according to this, something depressed his respiratory system. I think. I never was good at medi-jargon."

"That's what it says all right," Mrs. Lane murmured.

Derek flipped through the pages again. "Oh...here's a second lab result." He smiled. The lab order was given by Dr. Tomas. Dr. Tomas was the only person Derek knew who reassured his cadavers as he worked on them. Most people were freaked out by that. People like Derek made the conscious decision to take it in stride.

As Derek ran his eyes over the report, he frowned. "Heroin?"

"Heroin?!" Mrs. Lane repeated, leaning closer to him.

Derek swallowed and held the paper toward her. It was best she know everything. "That's what it says."

"I...I suppose that would explain. Heroin does depress the breathing; it's related to morphine. And injected intravenously it could take effect within seconds."

She shook her head, leaning her cheek on her hand. Derek glanced at her. He wished she didn't have to see these reports; at least there weren't any pictures attached. He knew she had a strong stomach to be a surgery nurse, but to see this kind of data on someone you knew and loved had to be different.

He turned his mind back to the problem. Mrs. Lane believed it hadn't been her husband's choice to take these drugs. Derek had to consider all possibilities, but it still looked pretty strange. Brian had taken too much for a first hit...and being DEA, he probably should have known that.

"Why take both together?" she asked, voicing Derek's next question.

He shrugged. Trying to explain it aloud to her might help him organize his own thoughts. "Well, it's pretty common to cut heroin with other substances; that way it —" He squeezed his eyes shut. "There wasn't any heroin in his car," he muttered.

"What?"

Derek straightened in his chair, bending over the papers. "I read the police report," he explained, glancing at the second lab result again. "They didn't find any heroin in Mr. Lane's car. Just meth. Curious for him to use all the heroin, but not all the meth."

She shook her head and sighed. "That sure doesn't make sense."

Derek traded reports with her and studied the preliminary descriptions. Hank had been right…the medical examiner had also noticed strange burn marks on Brian's face. Especially on the left cheek, but also on top of the nose.

"Can meth cause solvent burns?" he murmured, almost to himself.

"I'm not sure," Mrs. Lane answered, sifting through the documents. "I saw that, too. But Brian wouldn't have any reason to put it up to his mouth. There were no signs of meth near his mouth."

"That's weird. Very weird."

"You really think so?"

She turned her fantastic hazel eyes on him. *Supremely weird; why would a man with so much to live for go drug himself to death?* With an effort, Derek buried his nose in the reports. "Several things aren't adding up – yet," he answered. "Let's see: only one injection site – that's odd, too."

"That is odd."

"And on his right arm."

"Brian was left-handed."

"Oh, really?" Derek looked up for a moment and smiled ruefully. "That would have been too easy a screw-up."

There was a knock on the door, and a short, wizened man opened it.

"Dr. Tomas," exclaimed Derek, rising.

"Mr. Hayes," answered the doctor, shaking his hand. "Pleased to see you, yes!"

"You too, Doctor. Mrs. Lane, Dr. Tomas, county ME."

"Ah…Mrs. Lane? Lovely to meet you, ma'am, yes."

"Thank you," answered Mrs. Lane, shaking his hand. "I must have seen you before, but I can't place it."

"Well, yes, I've been around. Thank you, thank you. Yes, the clerk told me you were seeing the autopsy report."

She nodded. "Yes. Did you notice anything strange about my husband's body?"

"Please," he shook his head and smiled. "No, no, ma'am, I can't say. Sorry. I can't say; just what's in the reports, that's all."

"Was there really only one injection site?" asked Derek.

The doctor cleared his throat and glanced at him sidelong. "Very strange case, my friend. Very strange, poor boy. Healthy as a horse. What did you do to yourself, poor little man?"

Mrs. Lane glanced at Derek, who only smiled.

"No swelling, no muck," the ME continued. "Just one little mark, and the poor boy asphyxiated."

"So why did you come down here, Doctor?" Derek asked, cocking his eyebrows.

The little man shrugged innocently. "Why are you here?"

"My husband didn't do this to himself," Mrs. Lane murmured. "I know him better than that."

The medical examiner nodded. "Very smart young lady. Yes, yes. Let me know, Mr. Hayes."

"Will do." Derek cleared his throat. "It's good to see you again, sir."

"Yes, good to see you, too, Mr. Hayes. Long time since you hung outside my office to talk about my patients. Did this one's eyes look dilated, did that one have bruises in the wrong places. Yes, good to remember all our good times."

"Thank you, sir."

Derek looked up, and saw Mrs. Lane eyeing the two of them. She probably thought he had some morbid fascination with dead bodies.

"Back when I was a cop," he explained, shuffling his feet. "Plus, Dr. Tomas and my dad were friends. Uh…My dad was a forensic accountant."

"Wow." Cindy Lane smiled.

They were straying from the point, but perhaps it was good to distract Mrs. Lane from the case a little bit. It must be hard to forget about it when she went home to a huge, empty, silent house. Like after the accident, while Robbie was still in the hospital, and a four-person household had shrunk to one.

"I remember our first case together…" Dr. Tomas was saying, yanking Derek's mind back to the present. "Some bookie was found dead, I think, yes, in his bathtub. Mr. Hayes traced his accounts."

"My dad, not me," Derek clarified. "I was a kid."

"Curious thing about his pulmonary edema…"

"Uh…yes," Derek coughed.

Mrs. Lane smiled again.

"You know, Dr. Tomas, it's very encouraging to me to know that you aren't satisfied with my husband's case. Even if it's just little things, I know you've got enough experience to be able to smell when something's not right. It's like when someone walks into the ER, and everyone can tell there's another problem than what they're complaining of."

"Yes, yes, quite so. Tell me what the answer is, Hayes. It will be okay, yes?"

"Yes, sir."

"Nice to meet you officially, Doctor." Mrs. Lane shook his hand, and so did Derek.

Derek and Mrs. Lane signed out with the clerk and stepped outside.

"Listen," Mrs. Lane began, pausing at her car. "Thanks for doing this."

Derek shrugged and tried to smile. "That's what you're paying me for."

"Yes, but…You don't know how nice it is that I can see it's not just me. Do you really think there's something strange with Brian's death?"

"If I didn't, I'd say so," Derek answered. "Heroin is a strange 'first hit'. Plus, there are the solvent burns on his face. I'm pretty sure chloroform can do that if the contact is strong enough or long enough."

Cindy Lane screwed up her face and made a disgusted sound. "I just wish I knew who would want to do this to him! It's way too complicated to be someone just after his iPhone. I mean…his iPhone wasn't taken, but you know…"

"Right. Incidentally, was anything missing from his pockets, that you would have expected to find?"

She shook her head. "I don't think so. I've been trying to think, but I'm pretty sure everything was there."

"You said he claimed to be meeting someone, right?"

She looked up and nodded. "That's right. But there's nothing to show that anyone else was there…is there?"

"There are indications," Derek murmured, his eyes narrowing. He hadn't told her about the cigarette smell in her husband's car; it wasn't the sort of thing you could take to court. "Maybe not evidence, but indications. And frankly, I'm glad we spoke with Dr. Tomas. He's been in the business too long to jump at shadows."

Mrs. Lane shivered. "I just wish I knew what happened to Brian."

"We'll figure it out."

"Thank you." She reached over and shook his hand.

Even after she had pulled out of the parking lot, he could still feel her hand in his.

* * * *

Derek kicked the door closed behind him and strode into the living room.

"Whassup?" he called.

"There are 558 Brian Lanes in the U.S." Robbie answered, glancing over his shoulder. "As opposed to only 124 people named Derek Hayes."

"How nice." Derek dropped his briefcase onto the couch and walked over to Robbie.

"I think I found the one you want, though." Robbie turned back to the computer and tabbed dizzily through windows. "Wanna see?" He pulled up the website for First Baptist Church.

Derek leaned over Rob's shoulder. He could see a basement window in the background of the picture, and a plastic table in the foreground. Apparently the church had had a taco and game night years back; a young, dark-haired man sat behind the table, proudly displaying his workmanship in food, dripping salsa sauce and bulging with lettuce and sour cream. Cindy Lane stood at his shoulder, her face radiating laughter and smiles.

"Good guess," he said.

"I figured, since the caption is 'Brian and Cindy at *Friday Fellowship*'."

"That's her, all right," Derek muttered.

The live-action Brian was better looking than the one in the crime scene photos. He was stockier than Derek, with the musculature you'd expect in a federal agent, but his face was the pleasant, friendly type.

Cindy had her arms on his shoulders. No wonder she wanted his memory cleared, and his death explained; Brian wasn't looking at her, but Derek could tell by the set of his shoulders and the way his head was tucked back against her what he thought of his wife.

Derek frowned, patting Robbie's shoulder. How had a "nice couple" gotten mixed up in this – and what was "this"?

"Good job," he said.

"Thanks. There's a copy of the directory on the website, and the Lanes've been members for two years."

"Huh. A dedicated church-goer doesn't sound like the kind of person to be shooting himself up." Derek headed into the kitchen and pulled a Coke out of the fridge. "Had supper?"

"I put some burritos in the oven. Man! I bet I forgot to set a timer!"

Derek laughed and opened the oven. "They look okay to me."

In a matter of minutes he and Rob were bending over the coffee table with plates, saying grace.

"Say, Derek," Robbie began, sawing with his fork. "Was Brian Lane really a good church goer? I mean – so he was a member and attended their potlucks and stuff…"

"Right. Was it all superficial? I dunno – I didn't know him. I'd better talk to Mrs. Lane about him."

"And maybe his pastor?"

"Good thought. Why would a guy like that even want to do drugs? He wasn't about to be fired; his wife would have found that out by now."

Robbie swallowed a bite and cleared his throat. "I got your email. Why – I mean, why would he… Isn't heroin usually considered something you have to work up to? After the 'entry drugs' like marijuana or whatever they're called?"

"You'd think so. Yeah." Derek scratched his head and frowned at the wall.

"And then – heroin *and* meth… Why? And where did he get it from?"

Derek lowered his fork and picked up his can. "Maybe he wasn't trying to get high."

"Huh?"

"I don't know. Maybe he was trying to – you know…"

Rob shook his head. "Die?"

Derek nodded slightly. "Maybe he had access to the drugs from a bust or something, and figured it would be easier than, y'know, jumping off a bridge."

"But why? His job was steady… His wife wasn't going to, you know…"

"Leave him? That won't wash. Pay a bunch of money to find out why he died if she doesn't care anyway? I don't think so."

"Unless she's trying to fool someone."

"Who?"

"Dunno. What's that thing about – prefer the probable impossible to the improbable possible?"

Derek cocked an eyebrow. "Aristotle, right?"

"Peter Wimsey. But yes."

"Smart boy." Derek leaned back against the cushions and closed his eyes. "Something like that."

"Maybe he was having an affair and She was going to squeal so he did himself in."

Derek opened his eyes again and glanced at his brother. "No. You haven't seen his wife in person, have you?"

Rob snickered and shrugged. "Having an affair is dumb anyway. Having one when your wife is really cute just makes it extra dumb."

"No, I mean you haven't heard the way she talks about him. Even now, when he's dead, when she starts talking about him or his character, the things he did — man, she just starts to glow." Derek sighed and hugged himself for a moment. "If a guy's got a wife who treats him like that, and still goes looking for happiness elsewhere…Well, he's just got to be an idiot. And I don't think Brian Lane was an idiot."

For a moment, they both chewed their burritos in silence.

"I want to check out his church." Derek rubbed the back of his head. "So what's the next part of your theory – Brian's illicit lady doesn't actually squeal because he's dead anyway?"

"I don't know." Robbie shrugged, scraping bean sauce off his plate. "It's not a real theory; it's just brainstorming. But on TV, there's always an affair to cover up."

"You watch too much TV."

"Well, I did finish the chemistry curriculum."

"Oh, yeah, I remember you telling me that. I guess that means I have to grade all your tests, huh?"

"And figure out whether I'm going to do the physics course next or not."

"Yeah…" Derek rubbed his face and sat up. "You probably should start in on that, if you want to finish high school before you're 25."

"Ha, ha, very funny. I'm ahead in math."

"But you still haven't finished that history book, have you?"

"You said you'd read it to me."

Derek smiled. "Okay, yes, I did. We'll get on it." He sighed. "I'm glad Mom didn't throw out my old schoolbooks."

"That's makes one of us."

"You think I'd let you play on the computer all day long if you didn't have any schoolbooks?"

Robbie smiled. "Hope springs eternal."

"Nice try, bud."

5. "Angel of Light"

"I'm sorry, Mr. Hayes." Matt Crawford, DEA special agent, shrugged. "I think you're wasting your time."

"I thought you two were partners. Can you really see him shooting himself up?"

"Look, Hayes." Crawford took another bite of his burger and chewed over his plate for a moment. "It's not unknown for this kind of thing to happen. Being in the criminal justice profession is a stressful career, and some guys aren't cut out to handle it." The agent fixed Derek with a look before picking up his soda.

Derek chewed his tongue for a moment. "I'm not asking about generalities. I'm asking about Brian Lane. Was he really the type to deal with stress *that* way?"

"I've known plenty of guys," Crawford continued, waving his burger a little. "They're one thing at home, and something else on the job. Their wives see one thing, the hoods see something else. It wouldn't be the first time an agent went to the dark side and decided to try out the dope. He could have gotten it pretty easily."

"I thought you kept close track of that stuff."

"We do," snapped Crawford, jabbing at Derek with a fry. "We set the standard. But that doesn't mean a few bad apples don't slip in, and gum up the works."

Corruption? In the DEA? Tied to Brian Lane? Some of those things Derek could buy, with a little more evidence. But Cindy Lane was too passionate about Brian's innocence for him to write him off as a crooked agent. Unless *she* had something she was hiding…and Derek would take some convincing to believe that.

Derek sipped his Coke and swallowed. "So, you do think Lane was up to something underhanded."

"You don't end up shot full of dope by keeping your nose clean."

"Yes, but why would he do something like that? His wife thinks he had something on his mind. Do you have any idea what that might be?"

Crawford shifted and stuffed more burger into his mouth. For a moment, he avoided Derek's gaze, focusing on his food.

Derek narrowed his eyes.

"Look, don't think that just because we worked together we were all buddy-buddy and sharing our deepest secrets. Brian was just like anybody; he had stuff he didn't talk about with anyone."

"Like what?"

"How should I know?" The agent grabbed a napkin and glanced around. "He didn't talk about it. Sure, he had this 'private project' thing that was like all he could think about, but if he trusted anyone with the specifics, it wasn't mere mortals like you or me."

Derek leaned back, scratching his head. "So, you got the feeling he didn't trust anyone with what was on his mind?"

Crawford shrugged. "We did a few investigations together. He knew how to make a good show for the superiors, but..."

Derek waited, eyeing the other man. "But what?"

"Ever had someone else try to do your job for you?" Crawford cocked an eyebrow and finished his burger. "Brian had his good points, don't get me wrong. But when he did have issues, he had to deal with them himself – didn't like anyone on his back. Who knows if he got a bigger issue than he knew how to handle —?"

So Brian had trouble asking people for help – at least asking Crawford for help. That wasn't something to commit suicide over, was it? Derek shook his head thoughtfully…there had to be more to the story.

"Hey, I'm not denying we had our differences," Crawford insisted, leaning forward. "But if the police are satisfied, I'm satisfied. It's a heck of a way to go, but agents crack out of the blue all the time. And it's usually the ones who have it all together on the surface that go first."

Crawford seemed to realize how passionate he was sounding, and sat back, taking his elbow off the table. He was trying to convince Derek of something. Perhaps he was also trying to convince himself of something—?

"Agent Crawford, I believe?"

They both turned at the voice.

"Afternoon, sir," answered Crawford, shaking the older man's hand.

Director Stillman's distinguished grey hair was swept stylishly away from his face, and his tailored suit accented his rimless glasses. Same cut of suit as he'd worn at the Tough-on-Crime Summit.

"And you are…?" the director continued, turning to Derek.

"Hayes. Derek Hayes. Private investigator?" Derek prompted. Perhaps the director didn't remember their previous meeting. When you've seen one washed-up freelancer wannabe, you've seen them all –

"Have we met?" pursued the director as they shook hands.

"At the Tough-on-Crime Summit this summer, where –"

"Oh, yes! Mr. Innis gave that excellent speech."

Well, that was one opinion.

"Enjoying your lunch, Mr. Crawford?" asked Mr. Stillman.

"Well, sort of multitasking." Crawford gestured with his head. "Mr. Hayes is asking about Brian Lane."

"Ah, that awful tragedy." Mr. Stillman shook his head with a disapproving grunt. "I remember speaking with his poor wife about it. It shocked us all."

Crawford shot a glance at Derek. "See what I mean? Even the director is shocked by what Lane did. These things happen. You can't just –"

"With all due respect, you've lost an agent." Derek felt the two DEA members stare at him, but now he'd spoken. "From what I've seen in the police reports, and heard from his wife, I don't find the explanation very compelling."

"With all due respect," Crawford shot back. "It's not your job to explain Lane's death – it's the police's. And they've decided he took drugs for his own reasons. I've told you he had issues – maybe his wife isn't saying everything she thinks."

"Now, now, Mr. Crawford," Director Stillman broke in. "Mrs. Lane is in a time of stress. I don't think any of us could have foreseen this tragedy, but it's no use pointing fingers after the fact. Given the circumstantial evidence, the police are satisfied that no one else had a hand in Lane's death. Our best interests lie in focusing on the real crimes."

"But his wife isn't satisfied," Derek protested, glancing from one face to the other. "Are you telling me that you two, who knew Brian Lane so closely, are honestly convinced he killed himself?"

"*I* didn't say that," Crawford insisted. "The police did. And I for one trust the police department to do their job. I have enough trouble–" He glanced at the director for a moment. "I mean, I have my own job to take care of; I don't need to try to do the police's job, too."

"Well put, Mr. Crawford," smiled Mr. Stillman. "Of course, you, Mr. Hayes, as an independent professional, may do what you like with your time. Have you considered consulting the autopsy report?"

Derek narrowed his eyes. Did they really think he didn't know his job? "We've seen it, yes," he answered levelly.

"Then you must have seen how much of the drug was actually in his system."

Hayes and Hayes

Yes, he'd seen that. It'd been well over the typical amount used for a hit.

"Lane must have known what he was doing," Crawford shrugged, and drained his glass. "We don't have to like it for it to be true. And I can think of worse ways to go than death by meth. Anything else I can do for you, Hayes? I have work I need to get to – with all due respect, Director."

"Don't let me keep you," laughed Mr. Stillman, and shook hands all around. "Well, I wish you luck, Mr. Hayes — give my regards to Mrs. Lane, won't you?"

Derek watched Stillman walk away, and glanced back at Agent Crawford. "So that's it? You think that guy you worked with all those years –"

"Don't pull that routine," snapped Crawford, rubbing his hands on a napkin. "What's the first thing they do after a shooting? Interview all the perp's neighbors. And nobody ever has any idea – he was always a sweet kid who wouldn't hurt a fly. Or a weirdo who kept to himself and played video games, but whatever. It always hits you out of the blue – it's always the 'good kid' who flips out and kills himself, 'cause he can't take the pressure, or whatever. I don't care how long you make money off of Lane's lady, but sooner or later you're going to have to tell her the truth. And I don't envy you that."

Derek paid for his Coke and shoved the door open on his way out. Neither Crawford nor Mr. Stillman seemed to be aware of the heroin. There were worse deaths than "death by meth" – but whoever had killed Brian Lane had wanted it to be quick and sure. Was it really Lane who'd wanted himself dead…or was someone else involved?

In the absence of 19th century daily diaries, the best place to discover what someone had been thinking was their digital presence. The Lanes had a shared Facebook account, that had turned up nothing but old church acquaintances and a few puppy pictures from family members.

The only place left to look was Lane's personal computer – the one he took to work occasionally and kept separate from Cindy's things. If Robbie could open his files, they might find a clue to what had been bugging Lane. At this point, Derek would take anything.

6. "Sitting in My Kitchen"

Derek glanced at his watch once again. He was about exactly on time. He stepped out of his car, adjusting his shirt for about the fifth time. Cindy Lane had volunteered that he come to her house...that meant she trusted him. And not like that one woman who'd tried to "hire" him, the one with an extreme shade of lipstick and extreme drop in neckline, that he and Rob had nicknamed "Lawsuit Lucy" (as in, *Don't answer the phone – it's Lawsuit Lucy!*). That was a whole different category of air-quote "trust".

He tried to shut the door in a gentle, responsible way, but of course it decided to put up a struggle. Finally, he gave it a frustrated slam, and instantly regretted it. Only impulsive, immature men slammed their car doors angrily. Shoving his keys into his pocket, he strode up the walk.

It was a nice, middle-class house, with an attached garage and everything. The yard was actually big enough to do stuff in, like frisbee, or tag, or sparklers on the Fourth of July... What memories. He could almost see his dad running down the sidewalk with him, or himself giving Robbie piggy-back rides, back when... Back when life was normal.

The door opened in answer to his bell ringing, and he found himself being ushered inside. Cindy Lane had her hair back in just a pony-tail...it made her look even younger.

Derek adjusted his suit-coat. It'd been brand-new from the Goodwill just a couple months ago, and had always felt good enough for Mr. Hudson. Somehow, it didn't feel quite good enough for Mrs. Lane, though.

"Thanks for coming," she began, leading him back toward the kitchen. "Sorry about the inconvenience."

"No inconvenience," he answered, smiling. She was the one taking a chance on him.

They stepped into the kitchen. A dumpy woman stood at the kitchen table, rolling dough flat. Derek breathed in deeply of the warm sugar cookie scents. Suddenly, he was a little boy in his grandmother's kitchen, wondering whether she or his mother would win the argument of whether he got an extra cookie or not.

"This is Mrs. Goodwin, from church," Mrs. Lane explained. "Mr. Hayes, who's the investigator looking into Brian's death."

"Pleased to meet you, young man," Mrs. Goodwin exclaimed, waving. "Excuse me, I have flour all over my hands. Tuesday, you see, the ladies are serving lunch at the Rescue Mission, and Cindy, she can't be there, since she's one of these silly people who have a job they go to, you know, and I'm not going to be there, my husband and I have to be at the mission meeting, which, I'm not sure why they have it at the same time, don't ask me. Anyway, we can't be there to help, but we can definitely make cookies, so that's what we're doing this afternoon." She smiled and laughed.

"Ah," said Derek.

"Here...I have Brian's laptop all ready, like you said." Cindy appeared in the room again, and handed him a laptop bag. "Um...how long do you think you'll need it?"

"Well," Derek began, trying to smile competently. "The plan is that we'll only need it for 24 hours or so."

"Really?"

He suddenly realized her eyes had shifted to blue today. Inconvenient observation, which had no bearing on the case.

"Uh...yes," he continued, hastily looking down at the bag. "See, my...uh...business associate is going to mirror the drive onto his own machine, which means we'll be able to poke around in the data all we want without any fear of harming the original. You did say your husband kept it password-protected?"

"Yes; I might know the password, but I'd have to hunt around for it, probably. Brian gave the password to me a couple years ago, in case I ever needed to get on it for something. Actually, I wonder if he changed the password after he started his project... There's nothing on his laptop I need; all our banking stuff is on mine, too."

"Oh! by the way, we'll be completely confidential."

She shrugged. "I can only imagine what kind of insurance and disclaimers you have to have nowadays, when lawyers are a dime-a-dozen."

"I'm sure healthcare is the same, if not worse."

She rolled her eyes and nodded knowingly. She understood him; she understood his life. It felt good for someone to understand.

"Well...thank you," Derek began, clearing his throat.

"I really appreciate this," Mrs. Lane continued, opening a jar of sprinkles. "I just wish I knew who might want to do this to Brian."

"Leave that to us, ma'am," Derek assured her, waving his hand in the reassuring-professional-gesture. "With any luck, I'll get some help from this." He lifted the laptop bag.

"Good. Thank you so much." Mrs. Lane smiled. "Uh...are we burning a batch?"

"Oh! Yes, my fault! Don't you worry, I'll get it. I'll take these, it's my batch anyway, I burned them. I always burn at least one pan."

Derek smiled shyly and took a step toward the door.

"Oh, Mr. Hayes," Mrs. Lane exclaimed. "Before you go, do you like cheesy potatoes?"

Derek blinked. "Cheesy...?"

"I don't know what they're called. It's not exactly potato salad... Here, this." Cindy pulled a tupperware out of the fridge and handed it to him.

"Um..."

"You have a little brother, right?"

"Yes."

"Here." She set another tupperware on top. "These are sticky buns...like cinnamon rolls. You'll eat those, right? We just had a potluck at church, and a bunch of people sent stuff home with me before I could stop them."

"You need someone to look after you!" put in Mrs. Goodwin.

"I keep telling everyone I'm still learning to cook for one –"

"See? You want four days of all the same meatballs or whatever you make? No, this way you get all different things, and this way I'm not the one getting fat!"

Cindy laughed, still digging in the fridge. "Do you guys have any allergies?" she asked over her shoulder.

"Not that I know of," Derek stammered. "But –"

"Here." She put another tupperware on top of the other two. "This is like a cross between shepherd's pie and homemade pizza. Let me get you a bag for those."

"Um –"

"Don't worry about getting the dishes back, it's all my tupperware, so just whenever, you know." She shoved the plasticware into a grocery bag. "Does your brother like sugar cookies?"

"He's fifteen, but...I mean, yes, he...we..."

"Here." She stuck a ziplock of cookies into the laptop bag and smiled. "No one will notice a half-dozen one way or the other."

"Well...Well, thank you, Mrs. Lane."

"Cindy."

The room's temperature shot up five degrees. "Thank you… Cindy," he answered. "Mrs. Goodwin."

"Lovely to meet you," the lady called as he was shown out.

"Keep me posted, won't you?" Cindy asked at the door.

"Absolutely."

As he made his way down her walk, he pulled his key out. She had a lovely smile, and always spoke as though she was interested in him. Her case. What he had to say about her case. He chewed his lip and stuck the key in the car lock. Yes, she was very personable, but he was sure it was a professional thing. She was his client. Still, it felt good to feel like he had interesting, important things to say.

His cell phone started playing Larry Norman's "Lonely Boy". He pulled it out and tapped the answer button.

"Hey, Robbie."

"If you don't want the same thing we had for lunch, and you don't want to stop at the store, then we're having Ramen."

Derek chuckled. "How about cheesy potatoes?"

"Huh?"

7. "Speak Life"

Derek closed the door, whistling. Mrs. Lane had given him his first paycheck. That was nice, but more that that, he felt for the first time in years that he was doing something meaningful. Wearing a uniform and circling the mall for a few hours…it was harder to see how that was contributing to society. Mrs. Lane, however, had a real problem that *someone* had to make right. Maybe it would be him.

"Hi!" he called, dropping his jacket on the couch and stepping into the kitchen.

"Hi."

Something in Robbie's voice made Derek glance around the fridge door.

"You okay?"

"Yeah."

"Good." Derek cracked open his pop and walked to where Robbie sat at the computer, working with his hand weights. "Did you have supper?"

"Not yet." Rob glanced away from YouTube and rested his weights in his lap. "Did you?"

Derek smiled. "No, but I thought I'd ask."

"You're late again."

"Yeah, I know. Cindy Lane stopped by the mall when she got off work, and we were talking."

"I figured."

"I was going to call you, but then I forgot. Sorry." He set down his can on the coffee table. "Anyway, she got me a paycheck, so I thought we could order pizza or something."

"Okay."

Robbie's voice sounded strangely flat. Derek frowned and put the phone down.

"Do you feel okay?"

"Fine."

"Your back's bothering you, isn't it?"

"Not really."

Derek shook his head. He wasn't fooled. He could tell by the way Robbie was hunched over in his wheelchair. Well, he couldn't afford any new treatments and Robbie knew it. That was probably why he didn't want to talk about it.

Derek knelt beside the wheelchair, leaning forward to see the computer screen.

"Working on anything?"

Robbie shrugged and paused the video. "Just watching a tutorial for Blender."

"Have you started the physics book?"

"Sort of. I read the intro."

"Let's get on that. Maybe try to get the first chapter done by next week."

"Okay." Robbie did a curl with his left arm. "Are you going to do the experiments with me?"

"Sure, that sounds good." Derek stood up and headed for the couch. "I'd hate for Cindy Lane to learn I'm neglecting your education. She might fire me."

Rob cleared his throat. "So…Did you discover any new developments on the case with *Mrs. Lane* today?"

"Actually, it was really mostly background information." Derek leaned back against the cushions as Robbie rolled up to the coffee table. "She talked about Brian. He must have been quite a guy."

"Well, she liked him anyway."

"Did you know, they met at a funeral? Her grandfather's funeral, actually. Apparently her grandfather was Brian's Sunday school teacher when he was a kid – when Brian was a kid, that is."

"I know."

"Weird way to start a relationship, huh? But it worked for them."

"There are weirder ways. Like dating a therapist."

Derek sat up and stared at his brother. This was almost the first time in nearly four years Robbie had brought that mess up. Back when Derek was still raw from their parents' deaths, and he'd needed someone's sympathy – *anyone's* sympathy.

"Look, don't even bring that up, okay? That was then… I – I've left that behind."

Robbie rolled his eyes. "Well, excuse me. Just if all you want to talk about is girls, I figured I should mention the only girl I know."

"What girl am I talking about?"

"Cindy Lane."

Derek glared. Where did Robbie come off talking in that tone of voice, sunk down in his chair with his arms crossed? "Mrs. Lane isn't a girl; she's a woman. Besides, I'm supposed to talk about her; she's my *client*."

"You're supposed to talk about Brian Lane, not Cindy!"

"They're married; that sort of makes them connected."

Derek sprang to his feet and stalked into the kitchen. After several moments of staring blankly into the fridge, he shut it again.

"What do you want for supper?" he asked.

"I'm not hungry."

"You *are* feeling rotten. I should make you a doctor's appointment."

"I feel fine!"

"Then what are you yelling at me for?"

"What are you yelling at me for?"

The wall to the next apartment thumped several times. Mrs. Gibbons lived in the apartment next door, and usually gave her signal of displeasure when "Movie Night" got too explosive.

Derek crept back into the living room and slipped onto the couch.

"What would you like to do, Robbie?" he asked.

"I don't know," Robbie mumbled.

Derek rubbed his face and sighed. "I'm sorry for yelling."

"Me too."

Derek looked up, watching Rob fidgeting his fingers in his lap. Why'd he let himself get so mad at him? He was still just a kid, after all.

"How about *Call of Duty*?"

Robbie looked up and grinned.

8. "Country Church"

"Know what you want to wear?" Derek shouted.

"Doesn't matter."

Derek chewed his lip, flipping through his shirts. Not one of Dad's old shirts...he wanted one of the ones he'd bought himself, that fit him more neatly. He briefly considered that Mrs. Lane's living room and kitchen were mostly yellows and golds, then shoved those thoughts away. It was Sunday...he should be focusing on God. He pulled a mustard-colored shirt off the hanger and started pulling it on.

Stepping to the bathroom door, he knocked. "Can I come in?"

"Sure."

As he entered, he saw Robbie had gotten into his dress pants and was washing his hands. Derek picked up the razor and drew a deep breath.

"You mind if we branch out a little today?"

"What do you mean?" Robbie rolled to the medicine cabinet and pulled out his bottle of Lyrica, along with his daily pill-organizer box.

"I mean...like a different church. Did you want to try to talk to Mr. Mike this week?"

"I don't need to." Robbie's eyes flickered up at Derek's face before he continued filling his cup with water. "I...It sounds like he's pretty much made up his mind."

"Yeah...I see what you mean." Derek regretted bringing it up. He should have remembered what the deacon of technology had said when they'd button-holed him last week: *"Some members have—concerns about the church's professional website being managed by a—youth member. Nothing personal, just for propriety's sake"*. And all Robbie'd wanted to do was streamline the interface. That'd been a long afternoon for him.

"What did you have in mind?" Robbie asked, setting his cup back on the sink and looking up.

"I've heard good things about First Baptist," Derek answered, deliberately watching his reflection in the mirror. "They have an adult Sunday school class where kids and teenagers are welcome."

He switched the razor off and handed it to Rob. "That would be new and different," the teen agreed, leaning on the sink to see the mirror. Maybe he was thinking about what Mike had said, too.

Derek finished buttoning his shirt and smiled. "Well, their service isn't until 9:30, so we've got plenty of time to eat breakfast."

"Okay." Rob switched off the razor and set it on the sink, glancing over at his brother. "Hey, if you're wearing that shirt, I could wear mine that matches."

Derek grinned. "Sounds great." He stepped out into the hall, listening to Robbie's wheels on the linoleum. Why had he been so tense? Why would he expect Robbie to argue about trying a new church...even if it was First Baptist?

Maybe it was the prospect of seeing his client again. Derek really felt like he'd gotten to know the people of First Baptist over the last few weeks of talking to Cindy. He was looking forward to worshiping with them, and hearing their pastor. But it'd also be nice to see more of Cindy.

* * * *

Derek slid the hymnal back into the holder on the back of the pew in front. Glancing at Robbie, he saw him adding a few scribbled items to his sermon notes. Dad had trained them to take notes during service, partly by requiring a Biblical analysis of the sermon during lunch. Even at ten, Robbie had been good at tracing the narrative of Pastor Raul's argument. Growing up listening to

Derek and Dad go at it probably helped. Plus, Pastor Raul always had a very clear and understandable logic.

Sundays used to be crock-pot day, when Mom would plug something in before church and they'd come home to the house smelling glorious. Derek imagined himself and Robbie silently eating mac 'n' cheese at the coffee table, and his heart sank. He could try to cook something more exotic…but that wasn't what was missing.

"Good morning!" exclaimed a lady whose hair was either black or dark grey. "So glad you guys could make it this morning!"

"Thanks," Derek answered, taking the brake off on Robbie's wheelchair.

"I'm Cheryl Marchbanks," the woman continued, putting out a hand and shaking Derek's. "And who might you be?"

"Uh…I'm Derek. Hayes. This is my brother Robbie."

"Nice to meet you!" Mrs. Marchbanks exclaimed, shaking Robbie's hand, too.

"Thanks."

"So, you just passing through, or you have friends, or…"

"Uh…we're just visiting," Derek explained. "Trying something new."

"So glad you could be here."

"Thanks."

As Cheryl hustled off toward another member, Derek looked down at Robbie.

"You ready?" he asked, grabbing the handles of the wheelchair. "So, what do you think?"

Robbie pulled out his sermon notes and flipped them open. "I used two full pages," he answered.

"As opposed to last week?"

"I didn't even bother," Robbie mumbled, shamefaced.

"I don't blame you. It was the same sermon twice in a row, just different 'illustrations'."

"Yeah. I enjoyed Romans much more." Robbie smiled and breathed, "He sounds like Dad, doesn't he?"

"Funny you should say that."

"Morning, Mr. Hayes."

Derek spun around. "Good morning, Mrs. Lane," he answered.

She smiled. Wearing a skirt made her look taller. "It's nice to see you here."

Derek smiled back. "Thanks. We're just trying out new things. I…I hope it doesn't feel awkward to you…"

"No, not really." She turned to the middle-aged man who had walked up with her. "I just wanted you to meet Pastor Jones. Pastor, this is Mr. Hayes. My 'investigative counsel'."

"Pleased to meet you," Pastor Jones exclaimed, extending his hand.

"Likewise."

"And is this your brother I've heard so much about?" Mrs. Lane continued, smiling again. "I'm so glad to finally meet you."

Robbie made a pursed smile as he shook her hand, but said nothing.

"Yes, this is Robbie," Derek explained, gesturing awkwardly. "Robbie, Mrs. Lane."

"Derek has been very helpful to me so far," Cindy told the pastor, as he shook Robbie's hand.

"I haven't done that much, yet," Derek stammered. He *had* decided that Brian's dose had been intended to kill, but he still hadn't *proven* there was anyone else in the car, much less find out who it was.

"Well, we're very grateful for whatever you can do," Rev. Jones answered. "And I'm so glad you could join us."

Derek shrugged. "To be honest, our church hasn't had a pastor for almost three years. I think we both decided that we were tired of social actions and political correctness in the sermon."

"Uh!" Jones exclaimed, gesturing. "All these denominations changing their message for the sake of gaining favor with the world. It's a blemish on the name of the Church, and a hinderance to the true gospel."

Derek laughed. He could almost see Dad's face, saying basically these words.

"That's why Brian and I left our church in Grand Rapids," Cindy put in. "The leadership was acting un-Biblically."

"Mom and Dad left a church for that, too," Derek commented. He didn't want her to think he was mocking this kind of religious seriousness. "I was too little to understand at the time, but they said that the leadership wasn't respecting the Bible."

"False teachers are everywhere," the pastor sighed, putting one hand on his chin. "They're nothing new. Even the apostles had to warn their churches against various false doctrines."

"So…If your church hasn't had a pastor, what do you—do? I've never seen that situation before."

"Oh, we get interims from the denomination," Derek answered. "Which tells you a lot right there. The denomination has its own agenda to push, and everything."

"Sometimes it takes a lot to leave the church where you grew up." Mrs. Lane laughed. "My dad talks about how his family almost viewed him as apostate when they left the family denomination."

Everyone laughed. Derek relaxed his grip on a nearby pew and sighed. Mrs. Lane had said he had pluck. Not in those words, but she approved. It felt good to be approved.

Derek turned to the pastor. "So, have you been here long?"

"Almost fourteen years," Rev. Jones answered.

"That's a long time."

"Sometimes it feels like a long time, sometimes it feels like a matter of days."

"I know what you mean," Derek responded, rubbing his face.

"Oh…I think someone wants you," Mrs. Lane mentioned, pointing.

"Oh, yes, you're right. We're meeting someone for lunch. Well, excuse me; very glad to meet you." Pastor Jones shook Derek's hand and turned away.

"Thanks."

Derek glanced back at Mrs. Lane as she watched Pastor Jones leave. Now he knew why she'd borne up so well under this traumatic strain. He was glad she had an intimate, caring church family to support her. People needed other people they could trust, who could help them with the little things of life, who understood their lives and what was important to them, who could share their pain. He thought of Pastor Raul.

Cindy turned back and met his glance. Smiling, she dropped her voice slightly. "I don't suppose you've had a chance to look at Brian's hard-drive yet."

"Not exactly." Derek cleared his throat. "We're working on getting the drive mirrored, which is taking a little longer than we thought. As soon as it's done, though, I'll get it back to you and we'll start working on the image."

"The rub being it's encrypted," Robbie put in. "So it'll take longer."

Derek gulped and shot a sideways look at Robbie. Would Mrs. Lane think that Robbie knowing all about her case was a breach of trust?

"That sounds great. Thank you." She smiled again.

Derek heaved a sigh and smiled. If she was upset, she didn't show it. She was like the rest of her church...friendly, gracious, welcoming to everyone. Come to think of it, had anyone said more than "Good morning" to them last week? Joey Patel had talked to Robbie about *Halo Reach*, but that wasn't the same.

"Well, sorry to detain you," Mrs. Lane began with a gesture.

"No, thank you, I appreciate it. We really enjoyed the sermon this morning, and it's good to meet new people."

"I'm glad. There's a good bunch of people here. I...I don't know how I would have survived this whole thing without them."

Robbie cleared his throat and hugged his stomach.

"I know what you mean," Derek said. "You've got to have a support system."

"Right. Well, that just shows you God is still good. And I know Brian's with Him, now."

"That's got to be a big comfort," Derek nodded. "God gives us the strength we need to live in each moment."

Cindy beamed at him. "Day by day."

"Exactly." Derek noticed Robbie rolling one of his chair's wheels back and forth. Yeah, he needed to get him home. "Well, see you later."

"Take care."

"Thanks; you, too."

* * * *

As Derek started the car and backed out of the parking slot, he glanced at Robbie. "So...what did you think?"

Robbie shifted his Bible bag in his lap. "You didn't mention this was her church."

Derek frowned. He flicked on his turn signal. "Well...Does it matter?"

"Now I know why we came here."

Derek looked at him, but Robbie was facing out the window. "That's not it! We're just trying something new and different. Besides, last week you said you were tired of hearing the same old social activism sermon every week."

"I thought you said that."

"You said, quote, 'It'd be nice if every sermon wasn't about social inequality and making us feel guilty or whatever'."

Robbie heaved a sigh and leaned his head on his hand. "Puh-lease. You don't need to pull out the court recorder on me!"

"OK, I'm just telling you–"

"Don't. OK?"

Derek slammed on his brakes for a red light and sighed. "Okay, fine. What about the sermon? What did you think of that?"

"It was good," Robbie mumbled. "Better than we've been getting."

"What would you think if we went back?"

Derek waited for the snarky remark. Robbie had grown very snarky lately. It probably came from spending too much time alone.

Finally, Robbie answered, "The people were friendly."

Derek felt himself let go of a breath. "That's true. That's certainly true." At least they could agree on something.

They were both quiet the rest of the way home.

9. "What If I Stumble"

Derek pressed Cindy's doorbell and chewed his lip while he waited. She'd said she would be home by the time he got off work. He shifted Brian's laptop bag as he heard footsteps inside.

The door swung open and Mrs. Lane smiled. "Hello."

"Afternoon, Cindy." Derek smiled as he held up the bag. "I'm here to return your property."

"Thanks. Come on in."

Derek paused in the doorway, breathing in the aroma of tomato sauce and hot cheese.

Cindy laughed. "I thought I'd be lazy tonight, and just throw something in the oven. I'm still getting used to cooking for one."

"It's the little things that really get you, isn't it?"

She nodded. There was a moment of silence.

"Oh, by the way," Derek continued, holding up the grocery bag in his other hand. "I brought back some of your tupperware, too. We haven't finished the cheesy potatoes yet."

"No worries. Thank you." As she took the bag from him, she cocked her head for a moment. "Would you carry the laptop upstairs for me? You might like to see Brian's office."

"I...Sure."

"Second door on the right," she explained, gesturing up the stairs and turning toward the kitchen.

Derek drew a breath and climbed the stairs. A parade of suspicious situations flitted through his mind from the police academy's lawsuit-avoidance curriculum. But...Cindy would never be involved in a set-up like that. He pulled out his phone and tapped on the audio-record ap. Was this betraying her trust because of paranoia? Or being sensible? He could only imagine what Dad would have said about it. If only he was still around to say it.

Passing through a hallway lined with family portraits, running from black-and-white to Cindy and Brian, he pushed open the indicated door and glanced around Brian's office. Papers were stacked neatly on a desk to the right, while books lined a shelf to the left.

Straight ahead, under the window, Derek found what must be the computer desk. A wireless printer sat to one side, and a standard Apple laptop cord lay draped across an empty space.

Derek pulled Brian's computer out of the bag and laid it down, popping the magnetic cord onto the socket. Neat. Orderly. Was this Brian's habit, or had Cindy straightened things a little since his death?

Derek's ears tingled as he heard the sound of socks making soft thumping sounds on the carpet. He glanced over his shoulder as the owner of the house stepped into the room.

"Looks like you found it okay," she said, glancing around.

"Yeah...looks like he was pretty tidy."

"Yes, he was very organized," she answered, staying just inside the door. "I – haven't had the heart to go through this yet. I mean, I know where to find what I need for the bills." She sighed and brushed back her hair — a ponytail again. "Paying the mortgage and things like that."

"How is that going for you?"

"Fine." She gave a patient smile. "We really got a great deal on our mortgage, so we could cover it whether both of us were working or not."

"That's smart." Derek ran his eyes over the rest of the room, letting his mind fixate on each detail in turn. As he glanced back at the computer desk, he noticed a small silver picture frame.

He reached out and picked it up. Brian and Cindy were squeezed onto a bench in some kind of garden. Both of them were laughing and grinning like two kids on the first day of summer,

Cindy's lacy, white dress and veil completely overpowering Brian's dark suit.

Derek swallowed hard. He'd seen lots of wedding pictures. One day he'd get one. Dad had said there was a woman out there for him, somewhere – and that God knew where. He looked away from the happy couple and read the graceful, swoopy words that ran down the side of the frame: "Day by day."

"We sang that at our wedding," Cindy explained, at his shoulder. "That's why my grandma gave us that frame…He made sure it always stayed right there, by his computer."

"Nice," Derek rasped, and set the picture down right where it had been. He cleared his throat.

She gave a chuckle. "He was pretty sentimental in his own special way…but he was also very practical." She adjusted her shirt and sighed. "He didn't feel that…He didn't think we should have kids while his job was so unstable. You know – moving twice the first two years of our marriage…"

"Do you – I mean, did you want kids?" Derek stammered, remembering his audio recorder.

"Well, I enjoy them. I help in the nursery at church. I think they're very special." She shrugged. "But there you go…that's the way life goes sometimes."

"Yeah."

They returned to the entryway and Derek cleared his throat again. "Well, thanks for talking."

"Hang on." Cindy hurried into the kitchen again and returned with ziplock bag full of pizza slices.

"Here, I'll never finish all this," she insisted, handing it to him. "There's just one of me, I don't need a whole pizza."

"But–"

"And I've got plenty of other left-overs in my fridge. Share some with your brother."

Hayes and Hayes

Derek smiled. "Thanks…I know he'll appreciate it. He loves pepperoni."

"Did he enjoy Sunday school yesterday?" she asked. "I know he seems a little shy…"

"Yes…he's shy. And…he spends a little too much time alone, I think."

"That's got to be hard," she murmured. This from the lady who'd suddenly become single again.

"We make do. That's what you do in life," he answered.

"Day by day. God is good." She heaved a sigh and gave her shoulders a shake. "Say hello to him for me."

"I will. Thanks."

Back in his car, Derek pulled out his iPhone to stop the recording. He felt guilty about taking such precautions, but Dad would want him to be smart. And he had to think of Robbie. He set the pizza on the seat beside him and turned the key. Robbie would be waiting to eat supper with him, and he was running late. Later than he had expected. He glanced back at the Lane house. Time to leave.

10."Lonely Boy"

Robbie rubbed his head. Lyrica hadn't done much to ease the throbbing up the middle of his skull, and they were out of Ibuprofen. He glanced at the granola bars he'd laid on the coffee table. He still didn't feel like eating another one.

Derek must be off work by now, but he was probably talking with Cindy. There wasn't that much new on the case, but he had to give her the "update". Client? Yeah, right. Had he ever had this many "business meetings" with Mr. Hudson? You must be kidding.

He shifted slightly, wincing. At least moving didn't seem to intensify the burning tingle that ran up and down his legs. His nerves seemed to be indifferent to anything he thought or did. That didn't mean that moving was worth the effort.

"For crying out loud," he muttered. He glanced at the history book on the coffee table. Who really cared what the Ancient Babylonians had done, anyway? At least with the Egyptians, there were interesting things to learn about the Rosetta Stone and cryptology and stuff. The Babylonians were all dead, therefore all obsolete.

For the fifth time in as many minutes, Rob glanced at the clock. Derek was sure to be home any minute. It was already after 6:30. Derek would probably want supper; there were still some burritos, and plenty of Ramen. The teen drew the wheelchair a little closer, but didn't stir from the couch.

The front door rattled as someone fumbled with the lock. *About time.* Robbie crossed his arms and stared at the ceiling. Any longer, and he'd have begun to worry that something bad had happened.

Derek burst into the apartment and mumbled something about the landlord. The door closed loudly behind him.

"You're late," Robbie called.

"Yeah, sorry, traffic was awful. And I stopped by to talk to Cindy."

"What else is new?"

His brother seemed to take the remark as an honest question.

"Well, I learned more about Brian and Cindy, and their relationship. No one married to Cindy would ever think of suicide, unless he was an idiot. And Brian Lane was no idiot."

"That's not new," Rob snapped. "You already believed that *Mr. Lane* was murdered."

"True," Derek answered, leaning against the counter and opening his Coke. "But I'm getting more sure of it by the day. Sometime, I might find some hard evidence for it, too."

A stab of pain flashed in the area of Robbie's first surgery scar. He made a sound between a whimper and a groan.

"You okay?" Derek put his pop down and dropped to his knees beside his brother. "You don't look so hot."

"Just a bad day," Robbie mumbled. "I wanna take a bath tonight, Derek."

"Did you take any meds?"

"Just Lyrica…I couldn't find any Ibuprofen."

"You could've called me. There's some in my work bag — and I can stop at the store tomorrow."

"I'll be fine," Rob answered, as Derek rummaged in his bag behind the coach. "It only really flared up at lunchtime, anyway."

Derek appeared with a cup of water and a handful of pills. "Here. I'll leave my supply with you tomorrow, so I'll remember to stop at Walgreens."

"Okay." After he'd swallowed the pills, Rob looked up at Derek again. Why'd he let himself get mad at Derek? It wasn't like the accident was his fault. Now he was just trying to do his best to solve this case.

"Can you put me in the bath? I'm not really hungry for supper, I just want to get in some warm water for a bit."

Derek's face twisted up, and he pursed his lips. "Well...I sort-of promised Cindy...There's a Bible study tonight, at seven. I said I'd try to go."

Rob blinked. His shoulders slumped. Not Thursday nights, too. "Well, you can call her and tell her you can't make it. Come on, Derek, please?"

His brother scratched his head and chewed at his lip. "I...I can't just cancel at the last minute. That'd be like standing her up."

"You scheduled at the last minute. She can't be dependent on you. It's not like you were going to drive her anyway, right? She needs her own life, for goodness' sake."

"It's not like that!" Derek cried, standing up and pacing away. "And yeah, it's not just the two of us, but...but you like the other people at First Baptist, don't you? They like you. It's a good chance to get to know them better. It's not just Cindy."

"Really?!" Robbie almost shouted. "Don't tell me you've been spending afternoons at Pastor Jones's house for weeks and weeks."

"You just don't understand maintaining a professional relationship!" Derek exclaimed. "I've got to show people I can be responsible!"

"How many of your other clients have you dated?"

"It's not a date! It's a *Bible study*, for pity's sake!"

Mrs. Gibbons gave her signal of disapproval. The pounding on the wall from next door seemed to echo in Robbie's throbbing head. He laid his face in his hands, feeling tears welling up. Breaking down and crying like a baby...that would be the last blow.

"Oh, man," sighed Derek. "Okay. I'll put you in the bath, alright? Take it easy, it'll be fine. I'll put you by the end with the taps so you can make it hotter if you want. Okay? It's not like you have to come, if you don't want. I'll only be gone an hour…it'll be okay."

They wheeled into the bathroom. They started the water. Robbie slowly pulled his shirt off, wondering why getting his way felt like losing the fight. Derek knelt by the tub, struggling to fold down the legs of the bath seat so Robbie would be down in the water.

Robbie was stripped and down in the steamy warm water. It rose gradually up his back while the needle-pain in his limp legs seemed to leak out into the water. He looked up at Derek, who straightened to draw a deep breath. Derek always took good care of him; you couldn't call this neglect. Maybe it wasn't cheerful, but it wasn't neglect. It wasn't fair for Rob to have a bad attitude about it.

"There. I'll put your chair right here, and a towel and the phone here, just in case. You reach the taps okay? Good." Derek sighed again. "You want me to make you something to eat?"

"I don't know what I'm hungry for," Robbie moaned. "My stomach stills feels funny."

"All right." Derek checked his watch. "Maybe I'll just eat when I get back. I won't be more than an hour and a half. You going to be okay?"

"It's not standing her up, you know," Rob muttered. "You didn't promise to be there."

"Look," Derek sighed. "I'm sorry for losing my temper. I didn't mean that. But I can't afford to ignore a commitment like this. You know what happened the last time I didn't come through for a girl."

"You slept for two days straight."

Derek stiffened, and his eyes narrowed into a glare. After a few moments, however, he broke eye contact and walked slowly toward the bathroom door. "I won't be long," he murmured. "One hour."

"Promise?"

"Robbie…"

"Promise?!"

Derek rolled his eyes. "Promise." The bathroom door closed behind him.

Robbie swirled water against his knees and leaned his arms on the edge of the tub. Almost grudgingly, he admitted that the pain in his spine was less. His surgery scars bit into him less hard.

He pushed at the cold water tap with his elbow. "The last time I didn't come through for a girl." *Uh-huh. Michelle told you don't call again.* They'd had some fun with Michelle…he remembered her teaching them how to give Robbie a bath when he couldn't get in and out of the tub by himself. She'd taught Derek how to lift him in and out, how to help him dress while "encouraging him to be independent". She'd had a funny laugh, too…she'd laughed at almost everything, whether it was a joke or not.

Robbie twisted around and shut off the hot water. The front door slammed, making the whole apartment shudder. He shivered. The first time he'd had to be alone, he'd been so scared. Derek had called every hour to check in. Now it was a way of life. He'd left that immature, needy twelve-year-old far behind him. Now, he could probably live on his own if he really needed to…except for showers. Lifting out of the chair, over the tub wall, onto the seat was still a little complicated.

Squeezing his eyes shut, he dipped his face and sat up, shaking his wet hair. It wouldn't be the same. It wouldn't be enough. What would he do all day? Who would he watch Doctor Who with? Who would he cook Ramen for? He scratched his head and sighed heavily.

11. "Do Everything"

Derek felt his hands shaking as he pushed Robbie's wheelchair up the walk. For some reason, they just hadn't been able to get moving today. It'd taken them forever to get out of the house. Could they have been any later? Cindy surely thought he'd chickened out, and wasn't coming. His stomach turned over. Incompetent, undependable, immature. Michelle had been right about him…he couldn't do anything right.

With a sideways glance at Robbie, Derek pressed the doorbell and waited, chewing his lip. Several moments passed, as he rocked on his heels. Robbie shifted the bag of chips they'd grabbed at the last minute, and glanced up at him with a tiny smile.

Finally, the door opened and Cheryl Marchbanks looked out.

"Oh, hi! Glad you could make it! It might be easier to go around the side, we're all in the back. The sidewalk goes around that way."

She led them along the walk and through a wooden gate into the back. As they rolled around, a patio came into view, lined with the church's plastic folding tables.

Cindy Lane looked up from where she sat and smiled. Derek forgot the names he'd been calling himself; Cindy showed every sign of being happy to see them, not annoyed. He smiled back and rolled Robbie into the shelter of a portable awning.

"I'm so sorry we're late, Cindy," he began as she rose and came toward them. "I forgot we were going to bring something until the last minute, and Robbie was taking a while, and –"

"Never mind. I'm glad you made it." She smiled down at Robbie and reached for the chips. "The food's in the kitchen, through the sliding doors. Would you like me to put those away for you?"

Robbie said nothing, but handed her the bag and turned to look at Derek.

As Cindy walked away, Derek saw Pastor Jones beckoning to them. He parked Robbie at the end of the pastor's table and slid into the empty seat beside him.

"I'm sorry we're late," he repeated. "One thing and another, we just didn't get it together today."

"The important thing is that you're here," Pr. Jones answered. "Besides, the burgers aren't ready yet anyway, so you're not really late."

"We've been having problems getting the grill to work," Ellie Jones put in, leaning forward to hand her husband an iced tea. "I think they ran out of gas or something. I'm so glad we have men to take care of that, who enjoy fiddling with those things; it makes it so much easier."

Cindy reappeared and leaned on the table across from Derek. "Do you want me to get you something to drink while we're waiting? There's a cooler of soda in there, and a pitcher of lemonade, and another one of water."

"Robbie will be good," Derek answered, with a glance at his brother. "I might get something in a bit, if you don't mind."

"By the way," began Roger Thomas from the other end of the table (building contractor and one of the regular lawn-work volunteers at church; wife was fond of snap-dragons). "I've been meaning to ask you, Cindy, how your lawn's doing. It shouldn't be too long yet, but the weather's been so nice…"

"It has been gorgeous weather," Cindy answered, swirling her lemonade. "But Peter just cut it for me a week ago, and it's not too bad yet. You know," she laughed. "I was telling Mary-ann the other day, I don't think I've had to mow my own lawn since Brian died."

"Oh, my! That is funny, isn't it?" Mrs. Thomas laughed back. "I bet you still get lonely, though."

Cindy shrugged and dropped her eyes. "Sometimes. But that's life, you know. Day by day. God hasn't stopped being God."

Derek cleared his throat. "It is true, though, that...that God built us to need other people. To need *an* other person. Someone... who fits our slots and grooves, who completes us. For God's glory."

"Exactly right," Pr. Jones added. "*It is not good for man to be alone.* Don't I know it." He cocked an eyebrow at Mrs. Jones, who was setting up more folding chairs at the next table.

"My dad had a number of talks with me about that," Derek said, looking away from Cindy.

He nearly jumped as something thumped against his foot. Glancing secretly under the table, he realized Robbie's leg had fallen off the foot-rest. Spasms again, probably.

"Of course, some people are gifted with single-ness," the pastor continued. "The Apostle Paul says he wishes that all people could be like him, and be satisfied with God."

Derek reached out to grab Robbie's leg, and met someone's hands. He and his brother glanced up at each other, both twitching at the contact. Derek eased the leg toward the foot-plate while Robbie's face flushed.

Some people are meant to be single? What if that's me? What if there isn't a wife out there for me? Dad said there was, somewhere.

"I don't know," Cindy was saying. "I know God can sustain me through anything. He's certainly carried me through my grieving phase and onward."

Alone...on my own...Forever?! He watched Robbie's face as the latter rubbed his arm, staring at the table or stealing glances at people's faces. *Alone except for God. And Robbie. For good?*

"It could be that He's got a whole new field of ministry to open up for you, now," Pastor answered. "I've seen similar things happen."

"What's that saying? 'If God closes a door, He opens a window'."

"All the same," Cindy breathed, staring into her glass. "I'm sure glad he sent Brian into my life."

"I know what you mean. I feel the same," Ellie Jones responded, flashing a smile at the pastor as she passed, carrying a stack of card games.

Derek bit his lip. He mustn't allow jealous thoughts into him. He knew God would be enough for him...but he didn't feel like it. Still, he knew God was good. As Cindy said, "Day by day."

"Burgers are ready!"

"I think that's my cue," laughed the pastor, rising and moving toward a spot in the middle of the patio. "All right, everyone," he called, as clusters of the church family shifted their attention to him. "I'll go ahead and thank God for this meal, and this day, and our fellowship together, and then we'll dig in. Any instructions, Cheryl?"

"Buns and burgers by the plates, drinks on the side table."

"Everyone got that? Join me in prayer, if you would, please."

Everyone bowed their heads while Jones gave a brief expression of gratitude and praise. As he intoned the "Amen", there was a chorus of echoed "Amens".

"Come and get it," shouted Mrs. Marchbanks.

Chairs rustled and scraped as people rose to their feet. Cindy looked at Derek.

"Well? Shall we go? Or wait for the crowd to dissipate?"

"Whatever you like," Derek answered. His pulse had sped up, despite the warm day. 'Shall *we* go'...it sounded so...right.

"Well, why not? Gives us a chance to mingle a bit, anyway," she replied, rising to her feet.

Derek also rose, leaning down toward Robbie's level. "I'll bring you out something, okay?" he said. "Know what you want?"

Robbie glanced at Derek, but just shrugged. Cindy gave a laugh, and also leaned on the table toward Robbie. "I guess Derek probably knows what you like. Any special requests? I'm not sure what-all's there."

Still rubbing his arm, Robbie shrugged again, and mumbled, "Whatever. I don't know."

"Okay. I'll get you something good." Derek gave his shoulder a squeeze and turned to walk into the house with Cindy.

The kitchen was full of chatter and the aroma of well-done beef. Derek breathed deeply and handed Cindy a paper plate. She thanked him with a smile, and something warm surged in his stomach. She looked away to examine the asparagus salad, but his eyes followed her face, drawn...by something.

Why had she taken so much interest in a washed-up PI and his little brother? Was it really just Christian kindliness? There was lots of that at her church...surely it wasn't anything more than that.

She looked back at him to offer the chips, and her eyes sparkled with something. Happiness? Fun? Teasing? Something... He looked away. Mrs. Jones was talking. He put down Robbie's plate to hide his hand shaking. Whatever this was, he couldn't let it get in the way of the case. Clouding his judgement. He couldn't talk about this with Robbie...he already knew what he would say. *Just like last time, huh?* No; Cindy was different. He knew Cindy was different.

"Oh, is this your apple crumble?" asked the pastor's wife.

"Yes, that one's mine," Mrs. Goodwin answered.

"Mm...it looks delicious."

"Yes, thank you; I used the special recipe I got from, oh, you know, oh! Mrs. Marchbanks, she gave me the recipe for sugar-free apple crumble. So that one I made sugar-free, because you know, I have to watch my sugar, and I knew you did, too, so I thought, maybe, the two of us could eat it even if nobody else likes it."

The two ladies laughed. Derek smiled and scooped potato salad onto his plate.

"Well, I can't remember when I had apple crumble last," Mrs. Jones continued, serving up some. "I've got to be careful, you know, to keep the sugars and the insulin in balance."

"Exactly; when you say that I remember, you know, I'm so lucky compared to you, because didn't you tell me that part of what you have to do is stick a needle in yourself every day? Uh! I don't know how you do it, I don't think I could do that, ever, for anything. I think if I were to get diabetes like that where I had to, like you, stick myself every day I would rather just, instead of that, just die!"

"Oh, I don't think so," Ellie Jones laughed. "I'm sure you would get used to it, and it would become part of your routine after a while. Besides, I think John would miss you, if you went and died."

"All I know is, you are so much braver than me."

"Well, after all," Cindy put in, laying lettuce on her burger. "Different people are different."

"Needles are kind of creepy," Derek put in. "Especially if you've got to stick yourself, you can't even close your eyes."

Cindy laughed.

"You sound just like Brian," she exclaimed. "He didn't have a problem with potential injuries and blood, but he never liked to visit me in the hospital. He said even seeing a needle made him queasy."

"Hey, that's right," Ellie put in. "I remember, we were talking about marriage regulations or something one day, and he said he almost reconsidered marrying you when they had to do blood tests on him."

"I wouldn't put it past him," Cindy answered, smiling. "I wonder if they had to strap him down to do it."

Derek frowned. "Are you telling me," he began slowly. "That Brian was afraid of needles?"

Cindy looked at him and gave a little shrug. "Yeah, I guess he pretty much was," she smiled, making a small gesture with one hand.

"That he hated needles?"

"Oh, yeah."

"That he disliked visiting his own wife at work because he might see a needle?"

"Well, I mean, not exactly in so many words, but –"

"Did you tell the police this?"

She blinked, and frowned. "No. I didn't think of it. No, I don't *think* I told them that."

"I'm afraid I don't understand," Mrs. Jones said, gesturing with her lemonade. "Did the police ask you about Brian's phobias?"

Derek did a victory spin in the middle of the floor, while Cindy and Mrs. Goodwin both dove to catch the ketchup.

"Point being," Derek exclaimed. "If a guy terrified of needles wants to end it all, the *last* thing he's going to do is use a hypodermic."

"I can't believe that didn't occur to me before," Cindy whispered, stroking back a stray piece of hair.

"All of this meaning…" Ellie Jones murmured, frowning and looking from Cindy to Derek.

Derek grinned, gesturing with one of the plates and flipping a couple chips on the floor. "Obviously, Brian was murdered."

"Oh, my!"

Derek closed his eyes and drew a deep breath. "Whoever did it knew him well enough to know that he was left-handed, but not well enough to know that even if he had wanted to dope up, he would huff, snort, or swallow long before he would shoot. Don't worry, ladies." He glanced at the others in the kitchen. "You've got clear alibis, since you were mentioning Brian's phobia before Cindy was."

Ellie's eyes were wide, but she managed a chuckle. "I'm glad we're not suspects," she exclaimed. "But, my goodness! We knew Brian wouldn't have killed himself, but I was really hoping it had been some kind of accident. Who would do such a horrible thing?"

Derek smiled. "I don't know, but we're going to catch them if it's the last thing I do."

"Well, there are two of you being much braver than me, here."

Cindy laughed again; a subdued laugh, but still a laugh. "There you go," she sighed. "Working on Labor Day. Are you going to charge me holiday fare?"

He snickered. The flash in her eye showed she wasn't being serious. She was joking with him…and making him the butt of her joke. People like her only made their friends or themselves the butt of their jokes.

"Absolutely," he answered. "Which means I need to get an extra serving of whatever you made."

"I made fruit salad and brownies."

"Perfect. I'll do the brownies."

They laughed. She laughed and he laughed. Together. With a rush of warmth in his insides, Derek realized that he didn't feel as sorry for Brian as he should. And do what he might, he couldn't make himself feel guilty for that, either.

12. "Somewhere Out There"

Cindy had developed an established pattern of behavior. On clocking out, she would drive across the road to the mall and walk laps with Derek, often until he got off at six. Sometimes longer. Since passing on the information about Brian's phobia to the police, they'd been focusing on trying to find a motive for anyone wanting to kill him.

Armed with a McDonald's latte, she climbed the escalator toward the Sears outlet where Derek always paused in his rounds to wait for her.

As Derek turned his head and saw her coming, a grin filled his face. She smiled back, wondering briefly what his bosses thought of him walking around the mall with a woman. Well, he seemed to have taken her off-hand comment about ironing his shirts to heart...his uniform shirt looked extra sharp today. He straightened his shirt as she came up; it flattered his muscled shoulders. It helped for people in his profession to look impressive.

"Hi, Derek."

"Hi, Cindy."

They fell into step beside each other, and she took a sip of coffee.

"How have you been...since yesterday?" A chuckle broke from her in the middle of the sentence.

"Fine. How about you?" Derek stared into her face as he spoke, his head bent down closer to her level.

"Great. How is your brother?"

"He's...okay."

Derek paused to stare impressively at a group of tweens hanging around a vending machine. A couple of the preteens stared back at him. The rest avoided eye contact and shuffled away toward a clothing store.

Derek gave his shoulders a victory flex and looked back at Cindy. "Good news. We've been looking at the files we copied and decrypted from Brian's machine; apparently Brian was keeping notes on this 'personal project' of his, and there are some people mentioned that are now in the custody of the state. I have an appointment to meet with one of them later this week."

"Great!" Cindy swirled her coffee and took another sip. "What kind of people? Drug dealers?"

"Yes, the guy I'm going to see was a drug dealer. He's called Tokyo, and he was selling meth for the Blackhearts until the DEA got an anonymous tip about their set-up. Brian recorded that he couldn't find out who took the tip."

"Blackhearts, huh?" Cindy closed her eyes for a moment, waiting for the name to jog something. "The Blackhearts had a big operation trying to do business with rural users. But that was probably a couple years ago, when that was a really big problem."

She'd never forget the nights Brian had sat at the table, bent over his iPhone, hardly touching the supper she'd made him. Even when it was lasagna or his favorite shepherd's pie. Then one day he'd burst into the hospital waiting room, still smelling like a 12-hour stakeout, and kissed her, and said, "We're going out, honey; we got 'em!"

She gazed over the rail at the shoppers milling on the lower level, and tried to tell Derek. Tried to explain the significance of Brian letting his shepherd's pie go cold while he pored over the field reports. Show how it set up his excitement when they'd finally scored some major arrests against this gang.

"There was one gang leader especially, I remember. He was one of the chief coordinators, and apparently pretty ruthless. Brian's team were really happy when they caught him – a couple springs ago, probably. 'At least we got Shiv' – that's what Brian said. They didn't catch everyone in the gang, but they got Shiv. You know, Brian got a special letter of commendation from his superiors for that – he framed it and hung it in his office."

Derek nodded.

"He was so happy about that bust. Not because he got recognition, but because the city was safer with those criminals behind bars. He…"

This probably didn't relate to the current case, but she'd gotten carried away, thinking about Brian, and what was important to him – what made him light up. Even now, it was so hard to believe he was really gone.

Finally, she took a swallow of her latte and looked up.

She found Derek meeting her gaze, nodding seriously. What an awkward moment to realize his eyes were the same dark, chocolatey brown as Brian's had been…

"He was a good agent," Derek said gently. "He took his work seriously."

"That's true." She tore herself from his face and adjusted her bun. "So you can understand why his latest project drove him so crazy."

Derek made an encouraging sound in his throat.

"He was trying to nail the Assassin Squad. Did his files mention that?"

"Yes, there's a lot of material about the Squad in there."

Derek broke off and stepped into the path of a runaway toddler. The chubby little boy paused and stared bemusedly up at him while the mother, shouting commands and dragging a stroller full of shopping bags, staggered up to them.

When the child had been scooped up and toted off, Derek turned to Cindy again. "Tell me more about Shiv. Do you remember anything more?"

Cindy frowned. "It was several years ago, so not a lot. I — think that Brian went to testify at his trial, because he'd been at the arrest. I could be mistaken. Are those kinds of records sealed?"

"I'll find out." Derek chewed his lip for a moment.

Cindy took one last sip of her coffee. Was Shiv important? It'd been at least two years since he was sent to prison – was there some other connection to the Blackhearts that would explain what Brian had been up to? She hadn't heard him mention them very much before his death.

Derek cleared his throat. "Let's go back to the Assassin Squad. Did Brian say much about them?"

Cindy nodded. "He did seem interested in their movements. You see, how I understand it is: when you're selling meth, you either make it yourself or you smuggle it in from Mexico. Of course it's not as simple as that, but…"

Derek nodded.

"Well, anyway, apparently the Assassin Squad don't have any connections to Mexico…or not that the DEA could uncover." Cindy hurried ahead to drop her cup into a garbage can. "But Brian couldn't for the life of him find out where they were getting their raw materials to make their own meth. At least, that's my interpretation."

She smiled, even as a gap tugged at her heart. How strange, to be standing here discussing what her husband had thought, or known, or done… The memories made him feel as close as he'd ever been – like she'd just said good-bye on her way to work that morning. Yet at the same time, he felt very far away – like a character in a movie, or someone she'd known years ago.

"I heard him working in his office, one day," she breathed. "He said, 'Where are they getting the PSE, for crying out loud?'."

"Pseudoephedrine."

"Right." She nodded and glanced at her watch. They still had a couple minutes before Derek would have to clock out.

"Good thing to ask Tokyo about," Derek mused, scratching his head. "It's important for gangs to keep tabs on their rivals."

Weird – he did the same little squinting motion of his eyes when he was thinking as Brian did. In fact – when he wasn't talking, she could close her eyes and listen to his breathing and pretend…pretend that Brian wasn't dead. *What a peculiar little game to play with yourself!* Probably not a healthy game – Brian was never coming back. Still…

"Are you coming to Bible study Wednesday?" she asked, to think of something other than Brian.

"I'm looking forward to it."

"Think you'll get Robbie to come with you?" She wanted to see more of the reticent teenager. Ellie said he was one of the best students in the pastor's youth Sunday school class, but the last time Cindy had tried talking to him about his interests, his answers had been monosyllabic at best.

"I'll try." Derek didn't look at her, and his voice didn't sound enthusiastic. "I don't know. He…I don't know."

They walked in silence for a moment. Derek checked his watch.

"I guess I should get going," Cindy said. "I've got laundry to do tonight."

"Yeah, me too," Derek answered with a laugh. "Thanks for the tips," he continued as he shook her hand. He shook it several times, while gazing into her eyes. But that was okay. If she tried to block out everything except his dark, interested eyes, she could pretend… *Oh, my word.* She was doing it again.

"Take care of yourself," he said, and let go of her hand.

"You, too."

She was halfway to the escalator when she spun around. "You do know that…well, that gangsters and druggies aren't always exactly scrupulous."

"Sort-of by definition."

"Well…be careful, won't you?" That sounded silly. "Well, of course you understand the danger — it's inherent. I – just don't want anyone injured for my sake."

"Would I had an opportunity…" He cleared his throat, as though unsure where those words had come from. "But I promise to not be an idiot."

"Good enough." She laughed a little bit, and hurried down the escalator. Even over such a serious subject, he was so funny when he pulled that innocent, befuddled look…like Columbo, who acted as though even his own brilliant actions mystified him.

It must remind her of…but, no. Brian hadn't had an expression quite like that. He'd had a blank-politeness face, for when he couldn't get out of listening to the old man down the street who was convinced his calico cat gave him good luck. But Derek had a charm all his own…

13. "It's A Personal Thing"

Derek recognized Becky Foster from the group photograph in Brian's study. Although it was probably creepy that he'd followed her and her friend here from DEA headquarters, he was afraid of the "official" interview process that would be required if he wanted to talk to her professional-to-professional. In a bar like this, social barricades were usually – *usually* – a little lower.

He hovered at a table just on the edge of hearing, wondering how long it would take Foster's female coworker to powder her nose or whatever it was women did. He wasn't anxious to approach them together, but he might have to if he didn't get a better chance.

Finally, the blonde one rose and headed toward the back of the building with a murmured comment and a laugh. An opportunity not to be squandered.

Derek rose and leaned on the bar a polite distance from Agent Foster to order his soda.

When he saw her eyebrows go up, he smiled and explained, supposedly to the bartender, "I could use the caffeine."

Becky Foster chuckled. "They sell that at the McDonald's, you know," she commented, gesturing with her head in the direction of the nearest one.

Derek gave the smile of innocence and answered, "Oh, the people here are more interesting."

When she lowered her margarita glass and leaned toward him, he knew he'd won the first round.

The second round was talking about her work, and she won hands-down. As a DEA special agent, Becky Foster was appreciably discrete.

As they talked, Derek spotted her blonde friend come back into the main room. His pulse skipped a beat in panic, but she just smiled at Becky and started talking to a man at the other end of the bar.

There had to be some way to get the information Derek needed without blowing his cover of disinterested stranger. He started a circular progression of topics that would hopefully lead back to what he needed.

Personal relationships seemed to be a more approachable subject than DEA affairs – especially when Derek let Becky coax out that he was single.

"Now, the important thing to know about dealing with women is you have to show you understand what they care about." Becky angled her head seriously, staring at Derek. "You have to convince them that what's important to them is important to you."

"So, can you tell me what's important to women?" asked Derek. Not that he was trying to "make moves," but his romantic life to this point had been one catastrophic flop, followed by flatlining.

Becky shifted her eyes away, thinking. Her eyelashes couldn't possibly be that long actually – could they? He probably wouldn't know mascara if he saw it.

"Every woman's different…I think that's important to remember," his companion continued. "Ever noticed that when people ask for relationship advice, they're usually looking for a quick-fix thing?"

"They'd rather not hear that it'll take a lot of hard, unglamorous work?"

"Right," Becky laughed. "But at least I can tell you what's important to me."

"That'd give me a place to start," Derek answered. "Understanding what goes on in a woman's mind – the greatest mystery."

"It's not that complicated." She rolled her eyes and pushed her bangs out of her face. The lock of hair slipping across one eye looked cute – but impractical. Cindy would never wear her hair like that. Too annoying, always brushing at it.

"A woman wants honesty. She wants to know she can just take what you say to her. And a man's got to have character."

"How do you mean *character*?"

"Well...for instance." Becky shifted on her seat and sipped her drink. "There are these guys I work with, okay? Well, a couple years ago we pulled together a big case and made some major arrests in one of the local gangs. Well, one of our teammates worked really hard on that – really pulled his weight and brought the case together for us. He got a commendation from the higher-ups for that, and he really deserved it.

"Well, this other teammate got all mad, and started griping about how he should have gotten a commendation. I said to him, 'Matt, get a grip.' They only gave out one pat on the back. I know we all worked our tails off – that's what you do. So, our friend got special notice – that's no reason to get bent out of shape and start trash-talking him in the break room."

"I hear what you're saying," Derek sighed. That was a benefit of working for yourself and having no coworkers. And unless he missed his guess, the "Matt" she'd mentioned was Matt Crawford, one of Brian's teammates. (After all, she and Crawford had been standing next to each other in Brian's photo.)

"It sure isn't a reason to request a new partner," Becky agreed, with a roll of her eyes. "I can't believe he went and asked for reassignment over a silly thing like that."

"You're kidding."

She shook her head, swirling her glass before tipping it toward her mouth.

This was interesting. It seemed to explain some of Crawford's comments at Derek's meeting with him – though not everything. Was there a tactful way to find out *when* Crawford had made this request?

"When did he request that? Right after the incident?"

"No, actually it was this past winter or so. But I know it's because of their strained working relationship, and they've been strained ever since our teammate got the recognition and my friend didn't. I told him to relax and let it go, but they've been...oh, what's it matter, anyway? It's all over now."

So it was. Brian was dead, and couldn't be reassigned anything. Was a little recognition from the bosses really a reason to off him, though?

Derek made an encouraging sound, to see if she would produce anything else.

Becky was staring at the counter. She sighed. "So...how about you? You said you freelance – how does that pay?"

Derek shrugged and smiled. "Enough to pay the bills. You've got to work harder at picking up jobs, though."

"Is that why you hang out here? 'Cause the people are more *interesting*?"

"Sometimes. Sometimes I just want to relax."

Tonight he was working, though. And he'd pulled in a few tidbits.

Matt Crawford had asked to be transferred away from Brian – just a couple months before Brian died. It seemed a little extreme, but this whole convoluted case was extreme. At least he could keep his eye on Crawford...and see what else he could find out about that Blackhearts sting.

Perhaps Brian and Matt had been working on something together, and Crawford was afraid Brian would pull the recognition again. Still...Brian was six feet beneath a stone plaque. Did some people really take their recognition that seriously?

14. "FLOOD"

Coldness brought Robbie back to himself. And wetness. Shivering, he rubbed at his eyes, willing his consciousness back into the blank state it had been in. No use. He was awake, and when he drew a deep breath, the stench of a public restroom rushed into his nose, confirming his worst fears.

Struggling with his arms, he flipped over to his other side. No good. Now that he was awake, he'd never get back to sleep... not with the sticky, clammy sheets clinging to his legs. He let out a subdued groan. The reek alone would keep him up 'til morning. He bit his lip. There was nothing for it.

"Derek?"

Derek wasn't snoring, but he was breathing heavily, which was worse. It meant he was deep in his rhythm. He was going to hate to wake up. Robbie screwed up his eyes, reconsidering.

Another deep breath, and he grimaced. Life had to be livable. If he waited until morning, when the sun was high and shining in their window...that would give him a headache for sure.

"Derek?"

His brother shifted a limb, he wasn't sure which one, and sighed. He was really out. And he had to get up early to drive to the state prison. Robbie sucked on his lip a moment. Maybe he could change the sheets himself. He'd done it in the past. And he knew how much Derek hated dealing with wet sheets.

He hauled himself into a sitting position and yawned. If only he could just go back to sleep. He gingerly flicked the sopping covers off his legs and groped in the darkness beside the bed for the wheelchair. He clutched the armrest and tugged to bring it in. The wheels were angled wrong, and it rolled toward his feet instead of toward his head.

Suppressing a grunt, he yanked the fitted elastic off the head of his bed. He could untuck the bottom of the sheets from here, too, and did it really matter that the whole smelly mass ended up in his lap? He shuddered and began rocking to get it out from underneath him. No more liquids at supper. Ever.

Too hard a jerk met with too un-centered a rock, and Robbie grabbed for the wheelchair as he felt himself falling. He snatched a handful of sheet that came with him over the side; his elbow banged the wheelchair, which slid away from him and bumped against the bed.

The crash made Derek start up with a snort and a gasp. As Robbie rolled and thrashed to get upright, Derek fumbled for the switch on the lamp. They both squinted and grunted as the room was flooded with yellow light, and Derek shot his glance over the room.

"What are you doing?" he yawned, kicking his feet over the side of the bed. "You fall out of bed or something?"

"I...I'm changing the sheets," Robbie mumbled, leaning his back against the safe that they used as a bedside-table. At least he hadn't hit his head on anything. He let go of the sheet with a shiver and started rubbing his right hip, which was throbbing.

"Why didn't you wake me up?" Derek growled, grabbing Robbie under the arms and heaving him up into the wheelchair. "You trying to kill yourself?"

"I can get it!" Robbie assured him. Realizing his hands were shaking, he reached out to grab the sheets off the bed and bundled them into his lap.

"Uh," grunted Derek. "Got your T-shirt, too, looks like." He yanked the pillowcase off the pillow and started pushing Robbie out the door. "Man, that's disgusting. Let's throw you in the shower quick."

They rolled into the bathroom, Rob squeezing and un-squeezing the sheets in his lap. It was disgusting. He'd gotten it all over. Sheets, shorts, T-shirt... That's why Ferdinand sat on the bookshelf above Robbie's head now, instead of tucked into the crook of his elbow all night. Well, that and he was *waay* too old for stuffed hippos. Ferdinand had sentimental value, but that was all.

As Derek flipped on the bathroom light, they both let out exclamations. He flipped it off again and reached out into the hall for the hall light. That was slightly less intense, and Robbie began stripping off his wet clothes.

"Here...I'll throw those in," Derek muttered, grabbing the wet sheets. He took the sticky shorts that Rob slipped out of, too, and left the bathroom.

Rob shivered and rolled over to the shower. He could remember when he would bathe himself. He switched on the water and held his hand under it, waiting for it to get warm. He could remember...he could remember when he and Dad and Derek went swimming at the Y, and there was a public men's shower, and it was a big thing to shower along with Dad and Derek. Now, that seemed like part of a different world...a world he was barely connected to.

Derek came back into the bathroom as Robbie was reaching out to transfer himself.

"Whoa, take it easy. Let me get you."

He didn't need to wake Derek up. He didn't *need* Derek to transfer him into the tub. He was a big boy...he knew what he needed to do.

Robbie let out a snarl as his hand slipped on the wet tub. Derek caught him under the arm, and Robbie suppressed a wince. Alright...he couldn't quite do the tub by himself. Not without a risk of falling. And Derek wouldn't let him fall.

"Easy does it. Don't kill yourself," Derek said, switching on the shower part and standing up, flapping his wet hands. "I'll get the bed," he sighed, turning to leave the room again. "Man, that room is going to reek."

Robbie shivered as the hot water coursed over him. Of course it would reek. It pretty much always reeked. That's what happened when you lived with someone disgusting. It wasn't like Robbie tried to wet the bed! He rubbed his face, as something inside his chest seemed to sink.

Stinky bedroom. Extra laundry. Not to mention the prescription Derek had just refilled. Rob knew that cost a lot. And then there were the surgeries Derek had had to pay for, and the therapy. They'd sold Mom and Dad's house, and gotten this apartment, so it wasn't all out of Derek's pocket. But it was still a lot, when you added it up.

Robbie hugged his arms against his chest and leaned his head back to let the water run over the rest of his body. He could tell it was getting old to Derek. How many times this week had he needed new sheets? He didn't want to think about it. There'd been a period where the meds seemed to help…but not recently. What was wrong with him?

No way was it Robbie's fault, though. Of course not. Derek had been driving. And Derek kept saying it wasn't Robbie's fault. He rubbed his face again and shut off the water. What would Mom and Dad have said? He made a wry grimace at the shower wall. Derek kept talking about Mom and Dad like they were people with important roles in his life. How many years had it been? He couldn't even put a number on it.

He groped along the wall beside the shower for his towel and began to dry off. What if they had gotten a two-bedroom apartment. Would Derek use a different room? Would he leave him all by himself in a room? Not like he needed Derek's help to get out of bed. It was just faster. He could handle himself, it just made some things easier. But he could totally do it himself. He didn't need Derek!

His brother came back into the bathroom and lifted Robbie out of the shower. With a tremendous yawn, he handed Rob some new clothes and started helping him to dress. Robbie felt his hands shaking as he pulled his shirt on. They could totally have separate rooms, their own stuff, their own space. Once Derek got back on his feet and his career took off, the way it was bound to. That's the way it was when they were little, why not again?

As they rolled into the bedroom, Rob saw that Derek had already replaced the sheets on his bed...the brown stripy ones that they both hated.

"Uh...I've got an early morning tomorrow," sighed Derek as he lifted Robbie into the bed.

"Sorry..." Robbie mumbled as Derek tucked the sheets around him. Tucking him in...like Mom used to. Like Mom used to when he was just a kid, tucking the covers around him and kissing his forehead. Derek didn't kiss his forehead. He wasn't a kid anymore.

Derek yawned loudly and switched off the hall light. Rob watched him feel his way back to his bed, and hugged the covers against his chest.

"I'm sorry," he whispered again.

"I hope you can sleep okay, Robbie," Derek mumbled. "For what's left of the night. Sweet dreams."

"Sweet dreams." That old automatic phrase. Mom always said it, as she stood in the doorway of his room, just before she switched off the light. As though saying it made the light go out. *Sweet dreams.*

Derek's breathing slowed down. Robbie listened to the sound of the washing machine running in the other room, and lay down. He'd never thought about Derek not liking to share rooms with him. It was a lot of work to take care of someone like him. Derek shared his room, because that was what there was...because that's what he had to do. He couldn't like having to do laundry in the middle of the night. No one could. Rob didn't. If Robbie had a choice, he wouldn't share a room with himself. Disgusting.

He shivered. Now the pins and needles had started. He probably wouldn't sleep very well for the rest of the night anyway. Derek didn't like sharing Robbie's room. Derek's wife wouldn't like sharing Robbie's room. Assuming Derek ever got married, which was unlikely if it involved sharing a room with Rob. What if Derek did get married? Robbie felt his insides sink, as though he'd suddenly gotten emptier inside. He realized he'd never put it that way before. Derek might really get married. People did, sometimes. Especially if they were in love.

Robbie buried his face in his pillow and hugged it to himself. What if Derek got married? What would happen to him? He didn't need Derek! He could take care of himself all by himself. He could live off his disability, and live all alone and do his own thing and make his own rules.

What would happen to him? Who would want him? Where was there left for him to go? Not like he needed anything. He could do fine by himself. He didn't need help. He didn't need Derek. Much.

15. "Lose My Soul"

"I dunno, man."

Tokyo took another pull at the soda Derek had bought in the vending machine. Derek resisted the urge to pull his arms in and stayed leaning his elbows on his knees.

"Just talk. Don't stress it."

"We were selling ice down Lincoln," Tokyo finally went on, shrugging and staring at his tapping foot. "Lotta steady customers down that way. Still are, but not for me."

Derek nodded silently and waited. The gangster drained the pop can and set it on the floor by his chair.

"My buddies brought it in for us from our cookers. We bagged it up for buyers down there." His eyes slid up to meet Derek's. "You know the drill, huh?"

"Sure," Derek shrugged. "Go on. Lincoln Street. I thought…"

"Yeah. Our turf ends at the river." The convict stretched and rolled up his sleeves, revealing the bleeding, black heart tattooed to his forearm. It wasn't the ugliest design Derek had ever seen, but it still meant gang initiation rites, a life of crime, comradeship with murderers and drug peddlers. Definitely not worth the detriment to his appearance.

"We was branching out," Tokyo continued, glancing over his shoulder. A bald man with black and green bangles tattooed all up his arm was gently bouncing a toddler on his lap. A woman with raccoon mascara sat across from him, smiling.

"You're okay," Derek said. "Go on. Branching out."

"Lincoln is Assassin Squad territory," Tokyo muttered. "But we figured they didn't know who we were or where we was working from."

"What'd you tell the buyers?"

"That we'd sell to them for less." The inmate put his heel on the pop can and collapsed it with a sudden crunch. "I dunno how the Squad do it. We were majorly slashing our prices, and barely getting under them. Lester was getting antsy."

"Lester…"

The convict's eyes narrowed, but he smiled. "My boss."

"Okay." Derek shrugged. "Getting antsy. You weren't making money?"

Tokyo shook his head. "Nah…not really. A market is a market, and we were squeezing the Assassin Squad, but I'm not sure it was worth it."

Derek nodded again.

Tokyo glanced over his shoulder, and kicked at the flattened can. "I told Lester we were doin' our best. We'd gotten some users to switch, but some Assassin Squad were getting interested, too. Bad interested. They were coming to the end of the day with unsold product."

"Naturally, they were ticked off. What'd they do?"

"One of 'em came and talked to us," Tokyo frowned and looked up at Derek. "Marco Jung. He told me 'n Hack to clear out of their market or else."

Derek nodded. "Or else what?"

"Didn't say." Tokyo felt his shirt pocket and glanced at Derek. "They didn't let you bring in smokes, huh?"

"No. Sorry. Against the rules."

The inmate said something under his breath and heaved a sigh.

Derek stood up carefully. "I've got enough change for another Coke. Diet or regular?"

"Diet."

Tokyo followed him over to the vending machine and watched him push the buttons. The machine rumbled for a moment, and the can landed in the slot below with a clunk. Derek pulled it out and offered it to the inmate, who took it and popped the top open.

When they had sat down again, the former drug dealer took a deep breath. "It wasn't more than a week after that that the feds came down on our apartment, where we done our bagging and selling. Somebody musta sold us out...they knew enough to wait for Emo to come in for a load." He shook his head and gulped the soda. "Surrounded the block and knocked down the door. I'd only flushed half of the ice by the time they got through to the bathroom." He sighed and shivered. "Yeah...somebody squealed to them. I dunno. Couldn't a been one of our guys...that'd be dumb."

"That *is* suspicious," murmured Derek, watching a new inmate enter the visiting area with the tail of his eye. "Remember anything specific that Marco Jung told you?"

Tokyo shrugged and frowned. " 'Don't know what you're messing with.' 'Get out while you can.' 'We own this town, so stay out of our market.' I dunno. 'You'll be sorry by tomorrow.' "

Derek's eyes narrowed. "That's pretty specific. Think the Assassin Squad could've sold you guys out?"

The convict was quiet for a moment. After another swallow of Diet Coke, he answered. "Maybe. I dunno. Sounds weird."

"I'd sure like to know where the Assassin Squad get their raw materials."

"Me, too."

Derek gave a laugh. "So, you haven't any idea? I mean, surely it's pretty similar to where you guys get yours."

Tokyo raised his hands. "They move so much product they've gotta have a good system. That many drugstore buys has gotta attract some attention."

Derek nodded slowly. "Know anybody who might know?"

"Find Marco Jung. He roughed up Hack some; pay him back."

"If I can find him. Think he works on Lincoln?"

"Maybe now that we left." Tokyo drained the can and set it on the floor. "The fuzz grabbed all our product, but the Squad got their own." Crunch! The aluminum can bent under Tokyo's foot. "You can nail the Squad. Do that."

"If I possibly can." Derek threw a quick glance around the visiting room. "Are there any in this place, do you know?"

"Not that I heard," the inmate kicked at the two squashed cans, sending one sliding into the other. "Not that anybody's heard. One of my buddies," he glanced over his shoulder again, "Said a Squadster was in jail, got nabbed stealing a car. My buddy said the guy walked. Technicality or some crap like that."

"That I want to look into," Derek commented, scratching his head. "Got that guy's name?"

"He said he went by Beehive. Guess that won't be much good to the fuzz."

"I'll work with it. Thanks."

Derek drew a deep breath. "Can you talk about a guy called Shiv?"

Tokyo's eyes narrowed. "Don't get in his way. He was here for a bit – tough guy. Made sure the other crews didn't mess with us."

Derek had already found out Shiv's arrest and sentencing dates – and that he'd gotten parole a matter of weeks before Brian died. "Do you know much about him personally?" he probed, trying to sound casual.

Tokyo glared again. "Don't get in his way. That guy don't forget stuff. The DEA got him, just like they got me an' my buddies. All he could talk about 'til he got out was how he was gonna make those feds pay."

A chill ran down Derek's back. Brian had given evidence at Shiv's trial. Was this the strand he'd been hunting for? Brian had been up to his elbows in research on the Assassin Squad – but that didn't mean they had killed him. If Brian had known who was going to kill him, he presumably wouldn't be dead now.

"Well, thanks." Derek rose to his feet, grabbing the smashed cans and tossing them toward a near-by garbage can. Tokyo tracked his movements and stood, also.

"One more thing," Derek said. "Do you know Brian Lane?"

Tokyo frowned. "DEA. Asked the same kind of questions you ask. Said he'd nab the Assassin Squad. You gonna do that, too?"

Derek sighed and shrugged. "If I can. They sound a little above my pay grade — I don't know."

Tokyo wrinkled his nose and nodded slowly. "You do it, huh? Stop them. They wanna own the whole county, not just their side of town."

"I'll sure try. Thanks for the help."

Take over the county? What were the Assassin Squad, anyway? A rural gang with big-city aspirations? Or a city gang looking to expand into interstate traffic? Even if they weren't the ones responsible for Brian, they sure sounded like bad news. And what kind of gang sicced the DEA on its rivals, anyway?

16. "Curses"

Derek shoved the door closed behind him and hurried into the bedroom, calling, "Hi, Robbie."

As he stripped off his uniform shirt and grabbed another one out of the drawer, he realized something was missing. He hadn't heard Robbie's answer.

Stepping out into the kitchen, he glanced into the living room. Sure enough, Robbie was sitting at the computer.

"Hi, Robbie," Derek repeated, opening the fridge and pulling out a Coke.

"Hi."

"What do you want for supper?"

"I dunno."

"Well, you'd better make up your mind." Derek glanced at the clock. "There's a prayer meeting tonight at six-forty-five."

"Aw, man," Robbie exclaimed, leaning his head on his hand. "It's like you never get a night to yourself. You don't have to do everything, you know."

"I know. But there's only so much I can do about that," Derek gestured with the pop can and walked into the living room. "I know I've been really busy lately. I'm sorry about that, but the jail only allows visitors at certain times. Besides" – he sat on the coffee table facing Robbie – "I'm really enjoying this church. They…I don't know. They enjoy being together. I haven't gotten into the Bible this way since…well, probably since Pastor Raul left."

Robbie was leaning on his elbow, staring at the keyboard and avoiding Derek's eyes. Several moments stretched on in silence. Derek couldn't remember Robbie acting like this before… What was wrong with him? Had his back been acting up again?

Derek heaved a deep breath. "Did you do that math test today?"

"Yeah."

"What did you have for lunch?"

"I didn't."

"What do you mean, you didn't?" Derek stood up, watching Robbie's face.

His brother shrugged. "I wasn't hungry."

"Well, I'll make you some supper." Derek returned to the kitchen. "You in pain, or something?"

"No."

"You want any meds?"

"No."

Derek gave an exasperated grunt and closed the fridge. "Okay, fine."

What had gotten into Rob recently? Derek glanced at his brother again, and slipped into the bathroom. The pill box seemed to be on schedule: one more dose left for today, and three pills for every day the rest of the week, just like normal. He felt guilty for checking, but he unscrewed the cap on the bottle and peeked inside. He'd have to keep an eye on this…even though the bottle didn't list "grouchiness" as one of the side effects. Robbie was young, and still developing — maybe that was what was messing with him.

Derek returned to the main room. Robbie was still reading whatever it was on the screen.

There had to be a way to fix this; he considered a moment.

"I know," he announced. "We can make cheesy brats. We've got some of those. Okay?"

"Okay."

Cheese brats were what Robbie had always asked for as his birthday supper. They couldn't use the grill in February, but Mom always put them in the oven, which was the next best thing.

Derek flicked on the oven and pulled the package out of the freezer. As he dropped a number onto a cookie sheet, he glanced back at his brother.

"Look, I think you need to get out of this place. Why don't you come, too? It's no hassle to get into the church."

Robbie shrugged again, still not making eye contact.

"Hey, I think it'd do you good. Come on. We could...I don't know...go for ice cream afterwards or something."

Derek turned and slipped the pan into the oven. When he turned back, Robbie had rolled his chair to face the coffee table. He was rubbing his neck, his lips pressing together.

Derek smiled and leaned on the peninsula. "It's just an hour or so. And you know the people at First Baptist won't treat you weird or anything like that. As a matter of fact, Cindy asked about you the other day."

Robbie crossed his arms and turned his head to stare at the computer screen. "No thanks," he mumbled.

"Oh, come on!" Derek exclaimed, pulling the ketchup and mustard out of the fridge. "You really need to get out and about more. I'm sorry I've left you on your own so much, but–"

"No. No thanks," Robbie answered more loudly. "I'd rather stay here. I'm fine."

Derek sighed and sat down at the coffee table. "Okay, *fine*. I'll...I'll call Cindy. I'll stay with you. Happy? I'd better let her know...I just hope she isn't offended."

He grabbed the phone, watching Robbie. Cindy would understand...right?

After a pause, Derek drew a breath. "I just hope you snap out of whatever phase you're going through right now. You've got to admit you aren't being very good company right now."

He tried to laugh, but he saw Robbie's face twist up and his arms hug tighter against his body. Derek bit his lip.

What was the matter with him anyway? That's what happened when his "father" wasn't much older than he was. Derek bowed his head. Where was Dad when they both needed him so much?

* * * *

Cindy popped another Reece's into her mouth. Thursdays, her day off during the week, were for getting everything done that she didn't do on the weekends. Dentist appointments, appliance installation, less-crowded grocery shopping, house cleaning. Trouble was, there was nothing left to do. The laundry was done, the dishes were done, she did *not* want to vacuum or clean the bathrooms again. She didn't even go in any of the bathrooms except her own, except to clean. And when she cleaned, she didn't need to do anything but dust.

Her mom reveled in the mess and bustle of family holidays at home, when all the kids and spouses, and Mel's baby girl, crowded into the old homestead. She knew what she meant now. Brian's socks were in a black plastic garbage bag by the garage door. Some day, they'd make their way to the Goodwill with the rest of his clothes, but she hadn't had the heart to do it yet. Not yet. She'd never thought she would miss tripping over those irritating things in the kitchen, laundry room, on the stairs, everywhere. Now, socks were never anywhere they weren't supposed to be.

She forced herself off the couch and walked into the kitchen. She pulled a cookbook out of the cupboard and flipped through it absently. It was too early to bake cookies for the missions meeting…that would be next week, at the earliest.

She wouldn't mind being an old-maid-missionary-lady. Not if that's what God wanted for her. She knew plenty of people who'd been used that way. And God knew best. Just…she'd dreamed of something so different for herself. Brian would have been a great father, when the time came. She shook herself and pulled out the flour and sugar. She'd do dinner rolls…Derek's little brother always enjoyed it when she made rolls, or so Derek said.

The phone rang. It wouldn't be Derek; he was at work right now. She picked up the handset. "Hello?"

"Mrs. Lane? This is Director Stillman. You might not remember me…your husband worked for me in the DEA."

"Oh, yes, I remember you. We talked about Brian after his death."

"Exactly, ma'am, exactly. I'm so sorry to intrude on you."

"Not at all. Has anything come up?"

"I'm afraid there are no fresh developments, seeing as the police *have* resolved the case – but I thought I should check and see how you were coping. After all, as Agent Lane's supervisor, I feel at least partly, if not primarily, responsible for this tragedy."

"That's very kind of you," Cindy answered, leaning against the kitchen table. "But someday I'll find out who killed him. And I'm sure you couldn't have helped Brian. He didn't even tell *me* what he was up to before his death."

"I can sympathize with your shock," Mr. Stillman said. "I hope you won't take this the wrong way, but I don't mind admitting to you that my late brother had a drug problem. Some of his college friends introduced him to hashish, then meth."

"That's terrible."

"I know you'll understand how embarrassing this is to someone, especially a leader, in my organization, and that it won't go farther. But now you see how intimately I understand how you must feel about something so disreputable happening in your own family."

"I'm sure you were devastated when you learned about that," Cindy told him, pulling a mixing bowl out of the cupboard with one hand. "But, with all due respect, Brian didn't do this to himself – he was killed. Now that the police have reopened the case, I'm even more confident we'll find out what happened. I do really appreciate your interest in Brian, and your excellent recommendation of a private investigator for me."

"I'm glad he's working out for you. The last I heard, the police had closed the case — did you convince them to reopen it?"

"Yes; when I realized that using a needle was a silly thing for Brian to do – he hated needles, and avoided the doctor to keep away from them – Derek took that and a couple other things to the police, and they were convinced Brian's death needed further looking into."

"I hadn't heard that! It's good news for you – though, aren't you afraid it's just a postponement of the inevitable?"

Cindy heaved the sugar container onto the table. "Mr. Stillman, I know my husband would never kill himself. Whether we ever prove that to the authorities or not, I just want to find out who killed him and why."

"I understand your concern, and apparently the police think you've uncovered some valid evidence. If I may ask, do you have any direction you're pursuing in regards to who may have killed him?"

"Well, Mr. Hayes has been talking with several gang members who might have known Brian or known what he was working on. He seems to think Brian's death is tied to gang activity, since that's what Brian was working on when he died."

"Aha – trying to get inside his head, and see what he might have been thinking. What gang are you looking into?"

"Um…Blackhearts is the one I remember," Cindy answered. "Brian kept notes on his personal computer — I expect that if any of this turns out to be important, D– Mr. Hayes will let the police know about it."

"You say you have access to your husband's computer files?"

"Only the ones we had passwords to," Cindy explained, pausing as she lifted down the baking soda. "I know this must sound strange, but Brian had his email locked with a long, complicated password different from his other passwords."

"Did he really?" Mr. Stillman gave a chuckle. "Clearly he had something nefarious in his email."

"I doubt it," Cindy laughed back. "It's probably not important at all, since if he didn't even tell me about what he was doing, who would he email about it? It does feel convoluted, though."

"That's the word for it, Mrs. Lane," Director Stillman answered. "And it does make it more difficult to discover what was in your husband's mind if he didn't tell anyone about it."

"Well, I'm trusting Mr. Hayes to ferret out whatever information we need. He's done a great job so far."

"I'm delighted to hear it, and to hear you're in such good spirits."

"Well, I'm very grateful to my church family; they've been a great support."

"I'm sure," Mr. Stillman answered. "My wife and I belong to the River Valley Lutheran Church, as a matter of fact."

"How nice. Well, thank you for taking the time to check up on this case. I'm sure that, with your influence, you could do something to get my husband's memory cleared."

"I assure you, we're doing our best."

A few more pleasantries passed before Cindy hung up and popped off the lid of the flour.

It was flattering that the director wanted to check on her... but at the same time, he didn't seem convinced Brian was completely innocent.

Maybe that would take time. After all, the police had only taken the case more seriously once Derek uncovered Brian's severe fear of needles (and the chloroform burns on his face, among other things). Perhaps the director needed more evidence before he would commit himself.

She jerked flour into the bowl, spilling extra across the kitchen table. At least Derek knew what he was doing — and cared. Derek had believed *her*...not just the evidence, but her. When feeling very small and helpless and alone, it was nice to be believed. To be taken seriously.

Even if Derek did have a weird light in his eyes when he looked at her; like Brian's eyes, after two years of sitting next to each other in her father's adult Sunday school class. Before Brian asked her (and her dad) if she'd like to attend a day-conference for Christian young adults with him.

17. "Just Between You and Me"

Steaming hot French toast. Powdered sugar. Blueberries. Life didn't get much better.

Robbie put his fork in his mouth again and watched Derek skim down the line of six or seven syrups to find the maple flavored one. Derek didn't experiment with the syrup. When Dad used to take them out, he and Rob sometimes mixed the different syrups together, just to see how it tasted.

Mom used to make French toast and pancakes. It'd been so long, though. Derek didn't know how to make them from scratch, and they just weren't the same frozen. Besides, the blueberry syrup made the French toast better than Mom's.

"So did you make it past that temple thing after the dropship?" Derek asked, picking up his glass.

Rob nodded and swallowed his bite. "I got to the gravity lift under the *Truth and Reconciliation*, but by the time I killed everything before the hunters spawn, my health was so low I kept dying. Plus I only had one Marine left, so he wasn't a big help. I'll probably have to go back a couple save points and try to use less ammo."

"Well, I know when I tried it on Legendary, I didn't get past that first room in the *Truth and Reconciliation*. You know where the two hunters come out, and the cloaked elites?"

Rob laughed. "Yeah, I remember you playing that part."

Derek laughed, too, spearing a sausage. "Well, I'm sure you'll do a better job. Especially since you're such a pro with the sniper rifle."

Robbie grinned and looked down to stir his hash browns. "I dunno. If I get too frustrated I'll switch back to Medium for a bit."

"Good plan."

Derek swallowed the bite of sausage and began cutting his pancake. As he did so, he glanced back up at his brother, humor still sparkling in his eye. Robbie felt a warmness creep over his chest, and slipped in another succulent bite of French toast. There were good things to this case. They hadn't been able to go out like this in a long while. Really, since that time a year ago, after Derek finished serving some papers for Mr. Hudson. Derek couldn't spend as much time with him since he was out working all the time, but at least they could go out and do things together again. He closed his eyes for a moment to drink in the sweetness of the berry syrup, the warmth of the breading, the fact of Derek's being there.

"Hey, by the way," he murmured, dropping his eyes again. "You've been talking to a lot of – gangster people lately."

"Basically."

"What if – one of them won't talk to you?"

"That'd be too bad."

"I mean, didn't like you."

"You mean…"

Robbie swallowed. "You know — wanted to hurt you."

Derek took a long drink and set down his glass. "Well… that's sort of the life I've chosen. That's the training and preparing I've done for my career. That's what I signed up for when I became a cop."

Rob shifted in his seat. "I mean…"

"They train you for this in police academy, you know?" Derek answered. "I know enough about gangsters to not do anything stupid."

Robbie dropped his eyes.

"And if anything were to happen to me, you'd be okay. There *is* Dad's aunt and uncle –"

"I don't remember seeing them since the funeral. They live in Washington, don't they? Why would I want to go to Washington?"

"I don't want you to go Washington; I want you to stay right here." Derek made a tired sort of smile, and dropped a sausage onto Robbie's plate. "With me."

Robbie rubbed his face. Maybe he shouldn't have brought it up. Grandma Hayes was in a care facility in Wisconsin, but they hadn't seen her or the other relatives since Dad and Mom died. He didn't want to live with anyone else.

"Don't worry about it," Derek said a little louder. "You're a couple years from being an adult. The chances of something bad happening are a million to one. Besides, Mr. Hank is my power of attorney, in the event I have a stroke or something. You wouldn't mind staying with them, right?"

Living with Hank and Helen might not be too bad, but…

"They'll be your guardians for a couple years, then you'll take possession of whatever I can leave you. You'll do okay. You might not have a college fund –" Derek smiled "– but you'd do okay."

Rob nodded, pursing his lips. It wasn't like he had a college fund now, anyway. "Okay. Good." He still didn't want anything to happen to Derek, but talking about it more would just stress them both. "Just be careful, huh?"

Derek nodded. "Right."

Robbie fell silent while Derek's gaze wandered for a moment, as they both collected their thoughts.

Derek's face lit up and he rose to his feet.

"Derek!"

Robbie's stomach contracted and he lowered his head as Mrs. Lane stepped to their table and nodded at Derek's greeting.

"Fancy meeting you here," she exclaimed, glancing over and smiling at Robbie. "Small world, isn't it?"

Very small. Teeny.

"Robbie and I thought we'd get out of the house for a bit," Derek explained, gesturing.

Robbie. Rob-bie, as in diminutive form.

"So what brings you here?"

Cindy turned and indicated a booth under the windows. "Our ladies' small group is having a day out. Have you met them yet? That's JoAnn, in the green, and Mary-ann."

Derek smiled and waved. "JoAnn and Mary-ann. Got it. Don't tell me they're cousins."

"No, but a lot of people do get them mixed up. That is, get their names mixed up."

Derek grinned. "I'll do my best."

Robbie crossed his arms and stared at his plate. *Mr. When-I-first-met-you-you-had-a-band-aid-on-your-nose-and-I'm-glad-to-see-it's-healed-up-in-six-months would "do his best." Nice. Humble.*

Cindy leaned against the back of an un-used chair. "So…" she sighed, dropping her voice. "Not to bother you on your free time, but has anything come up?"

Derek smiled again, laying his hand on the chair she was touching. "We've actually had some good success. I've talked with someone called McCoy, who is part of the Assassin Squad gang. Sound familiar?"

She frowned. "McCoy rings some kind of bell. How did you talk to him?"

"Your pancakes are getting cold," Robbie put in without looking up.

"He's in the county jail," Derek answered, leaning towards Cindy. "Drug possession, trafficking, etc. I believe he was arrested by Brian just before Brian died."

"Don't mind me," Robbie muttered, pushing his plate away.

"You know, maybe that is where I heard the name McCoy," Mrs. Lane replied, shifting her weight to her other hip. "Brian got a call…that might be the call he got during dinner, one day, and he raced out into the garage almost before I realized his phone was ringing. He didn't want me to hear." She smiled and shrugged. "But he came back out and dialed someone else, and he said something about McCoy."

"That sounds good," Derek continued, scratching his head and raising his other hand to gesture. "Brian had some notes on him in his files. But here's what's really interesting."

"Hang on to your hats," hissed Rob, rolling his eyes.

"McCoy's convinced he's going to walk. Even though Brian and his team caught them red-handed in possession of the goods. I spoke briefly with his lawyer, and they're going to try to say Brian missed a step in obtaining the warrant, so it wasn't a lawful arrest."

"That's ridiculous."

Derek narrowed his eyes and nodded. "What's really ridiculous is this is the same defense lawyer who got off Beehive after he stole a car. Beehive and McCoy are both Assassin Squad."

Cindy shivered. "I'm starting to not like this. Did Brian ever meet this lawyer?"

"I'm still trying to track that down. I think they were both involved in Shiv's case, though. He's Blackhearts."

Cindy shook her head. "I'm so confused."

"I don't blame you." Derek glanced down at his plate for a moment.

"Your sausages are cold," Robbie mumbled.

Cindy glanced at the teen. "How are you taking all this, Robbie?" she asked.

Rob shrugged, and glared at the table. Why did she have to use the kid term for him? He was just a couple years from being an adult. And why should he care about what gangsters were doing what? It's not like it was his case.

Derek drew a breath. "McCoy told me one other weird thing," he went on. "Apparently there used to be an officer of the Assassin Squad named Jimmy Cann. Used to be, because he was killed in a firefight with the DEA. Prior to that, he'd been one of the highest ranking Squadsters, overseeing a lot of their territory and taking orders directly from their chief." Derek leaned forward as he dropped his voice. "From what I gather, he'd started putting together an elite bodyguard around himself, forcing people to swear allegiance to him, not necessarily his boss – even dissing some of his boss's orders."

"You mean maybe he got too big for his shoes, and his boss – sold him out to the DEA?"

"Or sicced the DEA on him — like they did to Tokyo and his Blackhearts."

Cindy frowned and shook her head. "How does that even work?"

"Beats me," Derek answered, shrugging.

"Wow…something the great detective doesn't know," Rob said under his breath.

"So – McCoy's counting on getting out of jail…"

"'Cause he's a Squadster, and they is da powerful."

"Right." She chuckled. "But then, why would he tell you anything? I mean, why would he even talk to you?"

Derek smiled and dropped his eyes, shifting his weight. "I do have an old buddy in the police force. And there are techniques for…I dunno, working someone up. You know how it goes… Emotional people are the easiest, because you just, you know, get them to feel like talking to you, and then they do."

"Mr. Hank put it stronger," Rob mumbled.

"Good for you," Cindy exclaimed. "I'm glad you're so good at this."

"Well…"

"No, really. I wouldn't know where to start."

"Hey…" Derek shrugged. "Not everyone has to be an expert at everything."

Mr. Humility.

"Well, I really appreciate it." Cindy glanced at the door and waved. "Uh oh, there's Stephanie. I'd better get back. Nice to run into you."

"You too."

"Thank you for talking."

"Enjoy your lunch." Derek grinned and shook her hand.

Cindy flashed a smile at Robbie and scrunched her eyes up, but he dropped his gaze. "See you Sunday, Robbie," she said with a wave, as she turned to join the three other women.

Derek sat back down and stabbed at his pancake, staring after her with a soft smile on his face. He stirred the bite around in the syrup, around and around, before he finally took his eyes off the lady and slipped it into his mouth.

Robbie pushed a blueberry back and forth on his plate. The sweetness in his mouth had fermented somehow, and his guts felt queasy inside him. Derek hadn't paid any attention to him, not even to get him in trouble for interrupting. Derek ought to have told him not to interrupt, or not to be snarky, or something. But he hadn't even heard. Robbie could have choked to death right there in front of him.

"You feel okay?" asked Derek suddenly, glancing over at him again.

Robbie swallowed hard and nodded. "Fine." The last thing he needed was more talk about his back, or his leg spasms, or something dumb like that.

"Okay. Well, where were we?" He chewed for a moment and continued. "I was going to say something, but I forgot."

You forgot. That's a laugh. Forget Cindy. Or you'll forget me.

18."Gumboots"

A light wind was blowing. Leaves rustled. Birds called to each other, riding the air currents past them. It was perfect.

Today was Tuesday. One of Derek's days off. So he'd waited until Cindy got off work, and they'd walked along the bike path out to the park behind the hospital. The little river that ran through town wound beside the path, and standing on a cement overlook, they could watch sticks and leaves float past. Trees had begun to change, and the opposite bank was tinged with color.

He knew Robbie was staring sullenly at a Physics book back home, but somehow he couldn't really think about anything else right now. Maybe it was selfish, but he could read the literature book with Robbie anytime. He and Cindy only had certain times they could both connect, and she needed him. She'd asked him to join her. He should be here.

Cindy stared out over the water, the liquid grey of her eyes almost seeming to reflect it. The breeze shifted loose strands of her hair around her neck and ears. Normally, her dark hair was just a fine accent to her fair complexion. Lit by the golden sunlight, it looked like streaming trickles of molten chocolate…except more poetic.

Derek squeezed his eyes shut and consciously loosened his grip on the metal rail. It was a good thing Brian was dead. If he hadn't been, he'd be throttling Derek right about now. Of course, Derek hadn't met Cindy until Brian was dead. So agonizing over these existential paradoxes wasn't helping anything. He was here to help *her*, not the other way around.

"Sorry…I was just thinking." She stirred and glanced his way. "Were you saying something?"

"Not really. I was thinking, too."

She gave him one of her softer, smaller smiles. "What're you thinking?"

He couldn't tell her. Derek bit his lip, feeling like when Mom asked him why he was looking at those magazines in the grocery check-out. He'd stood there with his mouth open while she waited patiently for him to come up with the answer she already knew. It'd been a good conversation in the car on the way home.

"Stuff," he evaded, rubbing his foot against his calf to fight the guilty feelings. "How about you?"

"Oh...stuff," she laughed back, and faced the river again.

What was she thinking? Same thing as him...No way. Girls didn't think like that.

"I was thinking...you know, Brian and I used to walk along a river like this. Before we were married." She glanced at him again. A lock of hair flipped into her face, and she swiped it away. "We weren't really dating, we were courting, so we went out to a public place to talk about theology, our life goals, what we each looked for in a spouse." She smiled as she stared unseeingly into the distance.

So the subject he'd been fighting had been laid in his lap. Maybe reminiscing about some good old times would cheer her up.

"So what were you looking for?" Derek asked. Character research for Brian.

"Faithfulness. Integrity. Someone who loved God more than he loved me." She looked up and smiled again, but her eyes had a droopiness about them. "I knew that if Brian ever stopped loving me, he would still love God, and so he wouldn't treat me any different. And he was always honest with me." She sighed and closed her eyes. "He wouldn't lie to me. I know he had secrets from me...I've told you about that. But...he..."

"I...I'm sorry. I see."

"He never lied about it to me. If he couldn't tell me, he told me that he couldn't..."

She put her hands up on her face and leaned against the railing. Derek reached out and laid his hand on her shoulder. No one should have to suffer like this. Especially Cindy. If only he could bring Brian back somehow...he was ready to do it. He stared out at the water, his fingers and stomach tingling. Something thick was trying to well up in his throat. Whoever had done this, he would find them and drag them to jail, with his bare hands if necessary.

"I...I'm sorry," Cindy gasped, as her shoulders shook. "It all came over me." Her voice rose in pitch as her sentence ended, and she turned away.

Derek stretched his arm across her back as her shaking slowly subsided. He couldn't take this...Why did she have to hurt so much? What could Brian have done for a murderer to take him away from Cindy? Someone had to pay for this. If only there was something he could *do*.

"I'm sorry." She swallowed and rubbed her face. "I don't know what came over me."

"It's okay."

"No...I'm sorry. I don't know what's wrong with me. Sometimes, you know...it just hits you out of the blue." She pulled a tissue out of her pocket and sniffed. "I think I'm past the shock of it all, and then...oh, I miss him so much sometimes."

"No...it's okay. You're not... I mean, a lot of people wouldn't be able to take it like this." Derek withdrew his arm, so he was just supporting her shoulder. Like any friend might do. Totally non-invasive. "Well...Look, you're doing it right now. You're pulling yourself together and straightening your back...You're amazing. You...You are so strong. You're one of the strongest people I know."

She gazed out at the water and drew a shaky breath. "Thank you."

"I mean it. You're fantastic. I... When my parents died, I think I was just numb. It's clear you're not numb, you're just in control...it's really...impressive. Inspiring."

She cleared her throat and gave a little laugh. Derek realized what he was saying. If only his mouth would slow down a little, maybe he wouldn't say such tacky things. *You're inspiring.* She could get better than that from a Hallmark card.

"It's weird, you know," Cindy murmured, wiping her eyes. "You go on from day to day, getting back into your routine... You start to forget about the pain, and then all of a sudden, it hits you like it just happened."

"I know what you mean," Derek breathed. "I know. Sometimes I'm driving down the road and I just *know* there's a car coming at me from my right blind spot. Even thought there isn't. And I've checked already, but I still feel it's there."

"A car accident has to be worse than what I'm going through," she gasped, trying to give a chuckle. "I mean, after all, at least we're assuming there's a rhyme and reason to Brian's death. Somebody had some kind of motive, even if it was just evil. But a car accident...that's like a natural disaster. There's no point or explanation...no reason."

"Except in the mind of God," Derek muttered.

She looked up and smiled into his face. Her liquid eyes stared straight into his, and he felt his insides melting into puddles inside him. God had made this part of him, too...even if he couldn't imagine why.

"That's exactly what I keep remembering," Cindy answered, reaching up to touch his hand that still rested on her shoulder. "It's not like Job had his trials explained, until the end. And all of the apostles faced torture and death for the sake of Jesus."

"Why should we think we're any better than they are?" Derek exclaimed, realizing the depth of his argument. "And we're not even suffering as martyrs. It's just sort-of average, fallen-earth suffering."

"You're right." She shrugged, letting his hand fall off. He pulled it back slowly, and watched her turn back to the water. "It helps to get things in perspective. Day by day," she sighed.

"What, like from dc Talk?" Derek smiled.

She laughed. "That's the one Brian usually sang when I said that. But I always think of the version my grandma taught me." She drew a breath and let the waterfront echo with her voice.

"Day by day, and with each passing moment, strength I find to meet my trials here."

"Trusting in my Father's wise bestowment…"

"I've no cause for worry or for fear."

They were just finishing up the second verse when Derek's cell phone buzzed. He snatched it out, and suppressed a grimace. Robbie had sent an email to his phone: "Are you dead or what?" *Very sarcastic, kid.*

"Well…I guess it's time to get on with life," Cindy sighed. "Is it anything important?"

"Not exactly," Derek muttered. For some reason, he didn't feel like telling Cindy about Robbie's recent grouchiness. Maybe he didn't want her thinking it ran in the family. Maybe he didn't want to think about how Rob was going to be a major part of his life for the foreseeable future, possibly for good…and anyone he married would have to deal with that.

"Well…thanks for taking time out of your day for me."

"I hope it helped," Derek answered, semi-consciously forming a smile in answer to hers. He had no right to impose his own messy life onto hers, especially as she had so much of her own trauma to deal with.

As they turned away from the rail, he reached out and touched her arm, as though almost by accident.

"Thank you, Derek. I do appreciate you just listening to me and letting me vent all over you."

"No problem."

"I'm not sure how my chatter today helped the case." She looked up again, her eyes twinkling.

"Regardless of that, it's worth it to spend time with you."

She studied his face for a moment, as though trying to gauge how much of what he said was sincere. It had been a little bold, but still…if she didn't take him seriously, his case and his career were in serious trouble, not just his emotions and self-esteem.

"Thanks."

They shook hands. After knowing each other so long, they might have been able to hug…just as good-bye. But he'd been too forward with her already. After all, she was just his client. And a fellow church attender, but what did that matter? He couldn't risk it…her…the feelings again. If he offended her now…

"I'll be in touch," he managed to say, though his throat was very dry.

"I'll look forward to your call."

Derek followed her with his eyes as she walked out into the parking lot toward her car. Just to make sure she was safe. He heaved a sigh. Yes, he was in trouble. Did she realize what he was thinking? If so, she'd been very gracious about it. He began strolling toward his own car, weighing his keys in his hand. If only there was someone he could talk to about it. Dad and Pastor Raul were both gone. Robbie couldn't sympathize…he'd never been there himself. If only…

19. "What Have We Become?"

Derek smelled his hot chocolate and eyed the man across the table from him.

"Well…thanks for calling me."

"Huh. Thanks for coming out."

Matt Crawford eyed his coffee mug. "Look, I think you might've gotten some wrong ideas last time we met. I wasn't trying to dis Brian like that – but when you bury a teammate, and the police close the case, and then some guy tries to come along and sort of un-bury him, it unsettles you."

Derek decided if they were going to get anywhere quickly he should try the direct method. "You two didn't get along, did you?"

"I'm not saying that!" Crawford shoved his cup to one side and leaned back in his chair, heaving a sigh. "Okay, so I didn't always say what I meant about him. He pulled his weight and he didn't talk behind people's backs."

"Unlike others."

Derek let Crawford take in his meaningful stare.

"Look, I don't know who you've been talking to," Crawford began again. "But it wasn't like that. I mean, I'd never try to hurt the guy. So what, he was the kind the higher-ups like to point out and brag on, but that wasn't his fault. Not really."

Taking a sip of hot chocolate, Derek raised an eyebrow. That's not the way it had sounded from Agent Becky Foster.

"Now, what's that look for?"

"Why'd you request a new partner?"

"'Cause he was getting on my nerves." Crawford swallowed hard and took a drink of coffee. Drawing a deep breath, he went on, "You wouldn't believe what he was like those last few months, with the Assassin Squad. It's like they consumed his life. I mean,

I'd seen him work hard before. That's why he got all those gold stars for the Blackhearts operation. But this was seriously a step beyond. A couple times, he called me and some other teammates up and we went to bust a joint just on his say-so. I mean, he'd gotten a warrant who knows where, but there weren't any orders or back-up teams involved – just us. That was freaky."

Crawford shook his head again and swallowed more coffee. Derek leaned back, ready to wait for the story.

"But I wouldn't hurt the guy. He was an okay guy. Well, Becky– I mean..."

He slid his glance to Derek. Derek tried not to give anything away.

"Okay, so my girlfriend's a teammate of ours. And she's been on my case about Brian ever since your last meeting with me – she said I shouldn't be so sour about it, and he deserved a better send-off — even if he did off himself."

Derek nodded for the agent to go on.

Crawford shook his head, frowning. "And that part's got me kind of shaken up. I know what I said last time – but I just couldn't believe it when they told us what'd happened. So, Brian was a little uptight – he wasn't the kind to do that. I mean, he wouldn't even go out with us after a shift if his wife was expecting him. You think a guy like that's going to leave without leaving something for her to know?"

No suicide note. What a good point. Derek nodded again. "I see what you mean. But the police had made up their minds."

"Right. And if he didn't do it himself..." Crawford shifted in his seat and ran a hand through his hair. "I mean...I said some pretty hard things, when he wasn't there to hear them. It wasn't just Becky who noticed, either. If Brian didn't ice himself – someone else did. But I'd never – so I said some things, but that doesn't mean I meant them. We didn't always see eye-to-eye, but I'm not the type to take things into my own hands like that."

Derek scratched his head. "Where were you, the night Brian died?"

Crawford half-rose, glanced into his coffee cup, and settled back down again. "I was supposed to go out with Becky, but she called to say she was sick. So I sat at home to watch the game. Didn't even order a pizza – just sat and ate chips."

"If you'd killed Brian, you'd have a better alibi than that."

"Yeah, that's what they say on TV, but I don't know…"

"Did you kill Brian?"

"No!" Crawford half-rose again.

"Good." Derek drained his cocoa cup and set it down.

Crawford rubbed his face and swallowed hard. "But then, who did?"

Derek scratched his head for a moment. Who indeed? The Crawford theory had seemed a little thin, but the Shiv theory would be even harder to prove, or disprove.

"How'd it start?" Derek sat up and leaned forward. "Why'd Brian take up this 'personal project'? What was bugging him?"

"Well, about, uh, a year ago maybe, we were working a sting with the Assassin Squad. Well, we'd set them up with about 40 gallons of PSE, which is usually the choke-point of production."

Derek nodded.

"The plan was to wait until they'd converted the stuff into meth, and then bust their producers, their distributors, their bosses, everybody. Their buyers. All of 'em."

The agent shifted in his chair and scratched his head. "But…I guess they caught wind of it or something. Don't tell anyone about this, but…when we went in to nab them, they'd cleared out: lock, stock, and barrel. I don't think anybody talked, so unless they figured out who I or Brian was…you know, saw through our disguise and realized we were feds?"

He shrugged, and Derek nodded encouragingly. The chimes above the door sounded as an older couple made their way into the coffee shop and up to the counter. Derek realized he and his companion were both sizing them up, and chuckled.

Crawford smiled, too, and cleared his throat. After a pause, he drew a breath. "Well, Brian really took that failure to heart. Nobody blamed him for it; it was a bad break. But it really bugged him. So he started digging into the Assassin Squad, like he was going to bring them down all by himself."

The agent tipped his coffee cup all the way back and swallowed hard. "Brian found an informant, I don't know where or how, but this guy told him about Assassin Squad movements. I know at least once, he got a tip about a Squad lab, but by the time we'd gotten the go-ahead from the director to raid the place, they were gone...vacated." He sighed and rubbed his temple. "A buddy of ours reminded me about that. Brian was pretty sore about it..." He gave a half-hearted laugh. "Maybe that's why he started getting his own search warrants, and not waiting for back-up."

"Any idea where I could find this informant?" asked Derek.

"All I know is his name's Cocoa, and he and Brian communicated mostly by phone. I mean, if Brian was paying for his information, they must have met sometimes, but I don't know anything about it."

"If Cocoa was an 'official' informant, Brian would have filed with the DEA so he could pay him organization money, right?"

"Yeah. I guess you might find out more if you talked to the accountants, but I doubt they'd be allowed to tell you anything."

"Probably not." Director Stillman might know something about it, though. He'd taken an interest in Brian's case, or so it seemed. Perhaps he'd be willing to help Derek out now.

The two men rose. "Well, thanks for everything."

"Thanks for trying to put this together," Crawford answered as they shook hands. "I know I said some things before that sounded weird, but I sure didn't want Brian to end up like this. I wish he'd trusted me more – but that's not really his problem, I guess."

"Regardless, someone who's bumping off DEA agents isn't healthy."

"You got that right." Crawford sighed as he shoved his hands into his pockets. "And I can see what Becky's been talking about, about not taking the chance to get stuff right before – you know, before Brian was gone."

"Yes, I know what you mean."

"It's creepy. Even he should get a better send-off."

"I'll do my best. We'll get whoever it was."

Crawford smiled. "Thanks."

As Derek pushed through the glass doors, he glanced at his watch. Cindy should be getting off work soon. He could swing by the hospital and give her the latest update. Simplified, to protect Matt Crawford's identity. Still, she might remember Brian talking about this informant "Cocoa".

Derek's phone vibrated. He whipped it out, and made a tired smile as he hit the answer button.

"Hi, Robbie."

"Hi."

Derek waited a moment. "Did you want something?"

"Just seeing where you are."

"I was in a business meeting."

"With a girl?"

Who had raised this boy? Derek didn't like his tone of voice, either. "With DEA Special Agent Matthew Crawford, if you must know. How's the password coming?"

"Nothing yet."

"Okay. Well, keep at it, huh? I'm going to run give Cindy an update. I'll be home in a bit."

"Can't you be home now?"

"I'll be there in a bit; relax. How's your back feel?"

"Fine." Robbie's flat tone didn't match his words. Derek rolled his eyes and leaned against his car door.

"I'll call the doctor's office today and renew your prescriptions. Okay?"

"Fine. I'll be here…"

"Sounds good. See you soon."

Derek heaved a sigh and swung into the driver's seat. Maybe Robbie was annoyed that he hadn't cracked Brian's password. Maybe his pain had spiked. Maybe something else Derek hadn't thought of. If only he'd come out and talk about it!

20. "What Is the Measure of Your Success?"

The receptionist's greying hair was swept up into a tight, neat bun. She stared at Derek over the top of her glasses as he approached her desk.

"Yes?" she demanded, like the Empress of India addressing a beggar boy who'd grabbed her elbow in the street.

"Excuse me...Mrs. Fielding?"

She glanced from the name plaque on her desk back to him.

"Do you have an appointment?" she continued, her fingers still paused in the midst of typing a memo.

"Not exactly. My–"

She rolled her eyes with short exhalation. "I'm sorry, you must have an appointment to see the director."

Derek drew a deep breath, crossed his fingers behind his back, and tried again. At the end of twelve minutes, they had discussed how much of a great politician or manager's work is actually done by secretaries, regretted the ingratitude of the modern youth, despised the depravity of the current motion picture scene, exchanged life philosophies, complemented each other on their respective competency and politeness, reminisced about the good old days when all young people were polite and all secretaries efficient, bemoaned the current drug crisis, which stemmed, naturally, from the lack of discipline in the public schools...

Derek slipped into a chair to wait until the director had a "free moment". Although Mrs. Fielding's clacking keyboard had a more amenable sound now, he overruled his body's urge to slouch back and cross his legs. In public relations, never take a good thing for granted.

After a time, Mrs. Fielding rose and went into the inner office. When she came back out with several sheafs of paper, Director Stillman looked out of the door after her.

"Why, Mr. Hayes!" he exclaimed, holding out his hand. "How are you doing? Of course I remember you — Come in, come in, I'm not doing anything important, just planning how the DEA, the state troopers, and the city police are going to eradicate crime. A simple matter, really – ha ha! By all means, come in…Thank you, Mrs. Fielding."

As Derek followed the director into the inner office, he flashed Mrs. Fielding his best business-like smile. The director was certainly being very friendly — he'd see where it led.

"Now, then," Mr. Stillman said as he slipped into his leather office chair and indicated another seat across the desk. "What can I do for you?"

"I know your time is valuable," Derek began, shifting in the captain's chair. "I have one question, and I believe it pertains to Brian Lane's death."

"Yes – I heard the case had been reopened," the director broke in. "As someone more closely tied to the case, could you tell me any of the specifics that convinced the police the case required more attention?"

"Well, for one thing, it would have been highly uncharacteristic of Brian – even if he wanted to commit suicide, he wouldn't have done it that way."

"It seems a little flimsy to me," the director mused. "Not to disrupt your story, but those in a depressed state of mind often do things that their friends and acquaintances would never suspect. Tragically, this is part of the reason suicides succeed when they do."

"There's also the heroin," Derek continued. "Whoever killed Brian planted meth in his car, and there was meth in his system. But it doesn't make much sense for him to die of heroin when the only heroin in the area was in his bloodstream."

"That does seem curious, if explainable."

Derek raised an eyebrow. "I sense you don't care for my explanation."

Mr. Stillman shrugged and smiled. "I acknowledge it's not my jurisdiction, but I would hate for you – and the police – to spend valuable time chasing a dead end."

Derek frowned. "Mrs. Lane believes her husband was murdered, and so do I. I just took what evidence I had to the police, and they made their own decisions from there."

Stillman raised his hands and smiled again. "I understand. I just want you to be forewarned that, as a piece of evidence, it's not much to base a case on. I should know…my whole life is based on constructing cases that will stand up in court."

Derek considered that given what Crawford had told him about the DEA's recent sting operations, "construct" was a very interesting word to use.

"I suppose this is rather irrelevant," the director sighed. "After all, as a private investigator, you may do as you like. I just think you have your work cut out for you. Now, what was your question?"

Derek closed his eyes momentarily to re-summon his train of thought. "Does the name 'Cocoa' mean anything to you?" he asked.

"Hmm…Cocoa? I can't say it rings any bells." Mr. Stillman flipped through a few papers on his desk. "No, I don't think I've ever met someone by that name. Friend of yours?"

"Friend of Brian's."

"Ah?"

"Yes – I'm trying to locate him."

"Now…how do you know this 'Cocoa' was a confidant of Mr. Lane?" asked the director, slipping off his glasses.

Derek shifted in his seat and shrugged. "I've talked to a lot of different people."

Stillman rested his elbows on the desk, leaning forward toward the detective. "Mr. Hayes, I'm afraid I'm going to have to ask you for some names."

"As a professional investigator, I'm afraid I'm going to have to ask you for a subpoena."

"Well played!" Stillman leaned back in his chair with a laugh; a strange, abrupt laugh that came from his throat, not his belly.

He slipped his glasses back on and cleared his throat. "I'm sorry; you're right. In this profession, confidentiality is always a consideration. I probably shouldn't discuss this further."

Derek watched the director's face for a moment or two, and rose. "I see," he answered, putting out his hand. "Well, thank you for your time, anyway."

"Not at all," Mr. Stillman began, also rising and shaking Derek's hand. "Now I come to think of it, however, it's quite possible some of Agent Lane's teammates have heard of this Cocoa. Just a moment…"

Sitting again, Mr. Stillman adjusted his glasses and did some more staring at the computer screen and flipping papers on the desk. "I don't seem to have gotten any data about this 'Cocoa'. I'll have to reread the reports. There must be something…"

"Well, I appreciate you trying," Derek began.

"If he was an informant, accounting ought to have some data on him," Stillman continued. "If I learn anything important, I can let you know."

"I'd appreciate that."

Derek wondered what Stillman had done with the business card he'd originally given him. Did Cindy have it? The director hadn't asked for Derek's info, in case anything did come up. "Here, would these be useful?" he asked, digging his business card case from his pocket and slipping a few out. "In case you need to contact me again?"

"Oh, why, thank you." Mr. Stillman smiled as he took them, tucking them away somewhere on the desk.

Derek rose to leave again. The director came around the desk and smiled at him.

"I know Mrs. Lane appreciates all that you're doing, and so do we," he said, shaking Derek's hand. "Anytime a federal agent dies, no matter what the cause, it is a loss to society. More than that, it's an indictment against his supervisors for allowing such a tragedy. We need every pair of boots we can get on the ground against the force of crime and drugs seeking to invade our communities."

Derek smiled, mumbling vague agreements. He wasn't sure the metaphor exactly correlated.

"The more the different branches of law enforcement work together, including the neighborhood watch and the people like you, the fewer criminals will be able to walk our streets," Mr. Stillman continued.

He must have his mind on the next "Tough-on-Crime Initiative" press conference. Oh, well…so far Derek was batting 0. What a drag of a morning.

"You will keep me up-to-date on your progress, won't you? I'm afraid I don't hear much about the official police investigation, and it would be a comfort to know someone out there is making progress."

"I'll do my best," Derek answered, the prime non-committal statement.

"Incidentally," Mr. Stillman continued, pausing in the middle of the doorway. "Since you've decided Brian Lane was murdered, what…er…motives have you developed so far? I'm afraid homicide isn't my particular specialty, but do you have any theories?"

Derek heaved a sigh and scratched his head. "I think it must be gang related, but which gang it's tied to and what their game is,

I don't know. And I hate to share theories before I have anything solid to support them with."

"I've heard Agent Lane's teammates mention a 'private project' of his. Does that sound important to you?"

Derek shrugged. "Well, Brian was too good an agent to chase down rabbit holes – I think he was on to something with that project. But did that something get him killed? That's harder to say. I have reason to believe he was in the sights of a Blackhearts enforcer who had a vendetta against the DEA, but that's not evidence of anything either."

"A vendetta sounds disturbing," answered the director with a terse chuckle. "I should warn our local agents to be alert. You, too, young man; take care of yourself."

"I plan to; thanks."

"Well, best of luck to you, Mr. Hayes. Honestly, I'd hate to be in your shoes – gang killings are often hard to pin down."

"You're right there. But I'm not giving up yet."

They shook hands again, and Derek slipped out of the office.

"Thank you for everything, Mrs. Fielding," he said on the way out. "I certainly hope your morning gets easier."

"Well, work is what makes the world go around," she answered, keeping her eyes on her typing. "Though you wouldn't know it from watching young people today."

Derek shut the door behind him as softly as possible. He certainly hadn't learned much from Director Stillman…Just more of the same hints about Brian's project, and more skepticism about the evidence they had turned up so far.

Brian must have been murdered. He *must* have been. And whoever had done it probably had gang connections. But that didn't help Derek find him. Which gang? And how had they known so very much about Brian to trap him like a sitting duck that way? He shivered.

Derek closed his eyes for a moment, filing the conversation into his mental vaults for future reference. At least he'd tried. He still had one more card to play in the search for Cocoa. He pulled out his cellphone. *Hank, don't fail me now.*

21. "Talk About Life"

Mrs. Goodwin scooped a slice of coffee cake off the platter. It slipped off the server and flopped upside-down on Cindy's plate.

"Oh! goodness!"

Cindy laughed. "It's all right." She picked up a fork and brushed the crumbs toward the center of her plate.

"Oh, good; you know, I'm so glad you're going to be there Thursday, to help out; I would help if I could but, wouldn't you know, the doctor scheduled my appointment right on top of that, but maybe it's all for the best, since I'm such a butter-finger anyway, you know!"

"Hey, I don't mind. Keeps me busy."

"Yes, how are you doing?" asked Mrs. Jones, coming up on Cindy's other side. "I haven't heard much how the case is going. Can I get you some tea?"

"Thanks. It's going well; we're finding out a lot. Derek's a very good listener, and that helps people open up to him," Cindy answered. "I think he's making good progress."

"I guess it's not the sort of thing where you can get an estimate how much longer it's going to take," Ellie Jones smiled.

Cindy tried to imagine what it would be like once the case was over. She wouldn't have any reason to go walk at the mall with Derek, anymore. For some reason, that made something inside her sink, and she took the teacup Ellie offered her gravely.

"That reminds me," Mrs. Goodwin burst out. "You know you gave me your camera for Joshua to take and do that thing, um, where he could make a movie of the pictures for the annual meeting; he was going to take the pictures of the missionary lunch, and do that for them, right? And remember I told you it was taking so long because something – I don't understand it – but it wasn't working for his computer, and wouldn't you know it, he said he was talking to Robbie Hayes and he went home and tried this little trick, where he had to do…something to the format or– I don't know that computer stuff (you know me), but whatever it was, he tried it and *zoop*: all the pictures went where they were supposed to, and don't let me forget, I have to get your camera back to you, and the CD – he put them all on a CD for you to take and play on the screen; but after that, I don't know what he did, but it all worked just fine."

Cindy sipped her tea. It was strange. Robbie seemed perfectly normal around other people, but whenever she tried to talk to him, he turned sour or something, and would just glare at his lap. She couldn't think what she'd done to him, but clearly there was something between them. She wished she knew what it was.

"He is a sweet kid," Ellie Jones was saying. "It's too bad he has to spend so much time in their apartment alone."

"Alone?" asked Mrs Goodwin.

"Yes, well, he told me something about it's just him and his brother left."

"That's right," Cindy put in. "That's why Derek's his legal guardian."

"Oh!" Mrs. Goodwin made a "there, there" sound. "Oh, dear, I can see that; that reminds me – oh, Mrs. Marchbanks…" Mrs. Goodwin stepped away.

Ellie Jones glanced at Cindy. "Are you doing all right?"

Cindy nodded. "I think so. The police are pursuing the homicide angle of the case, based on Brian's needle phobia and a few other things."

"I'm glad." Ellie squeezed a lemon slice into her tea. "I can't wait until we have some closure on this whole mess. Who would want Brian dead?"

"I don't know yet. I just wish he'd told me about it beforehand."

"Though, if that one theory of Derek's is true – that Brian was killed because he knew too much – I'm sure he didn't want you to be in danger."

Cindy smiled ruefully and shrugged. "As though a murderer would know for sure what I knew and what I didn't know."

"I don't know. It's also possible Brian wasn't completely rational."

"That's true," Cindy chuckled. The next moment, her face fell. "I'd still take him back, though."

Ellie reached out to stroke her arm. "We all would."

Derek had tried to get her mind off the case the past month or two. They'd talked about other things: mutual interests, their jobs, their families, the future. She enjoyed it, but it didn't solve the problem.

Sometimes – unable to sleep in the middle of the night – she'd sit in bed and stare, not at the book in her lap, but at the empty pillow beside her. It'd been nice to be able to turn the nightstand light on without disturbing anyone, but only the first couple times. She'd promised herself never to be annoyed with anyone she loved ever again. Why did she have to lose him?

"Is there anything I can do for you?" Ellie asked.

"You're doing it," Cindy smiled wanly. "I'm so grateful for you and the church family. I wouldn't have survived, otherwise."

"Hey, we're here for you, honey." JoAnn came up from Cindy's other side and patted her back. "So, when do we nail the criminals who did this?"

"It's got to be soon. Derek's found out a lot already." Cindy set down her plate and caressed her warm teacup. "He's very competent, and he's got great people skills."

She thought of the little old lady they'd met in the mall one day, and the way Derek had gently guided her back to the store where her husband was waiting. Apparently, they had dinner at the mall every Monday afternoon after doctor check-ups…and it wasn't the first time the poor wife had wandered off confusedly. But Derek knew exactly how to get her back to somewhere she recognized.

"He's no lemon, I'll give you that," JoAnn put in. "I wasn't sure what a real-life PI was supposed to be like, but whoever that was you talked to recommended a good one."

"Yes."

"He's not married, either," JoAnn continued, smoothing her hair back. "I wonder why. He's kinda cute…"

"Oh, really, JoAnn!" Cindy shot back. There wasn't any particular reason JoAnn shouldn't admire Derek; he was a good man. But…something in her rebelled at the thought.

"Did you know he's taken Brian's slot in the church mowing schedule?"

That just sounded wrong. There was something awkward about anyone taking over Brian's things or duties, even – or especially – Derek. But the mowing had to be done. Life had to go on.

Cindy would never forget Brian. He was a part of her, and that would never change.

All the same…it felt good when Derek made her laugh. Not many people could make her laugh like that. On the drive home from the morgue, she had thought she'd never laugh, or smile, or perhaps even move ever again.

But she needed to laugh once in a while, especially in this time of stress. God didn't make us to mope at home feeling sorry for ourselves. It was almost as though God had brought Derek into her life, not just to find justice for Brian but to help her through the grief stages. To make her laugh again.

* * * *

Trying to look like he was interested in the glass in his hand, Derek strained his ears. After spending weeks upon weeks wasting money and evenings in Blackhearts-territory bars, he'd finally come across some gangsters who were discussing something remotely interesting.

J-Dog and another Blackhearts member – "Catcher" Derek thought he'd been called – were snickering together further down the bar. And they were talking about Shiv.

The drunker they got, the more Derek questioned the reliability of their information, but he'd take what he could get.

"You know I was in the joint with Shiv?" said J-Dog for about the fourth time that evening. "Yeah…He packs a punch, all right, him. Didn't nobody mess with us while he was in there with us."

"He talks big," mumbled Catcher, tipping back his glass.

"He don't just talk," insisted J-Dog. "All the time in the pokey, he was talking about how he'd get back at the DEA pigs who collared him."

"Talk, talk, talk," droned Catcher.

"Nu-uh. He got his parole, like he'd said he would. He's gonna take some action."

"So he shot off his mouth about all those feds," griped Catcher. "But did he ice any? 'Member that one night you two got so sozzled, you smashed us into that guard rail…"

"You weren't so sober yourself that night," snapped J-Dog.

"And the next morning, we got on Shiv's case about that DEA agent who wasted himself," chuckled Catcher, pulling a cigarette out of his pocket. "If he wanted to ice that one, he missed his shot, we said."

"Talking about me again?" A scruffy-faced man with tattoos all up and down his arms stepped out of the shadows and leaned over the two gangsters.

"Shiv!" choked J-Dog. "Join us? Just remembering some good times."

Shiv glowered at them. Derek huddled over his still-full cup of alcohol. If Shiv was in a ditch the night Brian died, he couldn't have killed him. Could he?

"Can't you keep your mouths shut about anything?" Shiv snapped.

"Hey, not when I got a busted arm out of the deal," slurred Catcher, waving his left arm. "And I had plans that night. Then you two geniuses land us in the emergency room over a dumb game–"

"That's enough." Shiv smacked Catcher, making the Blackheart spin out of his chair. Shiv settled down in the vacant chair.

If it involved Shiv breaking parole, he'd probably make it hard to prove – especially for Derek. Hank *might* be able to get a hold of the emergency room records, but that was a big maybe.

J-Dog was talking about his time in the "joint" with Shiv, again. From Shiv's expression, it didn't look like he wanted to remember. Perhaps it was just as well Derek leave before another fight broke out. He'd had enough of that two weeks ago, at the place across the street.

And he still had the Assassin Squad theory to pursue. Provided Shiv didn't skip town, it should be safe to leave his case on the back burner. It sounded like this particular drunk driving episode was less serious than murder.

Derek reached into his pocket and pulled out his wallet to pay his bill. Maybe he'd even get home early enough to watch something with Robbie.

"You going to finish that?" asked the bartender, who'd been eyeing Derek for several minutes.

"I gotta drive home," Derek answered, and slunk toward the door.

22. "Sock Heaven"

"So that way, only you and the person you're sending the email to can see it," Robbie explained, watching Pr. Jones struggle to fold up the wheelchair. "Otherwise, it's like handing postcards down your street, where anybody who knows how can read it."

"My, my," the reverend answered, hoisting the chair up and sliding it into his trunk. "That does sound like a good idea. But I don't suppose anyone would be very interested in what my emails say."

"Yeah, 90, 95% of the time, people don't care whether other people can read their email or not," the teen continued once Pastor Jones had slid into the driver's seat. "It's really the principle of the thing. If I can keep other people from collecting data on me, why not stop them? It's not like it's any of their business what I'm doing, anyway."

"I see." Pr. Jones leaned over to open the door for his wife. "And you say this program is free?"

"Yep. It's basically written by people who are in it for the principle of it. Of course," Rob continued as the pastor started the car. "It's only really effective if everyone installs the keys. If you're sending an email to someone without a key, you can't encrypt it because then they couldn't read it."

"Don't tell me you're talking computers again!" Mrs. Jones laughed, glancing back at Robbie. "My lands...I can't make heads or tails of it."

"That's okay." Rob adjusted his seat-belt as the pastor pulled out of the parking lot. "Derek says not everybody has to be an expert."

"He's working again today, is that it?"

"Yeah. He flips Saturdays and Sundays, and he has to start at 12."

"I guess that goes with the job," Mr. Jones said. "It's nice he's got an afternoon shift, so at least he can go to service."

"Yeah...he tried to do that on purpose." Robbie leaned back against the seat and stared out the window.

"Will he be gone until tonight, then?"

"Yep. Eight-thirty or so."

Mrs. Jones shook her head. "Oh, dear. So you'll be alone all that time, then?"

"I don't mind." He didn't need another Mrs. Gibbons trying to be his mother and telling him what to do. Last night, she'd threatened to call the manager if they didn't quiet down. She'd kept Derek at the door a long time, asking nosy questions about how they were treating each other and whether Robbie was getting fed properly. As though he was a quad who needed to be coddled like a baby. If only Mrs. Gibbons didn't live on the end of the row, and there was *someone* else for her to "neighborhood-watch."

"I know you're very grown up for your age," the pastor put in, glancing in the rear-view mirror. "And especially if you have your computer to work on, I bet you do just fine keeping yourself busy."

"Yeah..." Rob relaxed against the seat, crossing his arms on his stomach. He wasn't being fair; Mrs. Jones wasn't anything like Mrs. Gibbons. And after all...it was sort-of his fault that he and Derek had been arguing. Derek had gone to the park with Cindy... all day long. He hadn't even offered Robbie the chance to go with...but it was true that Rob would probably have turned him down if he had asked. Still...Derek acted like he almost didn't care. It was so weird...

"I do have a project to work on," Robbie stammered. Anything to get his mind off last night. "I'm trying to find Brian Lane's email password."

"And how do you do that?" asked Mrs. Jones, smiling back at him.

"I have a brute-force program," Rob explained, locking his fingers together. "It systematically tries combinations of characters until it finds the right one. Of course...unless I get lucky, odds are it'll be doing that for years."

"Sounds like you need a stroke of luck," sighed Mrs. Jones.

"Do you think Brian used a random password, or a real word?" asked the reverend.

"Well, he didn't use a standard English word," Rob answered, and gave a half-laugh. "We tried those first."

"Oh, well," Pr. Jones laughed, checking his blind spot.

"Wouldn't Cindy know what Brian's password is?"

"No."

"Hmm," Mrs. Jones stroked her chin for a moment. "I think he must have written it down somewhere. Unless it was something easy like his birthday. How many times was he on lock-up, and he still couldn't remember the code to the alarm system, dear?"

The pastor and his wife laughed. "You're right...But then again, that's all numbers, and those are harder to remember."

"True," murmured Robbie.

"Well, I hope you're able to figure it out without waiting years," Mrs. Jones continued. "That must be very frustrating."

"Thanks." Rob frowned out the window. If Brian really and truly hadn't written the password down anywhere, it was less likely to be a randomly-generated password. Maybe he should tell his cracker to try pronounceable combinations. His left leg twitched, but he ignored it. What if, when Derek came home from work that night, Rob had Brian's password all ready?

He hugged his arms closer against his chest. Derek might take him out somewhere...maybe they would even solve the case. And then he would have no reason to go visit Cindy every spare moment of every day. Life would be...normal.

* * * *

"I'd have to ask Derek, to see if he could drive me."

"Okay. Does he work that Saturday?"

Robbie leaned back in his chair, the phone still pressed to his ear, and tried to see the calendar. Nope; it was too far away. "I dunno; I'll have to look."

"Well, it's at ten, so if he just dropped you off, I bet we could take you home. I'd have to check with my parents; I can't drive anybody who's not in our family, yet."

That's right. Joey was turning sixteen, now, too. "Oh… bummer."

"By the way, it's at LaserQuest, just so you know. Don't feel like you have to come, if you don't want to. I figured you could at least hang out and have pizza with us and stuff."

LaserQuest. *Laser*Quest. As in running around in the dark and fragging your friends again and again, in real life, except without the dying part. Or the running around part.

"Maybe let me think about it for a bit. I need to talk to Derek about it, too."

"Yeah, sure, just call me back anytime."

"Thanks, Joey."

"No problem. We miss seeing you guys at church."

"Yeah…how's church going?"

"Actually, we've started going to Trinity Free Church. I guess there's some sort of trouble brewing, you know, at the old place, and my dad decided we'd get out while the getting was good, or something like that."

"Cool. Well, take care."

"You too. Call me back when you can."

"Will do. Thanks for everything."

Robbie stared down at his wheels. The walls of his mobile prison. He needn't bother looking at the clock. He knew Derek was probably off work by now, but he wasn't coming home. He would swing by Cindy's house for some reason or other. At least two or three times a week, Derek had come home with the leftovers of whatever Cindy had cooked. Okay, it was pretty good, but still…

Where was Derek? Not here. Rob squeezed his armrests. He needed something nice and heavy to throw. Preferably against Mrs. Gibbons's wall. He sneered. That'd give her something to call the manager about. *I'm sorry, the principle resident is out right now. I'm the primary resident, since I'm the one who's always here, but he's the principle resident since he pays the rent.*

He picked up the hand weight from the desk and hefted it. It hurt more than it used to. They used to do stretches and exercises every night when Derek got home, while watching the news. He switched to the other hand and did a curl. Michelle had explained how he could work the muscles he still had, and strengthen his stomach so he wouldn't lose his sitting ability. Michelle had been really nice, and Derek had done everything with him back then, had always been right there. He flipped the weight back onto the desk. Why would anything change? Why should it?

Rob heaved a groan and rested his face on his hands. Peeking through his fingers at the computer screen, he glanced at the progress bar on his cracker. Nothing. Zilch. A wizard's touch, he had not.

He wanted to go to the party. He wanted to creep up ramps and dodge around corners and nail Joey with a harmless bolt of infra-red light. He wanted to play baseball. He wanted a brand-new iMac.

He wanted his brother to come home — and he wanted to be smarter than Brian Lane.

23. "Run to the End of the Highway"

Rush hour traffic outside St. James's parking lot was not much fun. Derek flicked his windshield wipers, watching the brake-lights of the cars in front of him flash like so many autumn leaves. If the bedroom window was still leaking, then his pillow would be getting wet. Unless Robbie had thought to move it, in which case his sheets were getting wet.

At least Cindy liked the way the case was progressing. She still hadn't found any clues to Brian's email password, but she'd corroborated that Brian sometimes had to go out on a bust at a moment's notice…and that once she'd heard him on the phone with a judge beforehand. Brian was a strange and enigmatic character… but he'd been on to something important. If only he'd kept a detailed diary of the day he was murdered, including the identity of his killer. *Dream on.*

Derek's iPhone started playing Steve Taylor's "Smug". Unknown caller. He pulled the phone out and hit the answer button.

"Derek Hayes."

"So you are."

"What's up, Hank?"

"This must be someone's lucky day," the cop continued. "Gornik and I were running a traffic check on Broadway, and pulled over a fellow doing over fifty back and forth between the two right lanes. Wouldn't you know it, he's loaded *and* got an open beer can in the seat."

Derek eased off the brake as the light turned green. "Man."

"Well, we booked him after finding some weed in his trunk…and guess who it was."

Derek checked his mirrors, and stepped on the accelerator. "I'm breathless."

"Jake Radcliff, commonly known as Cocoa."

"You're kidding."

"He's being checked in now, but come down tomorrow, he should have sobered up all right. I'll let you talk to him."

"You're amazing."

"Well, with perps like these, it doesn't take much."

Derek laughed. "I'll see you later. Gotta run to the drug store and pick up Robbie's prescription…I'm a little late, and he's going to be mad."

"How's he doing lately?"

Derek sighed. "Well…I dunno." He checked his blind spot. "He's been a little mopier than usual, but he won't talk about it. I know he's worried about this case, and he's helping me with Brian's computer. I wish he'd let me take him to the doctor."

"Well, you two take care, all right?"

"You, too. Listen, I really appreciate it, Hank."

"No sweat. Just doing my job. Besides, if you get him to talk, we might get some more arrests, and the fewer of these people on the streets the better."

"Sounds good. See you later." Derek killed the call and flipped on his turn signal. Cocoa Radcliff would surely have a unique perspective on Brian's case…he might even know who had killed him.

* * * *

"Fantastic!" exclaimed Sgt. Blake as Derek stepped out of the interrogation room. "I'd forgotten about your magic touch."

"Whatever," Derek answered, rolling his eyes. "That's called being nice to people and trying to address their concerns."

"I don't care what you call it...You got him talking. So, Cocoa was feeding Brian Lane info on the Assassin Squad's movements."

"Right."

"Why? I mean, I know he said Lane was paying him, but nobody works for that little. Not if they know what the DEA usually pays their informants."

"He's scared." Derek pushed open the door to Hank's office and held it for him. "He was even scared before Brian got wasted...I think he doesn't like that the Assassin Squad never get caught for anything. Even the gang world needs something to enforce the balances of power, and the Squad doesn't have any restraints at all. Monopolies lead to higher prices, which is bad for buyers."

"Are you telling me that druggie gave info to Brian because of economics?"

"No. But even druggies know that absolute power is only good for the people who have it."

"Anyway," Hank continued, flopping into his chair and gesturing at another one. "Where are the Squadsters getting their chemical ingredients? I had to take a call when you asked that question, so I missed that part."

"All Cocoa knows is, once, he saw a guy pull up with a semi full of goods at the abandoned warehouse they were using at the time. He didn't think the truck was from Mexico, but apparently you've got to be pretty high up with the Assassin Squad to find out more than that."

"Man, this is going to drive me crazy." Hank tossed the pencil he'd been fiddling with onto the desk and jumped up. "The chief thinks an increase in meth-related emergency room visits on the west side is linked to the Assassin Squad, and he wants me to figure out how to cut off their supply line. Easier said than done."

Derek scratched his head and chewed his lip. "I wonder what Brian Lane's angle was. You don't have to do much digging to find out the Squad is bigger than is healthy, but Brian was looking for something else. The way he talks in his files, he thought he was on to something really big."

"Pinning a name on the Squad's big boss would be big. Do you think Cocoa knows who this Big Boss is?"

"Nah…only the Squad officers are going to know that." Derek lifted his feet up onto Hank's desk and closed his eyes. "Besides, if Cocoa knew he could have told Brian."

"If he would have."

Derek rubbed his eyes. "Well, maybe that is what Brian was aiming for. The big boss is probably the one in charge of the raw goods."

"There's some big brain behind their movements. They keep moving their distribution hubs one step ahead of us, so it seems."

"What I wouldn't give to find Marco Jung. He's apparently the one who's filling Jimmy Cann's shoes now."

"The Squadster who was killed in a firefight with the DEA?"

"Right."

"After making some decisions without first consulting the Big Boss?"

"Exactly. Sounds like someone's jealous."

"And insecure."

"Sheesh, I would be insecure if I was a mob boss."

Derek sighed. "Well, at least I got you some more names of Squadsters. Not that that helps you find them, but it helps with the warrants."

"Hey, you did a great job in there," the cop answered, sitting on top of his desk and grinning. "I mean, getting him to confess to being connected to Brian Lane so we could keep him in custody was a stroke of genius."

"Well, he's scared of the Assassin Squad thinking he talked and then getting a hold of him. That's why he laid low after Brian got it. I gave him a simple way for the authorities to protect him."

"Yeah, but you didn't promise the state would shell out big bucks for witness protection; you had him confess to being a person of interest in Lane's case."

"He's a person of interest, all right, but he didn't kill him."

"What makes you so sure?"

Derek cocked an eyebrow and looked up at his friend. "Where's his motive?"

"You said yourself he was scared stiff of a hundred different things," Hank laughed, waving a hand. "You can twist the fear motive in all sorts of different directions, or rather, a prosecuting attorney could; I couldn't. But I asked for your reasoning; I didn't offer to give you mine."

"Exactly: his fear. He took Brian's death as a message to clam up, and until today he obeyed that message. Before Brian got it, his fear drove him to give information, doing what he could to sabotage the gang. Make sense?"

"Hn...I've got the same gut feeling," Hank consented, draping himself across a chair. "Then who did kill Lane?"

Derek groaned. "I've got a bad feeling it was a Squadster. I mean, it'd be so easy if we could just pin it to Shiv and be done with it."

"Didn't Shiv do it?"

Derek pulled his feet off the table and scratched his head. "I scored some info while eavesdropping the other night. Apparently Shiv and some of his buddies landed in the emergency room the night 'that DEA agent wasted himself'. How many of those are there – you know?"

"But you can't waltz into the ER and ask for year-old records on a stranger."

"Right."

"You've got a problem."

"Well, if those Blackhearts weren't *too* sozzled, I'm content to take them at their word and focus on this Squad thing. Nailing whatever Brian was after in the Squad is probably more important than Shiv breaking parole."

"I'll keep that in mind, though," Hank mused. "Unofficially, of course. Next time his parole officer's in the break room, I can drop the hint. Then he and the DA can decide whether it's worth a subpoena or not – Shiv is a big fish in the Blackhearts."

"Either way, we've got our work cut out for us."

"True. Have you opened Brian's email yet?"

Derek laughed, standing up. "Not yet, but Robbie's working a new angle on the password."

"That is some high-security spam."

They laughed.

"Well, keep your eyes peeled for Marco Jung," Derek said. "He sounds like the Shiv of the Assassin Squad."

"I'll call you personally," Hank promised, shaking Derek's hand.

"I'll count on it. Just don't get yourself shot, huh?"

"Haven't yet," Sgt. Blake answered. "I've been shot at, but I've never been hit. My wife says that's because she and the pastor's wife are praying for me every night."

Derek grinned. He'd always known the blonde, slender education major was exactly what Hank needed. Derek still remembered the way Hank and Helen's parents had winked and giggled at each other that day trip to the lake, the day Hank proposed.

"How's Helen doing lately?" he asked.

"Great! Just great. Her two nieces are spending the week, so Julie's been having the time of her life."

"She's gotta be, what, three now?"

"Yep."

"And ten months."

"Right…almost four."

"It was a Thursday…"

"Okay, buddy," Hank laughed, slapping Derek's back. "I get the point. Don't tell me that you know my daughters' birthdate better than I do."

"I – just have a good memory, that's all," Derek answered. "You asked me to file your paperwork so you could sign out early and run to the hospital."

"Yep…and Capt. Richter and my mother-in-law were upset for opposite reasons."

They both laughed. It seemed like just yesterday, and at the same time like a hundred years ago. Back when they were both young and happy, with their whole lives ahead of them. Derek drew a breath and glanced away.

"Hey, your turn will come, buddy," Hank told him, gripping his shoulder. "And you'll make a great dad, I know. Just look at the way you've taken care of your brother all these years."

"You need a wife before you get kids," Derek mumbled.

"There's plenty of girls that would love to marry you. You've just got to ask one of them."

"I've got to find them before I can ask them."

Hank put out his hand to stop Derek and stared him in the eye. "Did you or did you not call me up the other day and start talking about your client's case?"

"I — did."

"And did you or did you not begin discussing your client, the charming and talented Cindy Lane?"

"I...uh...Did I talk about her?"

"You did. Were you or were you not listening to yourself as you talked about that charming and talented young lady?"

"She's a widow," stammered Derek, backing away.

"Exactly! Listen, ask her out. Just do it. The worst she can do is say no."

"I don't think I can do that."

"Why not? There's no law against it. And it's not like she's married anymore. Look, give it a shot. If you talk about her to her face like you do on the phone, she's just waiting for you to ask her. And if it doesn't work out, well, better to find out sooner than later, right?"

"But... But..."

"And for pity's sake, stop blushing like that. You want people to think you're some girly wuss?" Hank laughed.

Ask her out. Ask Cindy – just out. Just to – hang out, just for the sake of it. Not for the case, just for them. He felt himself smiling in spite of himself. That sure would be nice...but would she go for it? It was way too soon after her husband's death...It would be disrespectful. But what if she went for it?

24. "Words"

"Cindy Lane?"

Cindy turned her head, and smiled. "Mr. Stillman. What a coincidence."

"Yes, what a pleasant surprise," the director answered, putting out his hand as his face creased into a smile. "How are you?"

"Fine, thanks. How are you? And your wife?"

"Shopping," he explained, gesturing at the nearby storefront. "I'm afraid I've been roped in for the day. You know how it is." He laughed.

"Well, that's sweet," she answered. She remembered that Derek had gone shopping for white shoelaces the other day… which were apparently harder to find than you'd think. She'd made another one of those off-hand comments about how the laces on her white work shoes were wearing through, and she wasn't sure if it was worth buying new shoes, since they were still in good condition. Well, he'd beat her to it and bought her new shoelaces. Men were so funny sometimes.

"Are you still pursuing your own investigation of your husband's death?" Mr. Stillman continued, shifting the Bath and Body Works bag in his hands. "It's been some time since he died."

"Oh, we're definitely still uncovering things."

"If you don't mind my asking, how is that coming along? The last time we spoke, it didn't sound like there was any conclusive evidence."

"Not exactly, no," Cindy answered. "But I'm satisfied that we're making progress."

"I did hear about your husband's phobia of needles, though that can hardly be called evidence of murder. Has your private investigator turned up anything else to support the theory?"

"As a matter of fact, he's been looking into the Assassin Squad gang, which Brian was going after before he died. Incidentally, I'd like to thank you again for your recommendation of Mr. Hayes. He's doing some fantastic work."

"Is he?" asked the director, leaning forward. "How so?"

"Well...I believe he's really gifted for this work," she explained. "He has a personable and relaxing way about him that encourages people to talk to him, which is important when he's interviewing people that might not usually be very communicative."

"I can see that. That is excellent."

"Plus, he has access to some, um, tech savvy associates."

She gave a laugh, thinking of Robbie discussing the church's computerized alarm system with Peter Green. Or encryption for the church's member database with Ellie Jones, the church secretary. If only she could figure out how to draw him out the way they did. Maybe it was that she tended to see him while Derek was around, and she could see a younger brother feeling overshadowed by Derek's impressive personality. He sure held his brother in high esteem, judging from the way he'd clung to him during their first few visits.

"Oh, really?" asked Mr. Stillman, bringing her back to the present.

"Yes," she answered. "They've been using some of the information from Brian's laptop to try and figure out what Brian was working on when he died, which we believe must be linked to the murderer's motive. Last I heard, we might even be close to cracking Brian's email password."

"Excellent! How do they do that?" the director pressed, cracking his knuckles suddenly.

"I'm not actually sure," Cindy answered. "I'm afraid computers aren't my thing. Seems like they've got some kind of cracker program that tries thousands of different digit combinations every second until it gets the right one. A little brute-force, but Derek's very optimistic about it. Good afternoon, Mrs. Stillman."

The director's wife was still a redhead, but not from youth. She nodded politely and shook Cindy's hand once her husband had explained who she was.

"Your husband's death was certainly a tragedy," she exclaimed. "Very shocking, and sobering. It must be awful for you."

Cindy thanked her for her sympathy.

"Well, darling, are you ready to move on?"

"How much more is there to go?" demanded the director.

"Oh, I need to return this, and I want to stop at Bergner's, to get some gift cards for your nieces, and then we need to – and stop cracking your knuckles like that, Gerald, you know it's bad for your joints. Pleased to meet you, Mrs. Lane. If there's anything we can do for you, do let us know."

"You're very kind."

Cindy watched the couple move off, and turned to find her own store. It felt strange to be in the mall without Derek, but she needed something for the baby shower this evening, and she'd put it off too long. Besides, Derek didn't have time to look in stores while he was working, anyway.

She glanced into the mirrored doors of a store, and paused for a moment. Strange…she thought she'd stopped caring about her appearance, after she'd married a man who loved her no matter what she looked like. Who loved her even when she first got up in the morning with her hair looking like a rat's nest. Brian had teased her, to be sure, when she staggered downstairs on a Saturday morning to find him dressed and combed and keeping her coffee warm. And they'd loved each other, even though he only stayed awake through the late movies for her sake.

Cindy imagined the scene to herself, she and her husband on the couch in front of the screen, he holding the bag of M&M's so she could crochet. Except…the only problem was they were watching *Doctor Who*…and, out of the corner of her eye, he looked a lot like Derek.

She hurried on, forcing her mind to focus on baby gifts. Life must go on; she didn't have time to day-dream. And God is always good. *Day by day*.

25. "Charm is Deceitful"

Cindy slammed her truck closed and smiled at Derek. "Looks like we got them all. Thanks for your help."

Derek wished she wouldn't smile at him. It was hard to think when she smiled at him. "No problem," he answered.

She turned to glance at the Rescue Mission. "Well, those boxes have been sitting in my trunk since the last Summer Club meeting, so it was time to get it done."

Derek cleared his throat. "Look...Cindy...I need to talk to you about something."

She looked back at him, and leaned against her bumper.

"I think maybe you should hire a different investigator."

Her face paled. "What? Why?"

Derek forged on. "I'm afraid I'm not doing as good a job as I should, or that someone else could."

"Nonsense –"

"Someone more professional."

"Stop," she protested, giving him a little slap on the shoulder. "You're doing a great job. We've learned a lot. And what are you talking about, more *professional*?"

Derek swallowed and licked the top of his mouth before continuing. "I mean...It isn't very professional to ask you to dinner, is it?"

Cindy drew a deep breath, her face regaining the color it had lost. Derek tried to read her gaze as she looked away for a moment.

"I see," she breathed.

"See, that's pretty casual, isn't it?" he mumbled.

She looked back at him and smiled. He reflexively smiled back.

"I'd love that," she said softly. "Where?"

Derek's mind scrambled a moment. "Pizza?" he asked.

Cindy laughed. "I love pizza."

Derek grinned. "I know. Deep dish, black olives, green pepper, extra cheese, meat optional."

She laughed again. "When?"

"Friday?"

"Friday."

* * * *

Twilight was falling outside the house. Cindy left the kitchen light on as she walked back into the living room. She couldn't get involved in this episode of *Law and Order*. Brian's favorite character was in the spotlight, and seemed to be the one who would solve the case.

As she flopped into the armchair, she grabbed the remote and clicked the TV off. Now the house was deathly quiet, and the living room seemed to be darker than it had been. She flipped the TV back on and started switching channels. Why did she even have this thing? There wasn't much on worth watching, and she got her news from the radio while driving to work, anyway.

She muted the TV and slipped some of her M&M's into her mouth. She could read the novel she was trying to work through. She should study up on the Bible story she'd be teaching in fours' and fives' Sunday school.

Cindy stood up and moved toward the end table where she'd left her papers. She didn't really feel like working on it. Maybe she should just take a shower and go to bed; it was another workday tomorrow. Another day, another night. And the house stood dark and empty. She'd never thought of Brian as being boisterous or noisy, but somehow…even the occasional clack of his keyboard upstairs or the creak of the floorboards as he shifted in his seat would be comforting.

If a floorboard creaked now, or course, she'd know it couldn't be Brian, and she'd worry. She held her breath half-consciously, listening. It was a still evening outside, so not even the curtains flapped in a breeze.

The phone rang. Cindy started, but after she glanced at the number, she smiled as she pressed the button.

"Mom?"

"Hey, honey, how are you?"

"It's good to hear your voice," Cindy answered, switching off the TV and slipping onto the couch. "How's Dad?"

"Actually, he said his back's feeling much better. The doctor recommended some therapy, so we're trying that; we'll see how it goes.

"Good."

"So, how's the case going?"

"It's going well," Cindy answered. She snuggled back into the sofa. "I can't give you all the details, obviously, but Derek's found out a lot. Apparently there's this meth gang in the area that's really hard to catch – like they're getting tips from inside the DEA or something. Anyway, Brian was getting close to the truth, it seems, and that something got him killed. And Derek and I are getting closer to finding out what, and who it was."

"I certainly hope you'll tell the police, once you figure it out, and don't leave your family to solve a mystery after your death."

They laughed. Cindy rested one leg on the coffee table.

"I haven't heard much about this Derek Hayes. Is he doing a good job?"

"I think so. He's definitely very competent."

"Mel said he was at your house the last time she called you."

"Don't worry, Mom; he was just picking up some lasagna. I still haven't figured out how to cook for one again, which is really funny if you think about it. Anyway, Derek and his brother are good at helping me clear out leftovers."

"One thing I have to say is, I raised daughters who know how to cook."

Cindy smiled. "You did all right, Mom. Derek says even his kid brother likes what I cook."

"Is his brother a picky eater?"

"No, he…" Cindy realized she wasn't sure how to explain it. "I'm not exactly sure. He doesn't seem to like me. I've tried to be nice to him. Maybe it is that Derek's been spending a lot of time with me, working on this case, which means Robbie's sitting home by himself."

"That does sound depressing. I thought you said they went to your church?"

"Yes, they're coming to First Baptist, but that's just Sundays. I don't know if Robbie gets out much the rest of the week."

"I know Katelynn would thrive on that!"

Cindy let out a chuckle. "How's she doing?"

"She was really excited: she got an A on her last exam. She's really enjoying all this graphic design stuff."

"That's good. You've got to find something you enjoy."

"So, how are you doing in other ways? Are you still in your small group?"

"Absolutely. I don't know how I would've survived this otherwise. I've also stayed in the Sunday school rotation, plus Wednesday night, and cooking for the Rescue Mission every month. I'm so busy, I barely have time to feel sorry for myself."

"That's sometimes the best medicine. What are you doing tonight?"

"Oh...just sitting home. I was watching some TV, but without anyone to share it with it feels a little flat. Brian...really loved this show."

"I understand. I worry about you, you know. No one your age should lose someone you love — unless it'd be one of your old geezer parents."

"Don't talk like that! You aren't trying to tell me something, are you?"

Cindy's mom laughed. "We're not going anywhere as far as I know."

Cindy chuckled, too; but her nerves were on edge. No one had expected Brian to go anywhere. Except his murderer. Who could get up in the morning, and eat their lunch, and go to a meeting, knowing they were going to end another human being's life? Who could look someone in the eye, and know they were going to deliberately destroy them? She shuddered.

"Oh, Mom, why did Brian die?"

"I wish I could give you a good answer, sweetie."

Cindy drew her knees up to her chest and cradled the phone against her cheek.

"I wish I could be there for you, honey. You sound like you need a hug."

"Yeah..." Cindy realized tears were spilling out of her eyes. "I thought I was over the hump. Why does it still hurt so bad?"

"You'll probably feel it for years," Mom said. "But that's not bad. Brian was a good man."

"Why–" Cindy's voice cracked. "Why would anyone want to kill him?"

"I hope they catch whoever it was."

Cindy sighed, rubbing at her face. "Yeah. I can't wait until we find out who it was. I mean, I know I'm supposed to be forgiving towards everybody, but sometimes it's hard to feel that."

"That's why love and forgiveness are a decision – not a feeling – made in God's strength."

"You're right," Cindy murmured, hugging a couch pillow. "I'm so grateful I have God. Otherwise, I'd feel *really* alone."

God...and Derek. When she talked with Derek, she could forget the hole Brian had left inside her. It put purpose in her life—not just with the case, but with someone else to worry about, someone else who needed help.

"Well, it sounds like you're keeping busy."

"Yes. It's kind of funny, though." Cindy smiled to herself. "Derek Hayes asked to take me to dinner. I feel almost guilty, but...I'm kind of looking forward to it."

"I suppose you don't have to go if it makes you uncomfortable. But I don't imagine Brian would want you to act like your life is over just because he's gone. And it's not like he can get mad at you, anyway."

"Exactly. Which, I don't know, almost makes it worse." Cindy gave a half-chuckle, half-sob. "How can I ever forget him? And yet, I agreed to go out with Derek. I've got this horrible feeling that my emotions are playing tricks on me."

Her mom was quiet for a moment. "I can see that. Take your time—you're still raw, and you might feel differently in a few months. If I were you, I'd lean on my church family. They're able to observe Derek without the same emotional fog."

"I'm so grateful for that, yes." Cindy's voice choked off as she thought of all the dinners Mrs. Goodwin had tried to push on her, and all the hugs and shoulder pats Ellie Jones had given her.

"If you didn't have First Baptist, I think I'd have stayed with you longer."

"I'm glad you didn't have to do that. I don't want to take you away from your commitments any more than necessary. I'm really glad you called, though."

"If there's anything we can do for you, you will let us know, right?"

"Of course."

"Well, unless there's anything else you want to talk about, I think I'll let you go. I just wanted to check in and make sure you're okay. Feel free to call anytime you need anything; we're not going anywhere."

"I will. Love you, Mom."

"Love you, too, sweetheart."

26. "Day By Day"

Derek was thumping in the bedroom, trying to find the *perfect* thing to wear. Robbie rolled his eyes. Just like a girl! It wasn't like this was the first time he'd met one-on-one with Cindy. So what, it was a fancy restaurant this time, instead of any of the other places where they'd gone on dates. Like the park or the mall. Yes, it was about time Derek admitted what he was doing…he was really and truly courting this lady.

"Hey, Rob, have you seen my nice shoes?"

"No. Check under your bed."

"I did…oh, there they are."

Robbie sighed and leaned his head on his hand. He was supposed to be watching the multimedia clips from the physics book's companion CD. Oh, the joy of animated parabolic calculations. He'd mastered sine and cosine years ago!

He clicked over briefly to his cracker program. Time estimated: thirty plus years. It was working through pronounceable combinations right now, but still nothing. He leaned his head back and grunted.

"No luck, huh?" Derek came out into the main room, winding a tie around his neck. *A tie! Oh, heaven preserve us.*

"Still chugging," Robbie answered, stretching.

"Man! I wonder if whatever's in his email is really worth it! I mean, it's probably 80% spam, anyway."

"Um…Didn't you say Brian didn't like to remember numbers? That he had trouble with birth-dates and stuff like that?"

"Right. Cindy said that."

No need to get persnickety. "Well, I figured he probably did something that he could remember without writing it down. Except not his own birthday, not his name, not their address, and so far not some mishmash of his or Cindy's name with anything else I can think of."

"Hum." Derek bent toward the screen, leaning on the desk. "Sounds like you've been pretty thorough. Hey, maybe it was related to something in his office."

"What do you mean?"

"I mean…something in his office helped him remember the password. That's pretty much where he sat, when he was on the computer at home."

"You mean like: yellow-pen-in-cup-holder-123? Dashes or no dashes?"

"No pens…" Derek muttered, pulling his jacket on and scratching his head. "Just a wireless inkjet printer, HP, and one of their wedding pictures in a special frame. Day by day…"

"Huh?"

"That's what the frame says. You know, the hymn? They sang it at their wedding, and Cindy's grandma gave them the frame. The picture's in a garden, and Cindy's on the right. They're…well…They'd just gotten married."

The longing look in Derek's eyes was pathetic. Or freaky scary. Robbie wasn't sure which he was feeling. He squeezed his arms across his stomach and looked away. If this went on…they'd wind up getting married. And then Rob would be on his own for good.

"That's what's on the computer desk," Derek continued, drawing breath and dropping to the couch to tie his shoes. "Over to the right's another table, with papers and bills and stuff on it."

Derek kept talking about the papers and the table, but Robbie stared at his computer screen, rubbing his nose. "Day by day." Cindy kept saying that, again and again. It was like her mantra. Like Pastor Raul and "God is good…all the time."

He closed his eyes, trying to envision Mom singing that song. She used to sing while she washed dishes in the kitchen, singing along with the radio, or the 2nd Chapter of Acts CDs. "Day by day…and with each *hmm*-ing moment…" Passing moment. "Day by day…and with each passing moment…strength I find…" Weird, how it'd been so long since he'd learned it, but it was still there, deep down inside him. He just had to remember how to drag it out.

"Well, I won't be long," Derek was saying, giving Rob's shoulders a squeeze as he headed for the door. "Be good. Eat one of those apples from the fridge, or they'll go bad."

"'K…"

The door closed, and the lock clicked. Rob sighed and hugged his arms. He could almost see what he was going to do… Day by day…

Derek's car engine started, and rumbled into silence as he drove away. Day by day…

Robbie pressed some keys on the keyboard, hiding the physics CD media. The cracker was still running, adding to the list of rejected passwords by the millisecond. He'd tried all the proper words already, so it wasn't that. Combinations of words?

His fingers flew over the keys. *Daybyday*. No. The password was thirteen characters long. *Day-by-day*…11, 12, 13. *Day-by-day-an*… Hm.

Rob put his hands behind his head, staring at the screen. He would get this cracked if it killed him. He was a two-bit programer, and a script-kitty hacker. *Redeem your honor, you sissy.*

Daybydayandwi. Da by da an wi ea p. Rob rubbed his eyes. He'd already checked Brian's recent web searches and files for something to do with password creation. Nothing. It was too long ago for the search history to be any use, and Brian hadn't copied any info onto his hard-drive. At least, not that a quick keyword search had turned up. Brian was way too smart, bad memory or no.

D b d a w e p m s I f t m. No…it probably contained some numbers, and probably some other symbols. Brian was good that way. He'd been pretty sharp about encrypting his hard-drive. What numbers?

Robbie racked his brain for what Derek had told him about Brian's habits, his likes and dislikes, his favorite numbers. He knew plenty of numbers that Derek might use, but this was Brian. What numbers would have been important enough to him to remember?

He punched in a few more combinations with 1234 stuck on the end. No go. He chewed at his lip, squeezing his eyes shut while his fingers hovered over the keyboard. He couldn't be bothered with sine and cosine now. He was going to get this if it was the last thing he did.

D b d a w e p m + five more characters. Keep punctuation? *D b d , a w e p m ,* _ _ _ _. Four places left. Perfect for…

Robbie rubbed his nose again, feeling his skin prickle over the back of his neck. Should he call Derek and ask…no, he remembered! His pounded on the keyboard for a moment, and held his breath.

Dbd,awepm0823

The computer made an electronic clicking sound. The window flipped up to reveal Brian's mailbox…full of unread mail. Lots and lots of unread mail. The last one that was marked as read was dated the day he died.

His hands shaking, Robbie grabbed the phone. As he started pressing in Derek's number, he peeked through the blinds on the front window. Funny…he didn't recognize those men. His finger paused over the call button as he stared out the window. He couldn't tell which apartment they were heading for, either.

27. "GONE"

He was late. Oh, so late. Derek thumped his head against his headrest to keep from honking at the idiot in front of him. Relax. He could roll down the window and yell something quippy at the guy. He imagined Cindy chuckling at him, if she were sitting next to him. He also imagined her rolling her eyes and ducking her head, half-amused, half-embarrassed.

Derek smiled to himself, drawing a deep breath. She wouldn't mind if he was a little late. Just a little. He could tell her about it when he got there. He smiled a little broader.

Larry Norman began singing "Lonely Boy". Derek rolled his eyes. He was at a stoplight...he should take the call. He pulled out his phone and hit the button.

"Derek, you gotta come home right now!"

"Rob–"

"Please, Derek!" The panting sound in Robbie's voice made him pause and listen more closely.

"What's wrong?"

"There are two guys outside, and...and they're walking back and forth on the sidewalk, looking at our door."

"So?"

"So...they look kind of tough. Look, can't you just come back–"

"No, I can't 'just come back'. Look, I'm running behind already. Just ignore them; they're probably neighbors–"

"They're not. I would know." Him and Mrs. Gibbons, the neighborhood watch.

"Okay, *friends* of neighbors, who are out for a smoke–"

"They're not smoking."

"Robbie! There's no law against walking around on a public sidewalk!"

Derek waited a few moments as the teen breathed into the mouthpiece. Was it possible to get prank calls from your own brother? Traffic was moving again...he should just hang up and–

"Derek, they're coming back this way. They've been out there for like ten minutes, and every time they go to the end, they turn around and come back toward our house."

"Like I said, there's no law against that." Cindy was going to think he forgot her. She would think he couldn't be on time for anything. He gripped the steering wheel harder to keep his hand from shaking. Not again. He was going to be there for her, to do what he'd said he would. Promise.

"Derek–"

"Listen, what do you want me to do, anyway? Would I say, 'You're freaking my brother out, go have your private conversation somewhere else'?"

"Derek, please." Rob's volume dropped as his pitch rose. "They're not talking. They're just walking back and forth, looking at our house. Please…"

Robbie had never sounded like that before. What on earth could two random guys do to scare him so bad?

"Fine. I'm coming back. I'll be a couple minutes. Really, though, if you're so scared, you should hang up and call the police."

"Okay."

"I'll be there, okay?"

The call hung up. Derek stared out the windshield for a moment, wondering what on earth he'd done. Hank was right…he and Cindy were on the verge of something. But now Robbie was going to ruin it.

Derek ground his teeth as he pulled a u-turn through an intersection. Someone blared their horn at him. Go jump in the lake.

Yeah, Cindy would be thrilled at having her whole evening cancelled because of his needy little brother. Only a jerk would suggest to his business client that she was more than a paycheck to him…more than someone to talk to…more than a sweet and beautiful sister in Christ…just to stand her up. She was probably sitting in the fancy booth right now, wondering if she should order for them…or if he'd forgotten all about her.

I understand, Mr. Hayes. Michelle's words echoed through his head. *Mr. Hayes.* 24 hours before, it had been Derek, but now it was Mr. Hayes. Because she *understood.* And nothing he could say could make her un-understand, that he wasn't just playing games with his brother's therapist, that he wasn't just trying to have fun, that she was the world to him, and…life had gotten in the way. He could still see her plastic, professional-to-client smile…her curt nods. He'd seen her face all the way home, as he crawled into the apartment, feeling like a beaten dog, and crawled into bed. Hiding from his problems. For two whole days.

It couldn't happen again. It was about to. He squeezed the steering wheel until his knuckles turned white. Robbie had better have a good explanation for this.

* * * *

Footsteps sounded in the living room outside. Robbie clawed under Derek's bed, one hand still clutching the phone where the police dispatcher was still saying calming things. Much good it did…the men, whoever they were, had made a thump at the door, and come right in. He just hoped they didn't hear him, here in the bedroom.

"Officers are on their way," the young woman said, from her safe little calling center. "Just stay on the line."

"Trying," Robbie whispered. He couldn't get a good grip of Derek's gun safe…not bending down from his chair. With his body folded in half, his chest was so cramped it was hard to breathe.

Squeezing his hand in a fist, he willed himself to focus. He lay the phone in the seat beside him, reaching down with both hands.

Their clattering footsteps showed they were walking on the kitchen linoleum, now. It wouldn't be long before they looked in here for whatever it was they wanted. He hooked the front of the safe with one finger, but the next moment it slid backward, further under the bed. If he scooched forward in his chair any farther, he'd fall right out to the floor. They'd be sure to hear that.

"I'm still here," he breathed, grabbing up the phone again. "Are you still there?"

"I'm still here," the lady answered soothingly. "It'll just be a few minutes…the squad car is close to your home now."

Abruptly, the bedroom door swung open. Rob heard the intruders' impolite exclamations even over his own yelp. One burglar lunged forward, clamping a hand over his mouth and neatly twisting the phone out of his grasp. As the thug pinned the teen against his chest, he reached over and dropped the handset onto the receiver.

"Oh, snap!" the other man hissed, still in the doorway. His dark eyes darted from Rob to his partner in crime. "The cops'll be here any minute!"

"Then you'd better find it fast!" snarled the other. His face, covered in a long, messy mustache, hovered just above Robbie's face. His big, calloused hand was so tight over the teen's mouth that he could barely breathe.

Twisting, Rob scratched at his face. Maybe he would let go for just a moment, so Rob could fill his lungs. All the thug did, however, was mutter curse words into Rob's ear. He grabbed Rob's fingers and bent them back the wrong way until he whimpered.

"Well?" he snapped, glaring at his accomplice, who was crawling under the two beds.

"Nothing," the other coughed, rising to his hands and knees. "Just that computer out there."

Hayes and Hayes

"Where's the laptop?" the mustache demanded, letting go of Rob's mouth and bringing his face around. Rob stifled a sneeze as he tried not to inhale the thug's reeking breath.

"Don't–" the teen squeaked.

"Hurry up! Where's the laptop?" The criminal repeated, giving him a shake that made his teeth rattle. Where were the police? Where was Derek?!

"No laptop!" Rob panted, trying to lean away from his captor. "We don't have one. We don't have a–"

The gangster's huge hand smacked across his face. "We know you've got it. Where is it?"

"Look, you want the coppers to see you working him over?" insisted the other burglar, plucking at his partner's shoulder. "Let's scram."

"And let him identify us? Is that really what you want, Jonny, you idiot?"

The second gangster took a step back, running his fingers through his black hair. "What do you want to do with him?" he murmured.

Ice-water pulsed through Robbie's veins as the big thug stared at him with much too thoughtful a look. He couldn't make a sound…he couldn't even swallow. Maybe he would retch. Maybe he would faint. Maybe his heart would climb right out his mouth and he would die of fear.

"Should we — call the boss?" whispered the thug called Jonny.

"What?! What for?" exclaimed the other one, sniffing and rubbing at his filthy mustache.

"Well…it ain't here. I can't find it anywhere. What else's we going to do?"

Jonny backed out the door, pulling his phone from his pocket and scratching at his forearm.

"Hurry up," answered his partner, grabbing a pair of Derek's socks and shoving them into Rob's mouth. At least they were clean. He was worrying about clean socks?!

Keeping hold of one of Robbie's wrists, the mustache-ruffian twisted Rob's arm behind his back and took the one step to the bedroom window. Tossing the lamp onto Derek's bed, he pulled up the shade. A loud curse broke from him when he saw the window air-conditioning unit. No quick escape that way.

Rob was just bringing his free arm around to loosen the socks when the goon dropped the shade and grabbed the arm. He twisted them both behind Rob's back so that the teen was bent over. Robbie trembled; the back of his shirt stuck to his skin as cold chills ran down his neck. The socks were too far back in his mouth, too…any second now, he was going to gag and heave. *Where are you Derek?!*

"Hurry up, Jonny, you moron," growled the big burglar.

The accomplice appeared in the doorway, pale-faced. "You'll never believe what he wants us to–"

"Enough yammering! Let's move it! What?"

"He said to…" Jonny pulled something out of his jacket pocket and held it out. Rob felt like his heart had forgotten to pump blood to his brain. A hypodermic.

28. "Fall Apart"

Derek had tried calling Cindy on the way back to his apartment. Twice. Either she had bad reception, or she wasn't answering his calls. He wasn't that late yet, was he? He pulled into his parking spot and drew a deep breath. Everything looked quiet. Robbie must have been overreacting again. How was he going to explain this to Cindy?

Derek hurried up to his door, and stopped dead. There were ugly scratches all around the lock, and the doorframe was gouged, too. No. Please, no.

Flashing lights filled the parking lot. Derek wanted to barrel through the door into whatever lay beyond, but he stood rooted on the front walk. He couldn't hear any sounds except the pounding of policemen boots. Not Robbie. This couldn't be happening.

"Excuse me, sir," began an officer, holding out a halting hand while his partner drew his weapon. "Keep your hands where we can see them, please."

"My brother," stammered Derek, reflexively raising his hands.

"Step back, please. Can I ask what you're doing here?"

"I just got home. He's home alone...I..."

"It's all right; he's good," came a familiar voice. A hand took Derek's elbow and eased him away from the door. "Go ahead and check the property, Hadley; I've got him."

The two officers who had arrived first pushed the door aside and crept into Derek's apartment, calling out their challenges.

Derek stood on the sidewalk, staring through the door of his own apartment. The afternoon light was reflecting off the kitchen linoleum, turning it the ugly yellow-brown it always turned when the sunset shone on it. Why wasn't there any sound? Why...

"Robbie?" he yelled through the door, feeling his pulse speed up in his wrists and neck. "Robbie, it's me!"

More police officers brushed past him and slipped into his apartment.

"All clear," muttered the voice at his elbow.

Derek followed the officers inside, taking in the radio chatter, the police examining a footprint on the carpet, the books dumped onto the floor, the kitchen cupboards standing open. No teenage boy; no wheelchair.

His pulse hammering in his temples, Derek pushed through to the bedroom door, glancing over another officer's shoulder.

"No!" he yelled. "What happened? He can't be–"

"Relax." Sgt. Blake grabbed Derek's arm again. "Paramedics are on their way. Just–"

"He can't be dead! What's wrong?! What–"

"Derek, chill!" Hank grabbed his shoulders and gave him a couple violent shakes. "Get a grip! We just got here; we don't know any more than you do."

"But…" Derek stammered, backing into a wall and peeking again at the form of his brother. They'd left him lying on his bed… on *Derek's* bed. The dingbats…it was higher than Robbie's bed was.

"I think he's asking for you," the cop by Robbie's side murmured, glancing out the door. "Derek?"

"Yes."

"Don't touch anything," Hank muttered as Derek slipped past the police in the doorway and knelt beside Rob.

"Derek?"

"I'm here, Rob," Derek whispered, reaching out to stroke the teen's arm. His stomach went numb…Rob's left sleeve was pushed up to the elbow. "Are you okay?"

"Fine!" Robbie gave an eery giggle. "Guess what, huh, Derek?"

"What?"

"They wanted a *laptop*!" He raised his free arm into the air, waving it vaguely at a spot on the wall. "I told them...that we didn't have a laptop," he slurred, hiccuping in the middle of his sentence. "But they...they still wanted one." Robbie rubbed at his face, his eyes roaming around the room. "Derek?"

"I'm right here, Robbie," he gasped again. Was that sirens he heard outside? Oh, he prayed so.

"I *told* them...we didn't have a...laptop," Robbie continued, waggling his finger at the air. "But they said we *did*. What laptop...did they mean?"

"I don't know, Rob."

"High as a kite," muttered an officer in the doorway, turning to leave. Derek wanted to slug him – anybody – but he kept rubbing his brother's arm. Whoever had done this would pay. Derek choked and swallowed hard. If he'd been home, doing his duty, none of this would have happened.

"What...did they mean...what..." Rob was repeating, gazing wonderingly at his thumb.

Derek turned his head, hoping that was the sound of paramedics making their way in the door. Moments later, an ambulance team appeared, while the sergeant gave them some quick instructions.

Derek backed up and sat on Robbie's bed to let them get at the patient.

"Yep...he's about as high as they come," the head paramedic commented, while his crew moved around the teen with their instruments. "How long since he injected?"

"Can't be more than five minutes," answered an officer. "He was on the phone with our dispatcher when the intruders broke in."

"Intruders?"

Robbie started mumbling Derek's name, staring about unseeingly. Derek rose, feeling like he might hurl.

"Hey, Rick...come tell us what's gone," Hank muttered, pulling on Derek's sleeve. "They'll take care of him, and it'll be a few minutes. Our forensic team is on their way."

Derek followed the cop into the main room and blinked around at his home. The bookshelves had been emptied. Kitchen cupboards had been banged open. Robbie's computer had been turned around, but not unplugged. What *had* they taken?

"What about the meds?" asked Hank, steering Derek toward the bathroom.

Derek rubbed his head, holding on to his stomach. The medicine cabinet hadn't even been opened. "I don't get it," he breathed, turning to his friend with a strained face. "There's nothing...Not that I can see. Robbie said they wanted a laptop. I don't get it..."

"Yeah, I heard him. They *said* that you had a laptop? Do you think they really said that? Or do you think he's just wired?"

Wired. High. Injected. Just like Brian Lane. Derek choked back the nausea and whipped his phone out of his pocket. Even if Cindy wasn't answering his phone calls, he had to warn her. He brought up text messaging and punched in a message.

"You think this is linked to the Lane case, then?" Hank whispered.

"Gotta be. Nothing's gone. They didn't even bother scratching at the safe." Derek glanced around the main room again, grimacing at the shards of casserole dish they'd left on the floor. "And they didn't shoot Robbie, or strangle him, or anything. They left a distinct mark. Like..."

"Like Brian," Sgt. Blake finished.

The paramedics wormed their way out of the bedroom, wheeling Robbie on a gurney. He was still mumbling under his breath, but his eyes had gone glassy.

"We need to get him to a hospital," the chief paramedic explained. "Can we contact his legal guardian?"

"That would be me," Derek rasped.

"You go with them — I'll handle everything here," Hank told him, patting Derek's shoulder. "You get Rob taken care of – I'll take care of everything else."

As they made their way outside to the ambulance, Derek looked at his brother's face again. Robbie's eyes had closed, and his breathing was shallow.

"Is he going to be all right?" Derek asked.

"We'll do our best."

* * * *

Cindy glanced at her watch again. After twenty minutes, Derek still hadn't shown up. Traffic couldn't be that bad over by his apartment, could it?

She sighed and stirred her Coke. She hoped nothing bad had happened. Had she gotten the right place? She must have — she remembered reviewing the directions with Derek, and this was the only sit-down pizza place on this road. And she couldn't have gotten the time wrong; it was right after she got off work.

Had she gotten the date wrong? She must have gotten something wrong. Derek would never… And for him to be this late…

Maybe he'd been held up? She smiled in spite of herself. There would be something impossibly ironic about Derek having another car accident. What if that was what had happened, and he'd been hurt or something? Her forehead creased and she glanced toward the door again. She didn't want him hurt. Still, she'd rather have it be something like that than – he just changed his mind. Could he really change his mind about her, about the case, about… everything tonight was supposed to be?

Well…wouldn't he have called her if he were able to? Of course he would have. He called her about everything, even little things. Like when he couldn't be at church events where she hadn't even been expecting him to show up.

Cindy grabbed her purse and began digging in it. After several minutes of hunting, she slapped her forehead. Of course! She'd woken up that morning with her phone as flat as a pancake—she'd forgotten to plug it in overnight for some reason. It was still sitting on her bedside table, and by now the battery light was probably green and full.

Derek must have called her, and she just hadn't gotten the call. What could it be about? Was she overreacting?

She rose to her feet and walked up to the hostess table.

"Excuse me…I've been at table four. But I need to run home and get something. I'm supposed to meet a young man here; if he shows up, could you tell him I'll just be a few minutes?"

As she drove home, she wondered what could have kept him. Maybe he really had been involved in an accident. She punched on the radio and switched to the news station, just in case. Maybe Robbie had needed help of some kind… What if he'd fallen and needed to go to the ER? That would be bad. She couldn't think of anything else that would keep Derek away…keep him away from her.

Maybe that was just her emotions, though. Derek had other things in his life that had to be important. She was getting way too invested over this thing. It was irrational — he was just late. But… why?

Cindy hoped there was a message on her phone that explained everything.

She pulled into the driveway and strode up to her front door. As she slipped her key into the lock, she glanced over her shoulder at a dark car that was just pulling onto her street.

Cindy closed the door behind her and dashed upstairs to grab her cellphone. Sure enough, it was fully charged. She flipped it open to check if Derek had left a message. Two missed calls, both from Derek, and he'd left her messages both times. A knot closed in her stomach. Maybe she wasn't overreacting, and there really was something wrong. At least he'd thought to call. Of course he had — why would she mistrust him?

Derek couldn't have called from the restaurant, unless he'd arrived exactly as she left. She moved her thumb over the button to replay the messages.

Almost subconsciously, she heard the sound of a car engine turning off. Walking to the front window and glancing out, she saw that the dark car, either a faded black or a nondescript grey, had pulled up into her driveway, behind her car. None of the neighbors were usually this rude.

Her heart pounding, she watched two men climb out of the car. They were dressed in shabby jackets and jeans…not the normal apparel for the locals.

The cellphone buzzed, and she glanced down at it. A text from Derek, now.

Thugs my apartment want Brian's laptop

Brian's laptop. Why would anyone want that, and why would they think it was at Derek's house?

The two men from the car were on the sidewalk, now, glancing this way and that. They sauntered toward her walk, and her front door.

Cindy pounded down the stairs and turned the deadbolt on the front door. Holding her breath, she peeked out the front again. The men, both ill-shaven, were coming up her walk while eyeing the first-story windows. One of them, with a big, black mustache hanging over and into his mouth, reached out and knocked on the door.

Cindy tore upstairs again. Her hands shaking, she shoved Brian's laptop into his computer bag, and moved across the hall to the bedroom. Was she being hysterical? She clicked open the safe under the bed and took out the gun Brian had bought her, strapping it on with the holster her dad had given her. Was she panicking over two poor guys who wanted to mow her lawn or something? They shouldn't have parked their car blocking her driveway, then.

Her hands froze as she was slipping her own laptop into the laptop bag. Her car sat in the driveway, trapped. What could she do? Tell them she had to leave, and ask them to move? That would be like inviting them to ransack her house as soon as she was gone.

They were knocking harder, now. She crept down the stairs and peeked through a front window once more, before slipping through the laundry room. Maybe the men were just innocent dayworkers, who had shown up at a bad time. Nevertheless, she could almost hear Derek's voice in her head...*I just want you safe.*

Her hand was shaking so hard, she could barely get the door open, but she finally stepped into the garage and locked the door behind her. Not that there was anything terribly valuable in the garage.

She unlocked Brian's car, whispering a prayer of thanks that she still hadn't traded it in. She'd chided herself a few times about the insurance expense, but now she was glad she'd delayed. If her view through the window had been correct, their car should be behind hers, leaving the second bay of the garage free.

As she started the car, she could hear the men still banging on her door. Would they knock it completely down? If they were honest insurance salesmen or whatever, surely they would have decided that she wasn't interested by now.

The garage door started to open. Cindy pushed down the door locks and put the car in gear, hoping the men wouldn't figure out what she was doing until it was too late.

The banging had stopped, but she hadn't heard them drive away. She pulled out her phone and punched in the number for the police. This was what she paid taxes for. As she pulled down the driveway and hit the garage door opener again, she saw the men glance around at her.

Her pulse quickening, she tucked the phone against her shoulder and stepped on the accelerator.

"Hello, there are two strange men knocking at the door of my house, and they've blocked my driveway with their car. My name is Cindy Lane..."

29. "You Are More"

The ambulance was slow. Way too slow. Derek huddled in his corner of the vehicle, chewing his lip. They were supposed to be a priority vehicle — didn't all those idiots who never pulled over for sirens realize someone's life was at stake?

Derek leaned his elbows on his knees and watched Robbie's face. His brother's eyes were closed, an oxygen tube running under his nose, his head to one side to keep drool from accumulating in his throat.

Derek suddenly realized that Mom had always been right. The boys had their dad's nose. And Dad was right, too. Robbie had his mom's long, dark lashes.

"Oh, Dad, I'm so sorry," Derek whispered. He'd sat like this, staring at what was left of his father's face, listening to all the machines beep and wondering what it meant. The nurses had begged him to let them check him for concussion. Take him away, and let the shock wear off. But he'd sat there, listening to the machines beep and watching the green line stop moving. Dad hadn't even woken up. But Derek had still promised him. "I'll take care of Robbie. I'll look after him. He's going to be all right; I'll take care of it." And he knew Dad was depending on him just as much as Robbie was.

He reached out and stroked Rob's thick, brown hair; it stuck together with sweat. Mom would say he needed a hair cut. She'd said that the day she died. "You know, you boys need a hair-cut," she'd said. "You're going to look like girls soon." And they'd laughed at it. Now it made him want to weep rather than laugh.

The paramedics murmured encouraging things. Static. This was probably their third call tonight. They didn't know Robbie; it didn't mean anything to them. It was a job, a paycheck, a way of life. Static; it just emphasized Derek's aloneness.

He buried his face in his hands, trying to tune out the ambulance siren. What had those rats given him? Meth, like Brian? Or worse…like Brian? At least Robbie wasn't dead yet — What would organ collapse even look like? Whatever it was, the drug couldn't have been in his system more than an hour or so.

Whoever they were, they'd better be miles away by now. Derek didn't care who they were, when he caught them... If. When. What pointless chatter. First Brian Lane, now his boy. And it was his fault, this time.

Finally, they arrived at the hospital. Fluorescent lights; people in scrubs. Gurneys and the reek of sanitizers. They rolled Robbie down the hall and into a room.

Derek leaned motionless against a wall while the nurses puttered around his brother, stripping off his shirt, sticking needles in him. Derek passed his ID and insurance card to a clerk, who whisked out with them.

Someone shoved a clipboard in his hands, and he found himself filling in boxes.

Name: Robert E. Hayes; Birthdate: Feb. 18...; Parent or Legal Guardian: Derek C. Hayes

And what a job he'd done of it, too. He hoped Hank would give him a good character reference. His ward ODed on an illegal substance...not something that would look good on his resumé. Especially in law enforcement. He realized he'd misspelled their street name...in pen. Mrs. Gibbons was probably right; he wasn't in any way fit to take care of his brother.

He looked up to watch them arrange ice packs on Robbie's body. Sixteen was too young to die. This couldn't be happening. This could *not* be happening.

"You done with that, sir?" asked a gentle female voice. Derek handed the forms over blindly.

"What's wrong with him?" he rasped.

"So far treatment is mostly symptomatic," she explained. "We've got an IV in to rehydrate him, and the ice packs should help lower his body temperature. He's probably in shock right now, but there's no sign he's had a heart attack or stroke at this point."

Derek nodded dumbly, watching a nurse draw a blood sample. The machines in this room were beeping. Derek hated beeping machines. Beep. Beep. Beep. How many beeps did you get? When would Robbie run out of beeps, and the machine would shut off?

Derek gripped the board at the foot of the bed, while the nurses moved around him with their gadgets and tools. He ran his tongue over the roof of his mouth, listening to Robbie's breath going in and out, in and out. It was labored and raspy, but it was still going.

He'd held vigil like this last time, too. He had sat and watched Robbie, waiting for him to wake up, dreading what he was going to tell him. Wondering how he would answer his questions…how he would reassure him.

Derek drifted forward and slipped into the chair by Robbie's head. "It's all right, Robbie," he breathed. *All right. All right.* How could it be all right? How had he done it that time? He'd patted Robbie's head, smiled at him. "I'm here. I'm here. You're going to be all right."

When he closed his eyes, the little boy's face stared back at him: wide eyed, pale, a band-aid on the right cheek, a bandage on the back of his head. Minor concussion. Nothing serious. The real damage was farther down.

As for Derek, he had a bruise on his left arm from the driver's side door. And muscle stiffness from the jolt. All the doctors and nurses called him a miracle… It wasn't fair. He'd still never broken a bone in his life.

And Robbie had never blamed him for it. There'd been pain and anguish, to be sure, but none of the psychiatrist's turning-against-your-caregiver-in-frustration. He'd always struggled on. Encouraged Derek in his career choices…all of them. Listened when Derek talked about Michelle. Been supportive when she told Derek to seek "other counseling options".

Michelle. And now Cindy. He'd never heard back from Cindy. She probably thought he was a self-centered jerk, like a stereotypical private eye, who'd been playing games with her all this time. He felt like all his guts had magically vanished, leaving nothing but an empty cavity. Should he call her again? He'd never be able to explain it...even if she gave him the chance. *Why me?*

Derek needed something to do with his hands, so he reached out and grabbed Rob's. It burned, like the rest of him. He squeezed it. Hard. *React, boy, react!* Do something...let me know you're still there.

Here they were again, just like last time. Derek in the chair beside the hospital bed, Robbie in it. Unconscious. How bad was it this time? "There's no sign he's had a heart attack or stroke at this point." Who had told him that...probably one of the nurses. How long would "this point" last? Derek squeezed Rob's hand again. He couldn't tell if it was getting cooler or not. Why wasn't he better already?

"Mr. Hayes?" Another nurse had come into the room, adjusting the IV bag and glancing at the monitors. "Admitting has some questions for you." She checked Rob's blood pressure. "Would you mind stepping out to the desk?"

"Uh...no," Derek answered weakly, staring at what her hands were doing. "Is he going to be okay?"

She looked up, and smiled. "We're doing everything we can," she assured him. "We'll probably need to keep monitoring him through the night. I'm not sure why he hasn't come to yet, but the best thing we can do is wait and respond to his symptoms."

Derek nodded, rising, and shuffled out of the room.

"Hayes?" the desk clerk asked, clicking something on her computer screen.

"Yes. I'm Derek, the patient is Robert."

"And the guardian is..."

"Me."

She clicked something on the keyboard, and grabbed the mouse again. "You're his..."

"Brother."

She raised an eyebrow.

Derek gritted his teeth. "The paperwork's back at my apartment, but I've got legal custody."

"All right." The clerk squinted at the screen a moment, and glanced up at him, holding out his ID cards. "We've got your insurance information. Any preexisting conditions we should be aware of?"

"Uh…" Isn't this what they had everything on the computer for – so they wouldn't have to keep asking these inane questions? "He's got a spinal cord injury."

"When did this happen?"

"Four years ago. June 27th. 2:08 p.m. Ish."

The clerk cocked her eyebrow higher. Derek glanced over his shoulder, then back at her. Robbie needed him. He envisioned his brother waking up all alone, no one beside him…

"Derek?"

Derek turned around.

Pastor Jones advanced across the waiting room, his hand out. "What brings you here?" he asked, shaking Derek's hand.

Derek looked at the clerk. "Are you done with me?"

"I guess for the moment," she answered.

Gesturing, Derek led Rev. Jones down the hall toward the room. "It's Robbie," he mumbled. "Long story. Meth OD."

They slipped into the room and stood next to the bed. Robbie lay in the same position the nurse had left him in.

"Some men broke in," Derek choked. "I was out. It wasn't his fault, it…it's my fault. I wasn't there. I think he's going to die."

"I don't care whose fault it is. God isn't done with you yet…either of you."

Rev. Jones watched them for a moment, while Derek stroked Rob's hand and tried to breathe. The pastor reached over and squeezed the two hands.

"Excuse me for a moment, if you please." A doctor, betrayed by his white coat and name-tag, had materialized at the foot of the bed. "This'll just take a moment."

He introduced himself and shook Derek's hand before he shuffled the two visitors away from the bed and took Robbie's pulse again. Derek watched him frown and turn to the nurse to ask a question. He started frowning harder and moved to Rob's other side.

He was going to die. His brother was going to die. Because he hadn't protected him. Because he hadn't done all the things a real father would do. Because he was just a kid, play-acting a dad, and that's not what Robbie needed.

The reverend was rubbing Derek's arm. Derek blinked and turned back to him, trying to focus. "May I pray for you?" Pastor Jones asked softly.

"Please. Please."

The pastor put his hand on Derek's shoulder and began murmuring to his God. Soft, patient requests. Thanks for continued grace. Requested blessings for others, with expectation of fulfillment. Dad. Dad. Just like Dad and Mom. They'd be doing the same thing, if they were here.

Derek smacked his hands into his face and held them there. If they were here, none of this would have happened. Robbie would still live with them, and Derek's life wouldn't be able to touch him with its deadly effects...

He felt his knees melting under him. He slumped against the wall, fighting the heaving in his chest. He clamped his hands over his mouth and eyes, lest anything flow out. He must not... not...

Rev. Jones slid his arm around Derek's shoulders to support him, still praying. The gentle words washed over Derek as his throat spasmed and he held his breath to keep from sobbing.

Not Robbie. Anything but Robbie.

Anything?

Not Robbie.

Or you'll do...what?

No...please...

Or what? My grace is sufficient for you.

Oh, man.

Well, it is.

Derek slid to the floor and buried his face in his hands. Not Robbie. Anything – well, almost any– no, anything. Anything but his innocent baby brother. Please. *Robbie...always there for me... always waiting for me, right there... Man! I didn't let him know how much he meant to me.*

Rev. Jones knelt beside him. Derek clutched his arms against his chest to hide their shaking. His heart was trying to crawl out his throat. All these years, Robbie had been his life. And now, in one fell stroke, everything he had left lay in pieces at his feet.

Where do you think I've been?

...Where?

Right behind you.

A father to the fatherless. A protector of widows.

"I know Robbie has professed to be Your child," Jones was saying, his eyes closed. "He has told us of his faith in You and his confidence in meeting his parents again, in Your house. Lord, You know what is in his heart, and I pray You will strengthen him and give him Your peace, which passes all understanding."

Pastor Raul had prayed for them, the day of the accident. Derek remembered his own emptiness, the blank incomprehension of what had happened, of what lay ahead.

"I can feel his pain as he agonizes over what might happen to his brother, and his own powerlessness to help him. Lord, touch his heart with Your peace, which passes understanding, and let him rest in Your hands. Because Your hands are big enough to hold even this."

My grace is sufficient. They'd never gone hungry. They'd always had a roof over their head. Even while working through Robbie's therapy, and the stone wall of Michelle's rejection…Pastor Raul had been like a father to them. Teaching them to rely on God.

Rev. Jones murmured an Amen, and pulled Derek to his feet. The doctor stood before them, with a clip-board.

"Well, according to the lab results, he's got a critical level of methamphetamine in his bloodstream."

We'd guessed as much.

"Any idea how this happened?"

"Some men broke into my apartment," Derek gasped, amazed that he could speak at all. "They wanted to kill him. I guess they go in for novelty hits," he added.

"Novelty is right. I've never heard of it being involuntarily administered before." The doctor cocked his eyebrows and handed Derek a clipboard. "We've administered something to bring his body temperature down. Rehydration is going well, and there's still no sign of a stroke, or heart attack. He must have good circulation. I think we'll transfer him up to ICU so we can monitor him at least 12 hours. If you'll just fill out these forms…"

As the medical staff filed out, Derek dropped into the chair again and began the paperwork. The pastor arranged a seat at the end of the bed, and sat also.

Derek looked up and blinked for a moment. "How did you get here?" he asked.

Jones smiled. "I was just visiting Mrs. Goodwin; she got her new knee today, you know. I was just going to go home when I saw you just now. I saw the paramedic team hustle through the ER, earlier; was that you guys, too?"

"Yeah…"

"Don't worry," the pastor assured him. "He'll be all right."

Derek heaved a sigh and stared blankly at the sheet of checkboxes. It took him a moment to remember how to spell "Lyrica".

Derek glanced up at his brother's face. "Do you think he's breathing easier?"

They both strained their ears as Robbie's chest rose and fell with his breathing. Maybe it was deeper, and more regular, than it had been. Derek grabbed his hand again. It still felt hot. Was the doctor right?

Rev. Jones stood. "If you'll excuse me, I should call my wife. I'd like to stick around, if that'd be okay with you, and she'd like to know." He started toward the door, and paused. "Do you mind if we tell the prayer chain? How much do you want us to say?"

"Prayer…uh…I don't know. I don't care. Whatever you think they want to know, I guess. I mean…make sure they know it's not Robbie's fault."

"It's not your fault either, you know."

"Well, yes, it sort of–"

"It's not." Rev. Jones laid his hand on Derek's shoulder again and leaned down to meet his eyes. "Break-ins happen all the time. Whether you were there or not has nothing to do with it. I know you would have done anything in your power to protect him, but there are some things you don't have control over. And you need to let them go."

Rev. Jones left. Derek felt the pen slip from his fingers and drop to the floor. Robbie's temples still glistened with sweat, but he definitely wasn't panting anymore. The machine beeps sounded less urgent.

You don't have control. It was a terrifying thought. And yet…it was just about the truest thing about Derek's life. He'd been driving the speed limit, through a green intersection, and someone had flown around a blind corner and run the red into him. Little consolation that he was as loaded as they come, and didn't survive what to him was a head-on collision. It'd taken Derek and Rob at least a year to pick up the pieces. They still weren't healed; Robbie would never be fully healed. Not all the way down.

But why had God protected Derek? He still had the use of his legs…and drove the streets of the city to this day. He hadn't been home when the thugs had broken in tonight…it could be him in the hospital bed, not Robbie. Why wasn't it? He was the detective, doing all the investigating and talking to people, the one who could identify all sorts of people. Robbie was just a kid. How was that fair?

"Life isn't fair". His mom had loved that saying, especially on chore day. Derek rubbed his face. Robbie had gotten the short end of everything. Derek had been acting like a little kid, focused on *his* wants and *his* dreams. A successful career. Investigative excitement. Important service to the community. A wife.

He swallowed hard. God had spared him so far for something. God knew what. He would focus on using the time for God's wants and plans. He let out a breath, thinking of all the time he had wasted; and God had still given him more time. Time to wait, to grow, to be more like the man God wanted him to be. To be the guardian Robbie needed him to be. If he survived the night. *Please, God. I know You're mighty and You know all things. But I need my brother. Please leave him with me for a bit longer.*

Derek glanced down at Robbie, and choked. His eyes had flickered; he knew it. He leaned forward onto the bed, staring with all his might. Long moments stretched together.

Robbie's eyelids dragged upward, and drooped down again. Derek's heart was hammering his rib-cage sore. There again: two glimmers of eyeball, while the pupils roved around confusedly.

Derek buried his face in the hospital blanket while hot water streamed down his face.

30. "Let the Rain Fall Down"

It felt like he'd been running 100 miles an hour, like his whole body had gone for a massive spasm party. It was worse than when he'd seen Dad and Derek watching a scary movie, late at night, when he was little and had to go to bed first.

His chest hurt, and his muscles quivered with tiredness. But he was breathing easier, now. His head felt hot, but there was soothing coldness all down his body. Maybe, sometime soon, he would feel a little chilly…but he didn't have the strength to shiver.

And now he was waking up. So tired. So…trembly. So…

Men! That's right…he'd forgotten about them. Men, in the apartment, and they were going to…

He forced his eyes open and swallowed. There were a lot of bright lights. His head ached, and his chest ached a little bit, and all his muscles felt used up.

His eyes focused on his arm. Something was sticking in it…a needle! A big, long needle dripping something clear into him! He couldn't let them do that…he had to stop them…

As he tugged his arm to free it, he heard someone say, "Robbie. Robbie, stop. Relax, stop it, Robbie."

Derek. Derek's voice. Robbie flipped his head over. His one arm was stuck, but he could use his other one… He groped into the clearing haze. Weird bracelet sliding on his wrist, getting in the way. Derek.

Derek's shirt. Derek's face. Derek's hands on either side of his head, stroking his hair. *Say it, man. Say it.*

"It's all right, Robbie."

He'd said it. Robbie let the rest of his body relax as he closed his fist on Derek's shirt.

"I gotcha, Robbie. You're going to be okay."

Robbie felt a smile pull at his face. Derek was here. Holding on to him. Just like last time. Of course it would be okay. It was last time. And Derek was there.

"Derek..."

"I'm here, Robbie."

"Where am I?"

"ICU of Saint James'. Don't worry; doctor's running some labs to check your blood again."

"What was it—they gave me?"

"Meth. But don't worry. You're going to be okay."

Somebody moved at the end of the bed. Robbie blinked until he recognized Pastor Jones, smiling at him.

"You're awake," he commented, coming forward and squeezing Rob's ankle. "Looks like you're going to pull out of it, buddy."

"Yes, he's going to be fine. You wouldn't leave me, would you, Robbie?"

You kidding?

"Oh, you're going to be all right," gasped Derek, leaning down and hugging Rob.

When he got that close, Robbie could see that his brother's face was a little red and swollen. He couldn't have been crying... could he? The last time Derek cried was when he got home from talking to Michelle the last time, and he'd tried to explain it to Robbie – and he'd suddenly staggered into the bedroom and shut the door. Rob had left him alone as long as he could; he didn't want to see Derek acting like a baby. That would be too embarrassing for Derek. And now – he hadn't been doing it again, had he? Had it really been...that serious?

"What happened?" he whispered.

"You tell me," Derek answered. "Those guys broke in, didn't they?"

Robbie nodded mutely.

"Well…you were right, I guess. Oh, Rob, I'm so sorry." Derek bent over and put his hands over his face. "I'm so sorry."

"Derek!" Rob struggled to sit up. It made his head spin, and his lungs feel squeezed, but he propped himself up with his arms. "Derek! You said everything was okay, right? Everything's going to be okay!"

"Of course it is," put in the pastor, stepping forward and putting a hand on Derek's shoulder. "But you see…Derek, as a man, feels like he's responsible for everything. He wishes he had been able to protect you, or done something to help you. It's very hard…for a man to watch someone he loves suffer and not be able to do anything. But you see, that's where we have to rely on God's strength."

Rev. Jones put his other hand on Robbie's shoulder. "We have to trust to God's protection, because He is strong enough to take all of this and turn it into something good, for His glory."

Derek was right. Pastor Jones talked *exactly* like Dad. Rob reached out and touched Derek's shoulder.

"Derek…You're going to be okay."

Robbie bit his lip as he thought of all the times Derek had reassured him that way, but he'd never thought about who would tell Derek that. Now that he thought about it, Pastor Raul had counseled Derek, but then he'd moved to Texas. And since then, it'd pretty much been him and Derek…until Cindy. And Cindy had introduced them to the people at First Baptist. And Derek had gotten all excited about something again.

Something sticky got in Robbie's throat. Either he was having trouble breathing again, or his body was trying to cry.

"Derek," he gasped, grabbing his brother's chin. "You need to look at me so I can tell you that you're okay." Mom was fond of telling people to look at her. "You're okay. It's all okay."

Derek put his hands down and met Rob's eyes. His face looked a little shiny, but it was doubtless just the hospital lights. That was all.

"I know, Rob," Derek whispered, squeezing Robbie's hand. "I'm just happy, that's all."

Someone cleared their throat. "Look, I'm sorry for busting in, but can somebody tell me what's going on?"

Everyone turned to stare as Cindy stepped forward. She glanced at the pastor and made a strained smile.

"Your wife told me Robbie was in the hospital," she explained. "What's going on? Is everything okay?"

"Yeah...yeah..." Derek nodded, standing up while keeping his hand on Robbie's shoulder. "Thank goodness you're all right. I tried to call you–"

"I forgot my phone at the house," she explained with a grimace. "But I got your text. What about Rob?" She looked straight at him, her face lined and strained, her eyes fixed on his. She really wanted to know.

"I think he's over the hump," Derek answered, stroking Rob's back. "We're still waiting for the doctor's word, though. He just woke up a little bit ago."

"But what did they do? I mean...you said men were at your house..."

"They...They had a needle," Robbie whispered. It might be the first time he had ever spoken straight to her. "They stuck me with something."

"Oh, no." She squeezed her eyes closed and drew a deep breath. "Just like Brian."

"Yes."

Robbie stared as Cindy put her hands over her face. The pastor moved forward to put his arm around her shoulders.

"You could be dead," she gasped. "I'm so sorry."

"It's not your fault," Derek exclaimed, reaching out towards her. "You can't be blamed for any of this."

"I'm still sorry."

Derek sighed and looked down at Robbie. "Me too."

Rob shook his head. "I'm fine. It's okay. Remember?" He summoned a smile for his brother. "It's okay."

Derek smiled, too. "Good boy."

Good boy. At least Derek was talking to him, still, instead of forgetting about the whole rest of the world.

* * * *

"That was the police," Cindy explained, coming around the privacy curtain again and closing her phone. "The officers that went to my house. They've found what might be jimmy marks on my lock, but they can't tell if anything's gone. I have to go back there."

Derek stepped forward. "By yourself? Do you want me to–"

"No. No. You need to stay with Rob. He needs you." Cindy heaved a deep sigh and rubbed her face. "I've only had a scare tonight — he almost died."

Derek glanced down at his brother and slipped his hand around Rob's wrist. "Yeah. Y...You're right." His face brightened. "Hang on a sec."

Derek whipped out his phone and punched in a number. A phone ringer went off in the doorway.

"Hang on," Sgt. Blake exclaimed from the doorway, glancing in at all the people in the room. "Someone wants me."

"I do. You're just the man I want to see," Derek answered, canceling his call. "What brings you out this way?"

"Well, visiting hours aren't over for a few minutes, anyway." Hank grinned and stepped forward. "Hey, good to see you with your eyes open, buddy."

"Thanks, Mr. Hank."

"Okay, spill it, what do you want?"

"Mrs. Lane was about to go back to her house to consult with the officers there," Derek explained. "Some people were approaching her house about the time I texted her, which must have been...7:10 or thereabouts. She called the police and left in the other car."

"Well, if you think these two events are linked, it makes sense for me to head over there," the policeman agreed, shoving his hands into his pockets.

"I'd appreciate you going over with her. To – make sure she's not followed and stuff."

"I get the picture, Rick," Hank answered with a wink.

"Do you really think Cindy is going to be in any kind of danger?" asked Rev. Jones. "If so, we'd be more than happy to offer that she spend the night at our house."

"It...I...Didn't sound like they were out looking to hurt people," mumbled Robbie. "Unless they think she could identify them."

"Which brings us to my real reason for being here," Sgt. Blake began, pulling a notepad out of his back pocket and feeling around his person for a pen. "Got any descriptions for me, Rob E?"

"I dunno," Robbie answered, dropping his eyes and adjusting the hospital gown. "There was a big mustache...the mean one had a mustache. He...He's the one that put Derek's socks in my mouth."

Derek smashed his fist into his hand and spun around to face the privacy curtain.

"I saw him," breathed Cindy. "I mean, one of the men at my house had a mustache – it almost covered his mouth…"

Rob nodded. "And smelled really bad."

"I wouldn't know about that."

Sgt. Blake cleared his throat. "Let's not adulterate the statement here. Go on; there was more than one attacker?"

"Two." Rob cleared his throat. "The other one was Jonny. He's the one who talked on the phone."

"The phone?" pressed Hank, scribbling with his pen.

"Sorry. One…one of them… Well, I'll start at the beginning." Rob shifted his left arm, then reached over with his right to scratch the left side of his head.

After a brief summary of his experiences, he drew a breath and rubbed his face. Derek was pacing back and forth by the door, whacking his palm with his fist. Cindy, her face drawn, shuddered and reached over to give Robbie's hand a squeeze.

"Well, those descriptions aren't much to go on…" the cop muttered, making a few extra jots in the notebook. "But in the next few days, Derek can bring you down to the station and we'll show you some mug shots. Copeland does really good sketches; maybe you can work with him, too."

"Okay."

"You're a good man. Glad to see you're pulling through okay."

"Thanks."

Hank shook hands all around, and waited at the door while Cindy hugged the pastor and Derek and brushed a kiss onto Robbie's forehead.

"Call me when you guys get home, no matter what time it is," she told them. "I want to be sure you're okay."

"Likewise," Derek answered. "Sorry about dinner—"

"Not your fault."

"Be safe."

"You, too." She smiled and slipped out the door while Rob stared after her, rubbing his cheek. She hugged Derek, but she kissed him.

"Do you think they'll release him tonight?" asked Rev. Jones.

"I have no idea," answered Derek, sinking into the chair by Robbie's bed. "Oh, man, and my car's still back at the house."

"Why...?"

"I can be around to give you a ride," Jones answered with a smile. "Just let me call my wife. We'll make sure you guys get home just fine."

As the pastor left, Derek answered in a low tone, "I rode with you in the ambulance. You were probably too whonked out to notice."

Robbie sat silent for a long moment. "You came back to the apartment?" he whispered.

"I told you I would."

"Did you call her?"

"I tried." Derek smiled. Right now, he looked a lot like an old man...wrinkled and tired. "Her cell phone was at the house, she said."

Rob closed his eyes and drew another breath. "Derek, guess what."

"What?" Derek rested his head on one hand.

"D - b - d - , - a - w - e - p - m - 08 - 23."

"What?!"

Derek was sitting up now. Robbie grinned.

"Capital D, lower b, d, comma, a, w, e, p, m, digits oh-8, 23."

"But…what…"

"Day by day," Rob continued, nodding his head and waving an index finger. "And with each passing moment. Keeping the punctuation and capitalization, and adding the numerical date of the wedding. August 23, you said, remember?"

A long, crazy grin slid across Derek's face. "You…sneaky…conniving…genius!"

Rob laughed.

"You sleuthhound of a techie. I'll have to cut you a commission for this."

"I'll take it in brownies."

They laughed so hard a nurse stuck her head in the door to tell them to stop disturbing the other patients.

31. "The Finish Line"

Derek paused in the doorway and stepped to one side as a nurse headed out of the room. The woman glanced at him over her armful of gadgets and papers, frowned, and swept past. Derek raised one eyebrow and continued into the room, throwing his brother a smile.

They'd let Robbie change into his civvies since Derek was there Saturday night, which was encouraging. He was rubbing his face, and smiled with half his mouth as Derek took a seat beside the wheelchair.

"Hey, buddy," Derek began, handing Rob the jacket he'd brought from the apartment. "I think we're going to make this escape good. It sounds like we've reached the administrative-formality stage." He flapped the clipboard in his hands.

"I hope so," Rob gasped. "I don't think I could take much more of this."

"Well, what on earth happened to you?" asked Derek, leaning on Rob's armrest and brushing his bangs off his forehead. "I mean, besides the obvious. You do look like you've been through the wringer."

"Derek, they think I did it myself."

"Who? How could they?"

Robbie drew a breath. "A couple of the nurses. They got all *you know you're going to kill yourself one day* and stuff like that. I told them it wasn't my fault…"

"Of course not!"

"Telling me all about this program, *Thirty Days to Freedom* or something…" Rob's face twisted.

"Hey, it's okay. The police know what happened, and they're the ones who matter—"

"But they still had some psychologist or something up to talk to me."

Derek rolled his eyes. "Sweet. Well, don't let it bother you. You told them the truth."

His brother nodded, staring at his lap.

"It's just procedure...nothing to do with you." Derek slipped his arm around his brother's shoulders. "They're just trying to cover themselves; you know, in case Child Protective Services comes down on them or something. It'd look bad otherwise. Hospital psychologist...he just ask routine questions?"

"Yeah. Lots of questions about what I do all day, how I'm doing in school, how you treat me."

"Aha...They probably wouldn't want me there, then, anyway."

"I wanted you here."

"I know, buddy," Derek sighed. "Look, I'm real sorry about the past few months. I don't think I ever said it, but...I'm just sorry."

Robbie looked up. They watched each other's eyes for a moment.

"Me, too," Rob muttered.

Derek cleared his throat and looked away. "I, uh, have a little more bad news."

"Am I–?"

"I have to–"

They both stopped and stared at each other.

"Go ahead," Rob prompted.

"No, you first."

Robbie swallowed. "Am I...Am I going to have any dependence issues?"

"I don't know why you would."

"I heard meth was...really..."

"Addictive? I don't think you'll experience any craving after one hit. Not in such a way that you could tell it's different from just still feeling sick. How are you feeling?"

"My back aches..." Rob answered with a rueful smile. "But she said – Nurse Karen said my pulse rate was good. Within parameters."

"That's something to be thankful for," Derek said.

"She's nice."

Derek smiled, and straightened. "Well, I'm afraid I still have to work this afternoon. I tried getting a hold of the supervisor, but the one guy's phone goes straight to voice-mail and the other guy I tried said I'm the only one scheduled, so they kind of need me there. He agreed I could be a little bit late, but he didn't sound happy about it, so I'm going to try not to be."

Rob drew a deep breath and hugged his jacket to his chest. "I guess it's a wage."

"Yeah."

A machine on the other side of the curtain started beeping. Robbie smiled.

"That monitor's been having a fit all night. Remember how I used to set them off all the time?"

Derek smiled back. "Especially when that one old lady nurse was on duty; the one who always kissed the top of your head, remember?"

Robbie flushed.

Derek looked up and rose to his feet as a nurse and doctor entered the room.

"I understand you're anxious to get home," the doctor began with a smile.

Rob nodded.

"Well, your latest blood-screen came back okay, so I guess I could let you go," the doctor continued, sifting through the papers he held. "Blood flow seems to be all right, temperature is controlled, psych evaluation came back normal."

Derek felt Robbie heave a sigh beside him. He laid a hand on his brother's shoulder.

"Are there any long-term risks we should be aware of?" he asked.

"Just, uh, clustering behaviors," the professional murmured, gesturing Derek aside with his head. "I understand you're the guardian?"

"Yes." Derek's eyes narrowed. *Here it comes. I've been neglecting him? Abusing him? Clustering behaviors, my ankle.*

"I would suggest that Rob not be left alone any more than necessary for several days. I'd really prefer to keep him under observation for a while longer, but his organ function is good, and I guess he'll be all right. You can set up a follow-up appointment on the way out."

"Thanks." Derek let out an unintentional sigh. He was overreacting again. *Everything's fine.*

"Just make sure someone's around in case his symptoms start recurring. The poison – and that's what meth is…poison – won't completely clear out of his system for some little time yet."

"I understand. I'll see to it."

"Good." The doctor handed Derek some of the papers and smiled at Robbie again. "Just see the receptionist on the way out, and the financial office will get something mailed to you."

Oh, happy day. Derek suppressed a groan and gave Rob's shoulder a squeeze. He'd make sure *he* got that envelope before his brother did.

* * * *

Derek pushed Robbie into the apartment, dropping the discharge papers from the hospital onto the coffee table.

"Ten minutes...plenty of time," he exclaimed.

Rob was already at the computer. "We don't have to do this now," he began, punching in his screen-unlock password.

"I'm sure you're itching as bad as I am," Derek answered, grabbing a chair and dragging it up to the desk. "Let's see if there's anything worthwhile here."

"I didn't touch any of the messages," Robbie continued as he clicked over to Brian's mail client. "So all of the unread stuff is still marked as such."

"Thank goodness the thugs didn't decide to take off with your computer."

"Eh...it's old."

Derek leaned forward toward the computer screen, chewing his lip. "Let's see what he read before he died. Crawford, First Baptist, Cindy, ad for...I can't even tell what they're selling. And then there's—" Derek drew a breath and straightened to run his fingers along his scalp. "Mr. Stillman," he murmured.

"Who's that?" Robbie asked, frowning and cocking his head.

"The director of this sub-area of the DEA. The ultimate boss of Crawford and Brian and their teammates."

"The guy who was mad at Brian for not clearing those raids with him?"

"Right..." Derek rested his elbow on Robbie's armrest. "The raids where they arrested McCoy."

Derek double-clicked on the list item with Stillman's name on it. The email, dated the day before Brian died, popped up in a larger window. Scrolling down, he read the blue text that showed what Stillman was replying to...an email from Brian to the director.

Dear Mr. Director: I'm afraid I must report that something corrupt is going on inside the DEA organization. I've been gathering information privately from a number of sources; see a summary of this below.

I am a trained DEA agent, and in my professional opinion, there must be someone in the organization who is not only leaking information about agent movements to the gang known as Assassin Squad, but also directing this gang's movements and helping them to evade law enforcement.

I'm sure you must be skeptical, but please take the time to review my evidence. I don't know who could be doing this, though it's obviously someone with a lot of authority, and possibly someone who has had opportunity to interact with gang members. I'm convinced that this double agent is also connected to the recent deaths of two of our undercover agents, Bradford and Smith. I'm sure you've been briefed about them, but I knew them personally. Please consider the facts I've gathered, as this matter is much too important to be ignored.

If you know any other supervisors who should be alerted to this, please pass this file along. I realize this has the potential to damage the whole district, not to mention the general reputation of the DEA, but we can't afford to ignore this issue. I'm sure if you examine my document, you'll be convinced of the truth of my claims.

Derek scrolled up to the top of the window again and glanced at Robbie before reading the director's reply.

Agent Lane: I understand your concern over this issue. This is a very serious matter, and I appreciate the discretion you have exercised in addressing it.

Although I had had some suspicions of this very situation, you have provided some very valuable evidence toward the final resolution of the issue. However, if you would be willing to pursue the investigation further, I would appreciate your assistance.

I've made contact with a member of the Assassin Squad who might know the identity of this double agent, but I haven't had the opportunity to officially interview him. His name is Jonny Santos. We don't have any excuse to bring him in to the station, but I can convince him to meet with you in private. If you can convince him to tell us what he knows, we might be able to collar this traitor once and for all.

The meeting place was the abandoned parking lot, where Brian's car had been found later that night...and Brian was found dead.

Derek scooted his chair back, bumping Rob's wheelchair, and ran his fingers through his hair. He drew a breath, and let it out.

"What does that mean?" whispered Robbie.

"I want to talk to Jonny Santos," Derek muttered.

"You wanna meet the guy who killed Brian?!"

"He might help us corner the guy who gives him orders." Derek's eyes narrowed, and his hand closed in a fist.

32. "Me Without You"

Robbie didn't know why Derek thought this was a good idea.

He got that Derek had to go to work, especially with the hospital bill coming. And doctor's orders were doctor's orders. And he had to admit that the apartment felt a little silent and creepy after what had happened Friday night. But did Derek really have to ask *Cindy* to come and babysit Robbie?

Baby-sit. Like he needed someone to watch him and make sure he didn't choke on any marbles. Robbie glanced up from his book and sighed. Right now she was in the kitchen, sweeping, while the dishwasher rumbled and gurgled. Squeezing *The Works of Mark Twain* a little tighter, he shivered and ducked his head before she saw him staring at her.

Cindy walked to the hall closet and put the broom away. Glancing into the bedroom, she asked, "Can you really tell which clothes in here are clean and which ones are dirty?"

"Yeah…kinda," Robbie muttered, putting the book between them.

She turned her head to look at him. He hastily bowed his head and tucked his chin against his neck.

"Okay…we need to talk." Cindy walked over and dropped onto the couch in front of him. He pressed down into the wheelchair, but she grabbed the literature book and laid it on the coffee table.

"Look, I'm not very good at beating around the bush. Is it true that you don't like me? Did I do something to offend you?"

He couldn't tell her. He couldn't tell anyone. He didn't even know what to say. All he knew was there was this strange little knot in his stomach… Like being in the presence of your executioner.

"I've seen you talk to other people at church. I can tell you're very smart, and you're very mature and well-spoken for someone your age. So I'm kind of hurt that you ignore me when I try to talk to you, or try to interrupt when Derek and I are talking."

Rob crossed his arms and hugged them close against his chest. He knew it wasn't fair. Just because Derek was in love with her wasn't a reason to be mean. But he didn't have to like her. Why should he have to like her? She made him feel quivery just being there.

"Listen, I know how important Derek is to you." Cindy put her hand out and laid it on his knee. "He's funny, and considerate, and great at listening to people. I know; he — he's become very important to me, too."

He gave a stiff, awkward nod. He could tell. He could tell by the way she smiled at Derek, by the way she called him to make sure he was doing okay, by the way she spotted him across the whole sanctuary and started smiling, even seeing him at that distance. He knew Derek was important.

She was leaning forward, but he didn't want to look at her. He knew all the good things she'd done for Derek, like getting him to comb his hair every morning. Derek whistled a lot more than he had before, too. Robbie wouldn't mess it up, but that didn't mean he had to like it.

"Listen." She touched his face, forcing him to look at her. As their eyes met, he realized, as though for the first time, how cute the smile-sparkle in her eyes was. Derek was really lucky. Derek…deserved something like this.

Something was trying to crawl out of his throat, and he was afraid it would push on the back of his eyes and make tears come out.

"I know how much Derek cares for you. And I promise that will never change." She cocked her head in a serious expression, waiting a moment. He should say something.

He opened his mouth, but nothing came out. Derek was good at remembering things. He'd be good at remembering things for Cindy. Cindy would be happy with the way he remembered things that needed to be done.

"He'll never stop loving you. He'll always take care of you. I promise that, okay?"

Robbie opened his mouth again, but could only nod. Wasn't she going to marry Derek? Wasn't she going to let him take care of *her*?

"You aren't going to walk away from him, are you?" he breathed. "Like Michelle did? Don't walk away; that killed him."

Cindy raised her eyebrows slightly, but smiled and shook her head. "I won't. Never."

Rob dropped his head, fidgeting with his hands. As long as that didn't happen again. Whatever Michelle had done had ripped Derek's heart out, and he couldn't let that happen again. No matter what it took.

"He needs you," Robbie whispered. Derek sure needed something; something Robbie couldn't give him.

The doorbell rang, saving him from any more "heart to heart" business. Cindy got up and peeked out the front window while he rolled to the door.

Derek had installed a hook-and-chain on the front door. On the drive back from the hospital, he'd told Robbie about it, and then he'd made sure Rob could reach it before leaving for work. "Make sure you lock that. I trust you to let me in," he had said, with a half-hearted smile.

"Two women," Cindy told Robbie, coming back from the window. "I don't know them."

Trying to make his hand not shake, Robbie unlocked the doorknob and peeked through the crack of the door.

"Good afternoon, my name is Pamela Novak," said the woman with straight bobbed hair and a folder in her hands. "This is Jessie Taylor. We're with the Department of Child Services."

Oh no.

"We've received some allegations of neglect," she continued, pulling a badge from around her neck and holding it up to the door for Robbie to see. "May I speak to Mr. Derek Hayes?"

Derek, why aren't you here?!

"He..." Robbie began, and cleared his throat. "He's at work. You could come back later..."

"Are you in the home alone?" asked Jessie Taylor, giving her bottle-blonde ponytail a toss and stepping forward. "Can we come in?"

"Um...I'm okay," Robbie stammered. *Not this, too.*

"I'm afraid we need to come in," Ms. Taylor pressed, taking another step forward.

"Excuse me," Cindy put in, squeezing between the wheelchair and a bookcase to see out the door. "I'm a family friend. Do you have a court order?"

"No. We're not here to cause problems," Ms. Novak insisted, putting a hand out toward Ms. Taylor. "We have no intention of removing minors from the home, unless an emergency arises. We're only here to investigate the allegations. If there's no grounds for an intervention, we'll leave immediately."

"We need to make sure all minors in the home are receiving adequate care," Ms. Taylor insisted.

"That would be me, and I'm not very minor," Rob growled.

"We also need to speak to your guardian. I understand your relationship with him is strained."

"What?!"

"Look," Cindy murmured in his ear. "If they don't have a court order, they can't take you…except by force. If we let them in, then all the neighbors won't have to listen to our discussion."

She was right about one thing…the last thing they needed was Mrs. Gibbons getting the full scoop on these allegations. Speaking of which, Robbie bet he knew where they had come from.

He stretched up and slipped the hook out of the eye-screw to unchain the door. He and Cindy backed away from the door into the living room, while the case workers came in and shut the door.

Ms. Taylor gave a loud sniff as she glanced around the apartment. "Has this home been cleaned regularly?" she asked.

"It's a couple of bachelors!" Cindy laughed. "What do you expect? It's not going to be *Better Homes and Gardens*, but it's not like they have roaches."

They didn't, which was really saying something in that part of town.

"You don't live here?" asked Ms. Taylor, as Ms. Novak made herself at home on a chair and Cindy brought the other one in from the kitchen.

"No. I'm just visiting Robbie. I'm Cindy Lane," Cindy explained as she shook the two women's hands and sat on the couch by Rob.

"*You're* visiting Robbie. You're Robbie?" Ms. Taylor continued, turning her sharp eyes on the teen.

"Yeah." Robbie crossed his arms and sank down in the wheelchair.

"All right," Ms. Novak sighed as Ms. Taylor settled on her chair. "To start out with, this is just an evaluation. We're just investigating some allegations. Whenever we receive a call, we're required to respond to it, no matter how much sense it makes. It's just how the rules work."

"I understand," Cindy answered, nodding. "Just what were the allegations?"

"General neglect," Ms. Novak said, referring to her folder. "Leaving a minor unsupervised for long periods of time. There have also apparently been loud arguments? Loud enough to disturb the neighbors?"

"There's only one neighbor who's ever disturbed," Robbie mumbled. "And she's disturbed by loud movies."

"Do you always get along with your parent?" demanded Ms. Taylor.

"Well…I mean, sure we…uh…I mean, sometimes we argue a little, but it's nothing big. I mean, he'd never hurt me or anything."

Ms. Taylor nodded, squinting one eye. Before she could say anything else, Ms. Novak spoke up.

"What did you argue about, Robbie?" she asked.

He shrugged. He couldn't talk about it in front of these strangers, and especially not in front of Cindy. "Stuff…" he evaded, ducking his head. It was too embarrassing.

"Uh huh. What kind of stuff?" She leaned forward a little, smiling and trying to catch his eye.

"Just…dumb stuff. You know. Stuff between the two of us."

"What kind of stuff between you?" asked Ms. Taylor. "How does he treat you? Derek Hayes is your guardian, correct?"

"Yeah. He's my brother. He takes good care of me."

"Does he ever hit you or handle you roughly?"

"He's my brother!" Robbie cried, feeling clammy, cold sweat soaking through the back of his shirt. "Why would he do something like that?"

"You can tell us. What's making you so nervous?"

"You can't blame him for being nervous," Cindy interrupted, scooting forward to the edge of the couch. "This has been a hard week for him, but he loves his brother very much and doesn't want you to remove him. Believe me, Derek Hayes is a very competent caretaker; he's been providing care for Rob for many years now, and he's sacrificed a lot of his own wants and needs to make sure Rob's condition is properly treated."

"We received a complaint," Ms. Novak put in. "That there was a home invasion while Robbie was home alone."

"There's no way Derek could be blamed for that," Cindy answered, putting a hand out to stroke Rob's knee. "If he'd been here, he might have been able to do something to stop them, but even as it was he did everything in his power to get Robbie the help he needed."

"We also received a report that Robbie was admitted to the hospital Friday with an overdose of an illegal substance."

"I'm better now," Rob stammered.

"Obviously. You were discharged from the hospital. Where did you get the drugs? Did someone give them to you?"

"I didn't...Yes." Robbie swallowed and let out a short breath. "It was the guys who broke in–"

"Did you know them?"

"I – no." Robbie shot a glance at Cindy. "They – gave the meth to me."

Ms. Taylor was frowning. "What sort of history do you – and your brother – have with drugs?"

Robbie leaned away from Ms. Taylor, inadvertently leaning toward Cindy. "None! Neither of us have ever done that! We believe it's wrong."

"Trust me, there's nothing like that in this family," Cindy exclaimed. "It's a long, complicated story; I really suggest you consult the police report for the details, if you need them. The police officers who were here that night know Robbie's telling the truth. It was administered involuntarily."

"That is interesting," Ms. Novak put in, jotting things in her folder. "It must have been very scary," she added, and looked at Robbie.

He twisted his hands in his lap and nodded. He sure didn't want to rehash it in front of strangers. Again. He'd had enough of that at the hospital.

"Do you have prescription pain meds in the home?"

"Oh, please," laughed Cindy. "Let's not turn this into a HIPAA suit."

Ms. Taylor blinked, but Ms. Novak chuckled.

"I'm sure if you do need to know that," Cindy continued, "Your department can send the Hayes's doctor a subpoena. But I'm afraid I don't feel comfortable disclosing that information. I do work in healthcare, after all."

"I completely understand," Ms. Novak answered. "And I appreciate your suggestion of the doctor. I'm sure he could confirm how Mr. Hayes is keeping up with Robbie's medical needs. I do have to ask, though," she added gently. "Was Derek at work at the time of the break-in, and the overdose?"

"He's at work a lot," Rob said. "But he has other things he needs to do, too. I'm used to it. I'm almost an adult."

"Yes…how old are you, Robbie?" asked Ms. Novak.

"Sixteen and a half."

"He's very competent in his own care," Cindy insisted. "In another year and a half he'll be a legal adult, able to make his own decisions about where to live. Even now, he's pretty good about communicating his wishes and speaking his mind."

No need to be sarcastic.

"So…you feel satisfied with your living conditions?" Ms. Novak asked, facing Rob and moving her head forward.

"Absolutely." Robbie hoped his voice didn't sound as dry as it felt.

"I've seen what a great sibling relationship they have," Cindy said. "If you want, I can give you their pastor's number, too, and he'd be glad to talk about it. We go to the same church."

"Hm." Ms. Taylor cocked her eyebrows.

"In fact, if you wanted I bet the pastor would be willing to come down to the apartment so you could talk to him here," Cindy continued. "It might take him a few minutes to get here, though."

Pastor Jones knew it wasn't Robbie's fault, and so did Mr. Hank. Surely no one could yank him without Mr. Hank standing up for them.

"I don't think that will be necessary," Ms. Novak responded, rising. "I've seen that Robbie is mobile and independent, and I'm sure if he needed help he would know whom to call. The police were here the other night, so he knows how to respond to an emergency."

"Are you getting adequate nutrition?" asked Ms. Taylor.

"There's plenty of food in the kitchen," answered Cindy, with a wave of the hand. "You won't starve very fast on tater tots and frozen pizza."

"If you don't mind, I'd like to take a quick look around the rest of the apartment, just for due diligence." Ms. Novak moved toward the closet. "I don't think this is a case that would concern the state, but I need to cover all the bases."

Cindy smiled. "By all means."

Robbie and Cindy glanced at each other. She winked at him and rose to join the case workers as they peered through the bedroom door. Robbie crossed his fingers that they wouldn't take a deep breath while they were standing there.

Ms. Novak made a tour of the kitchen, opening a few random cupboards and nodding with approval—the breakfast cereal, canned soup, and other essentials were all stored below counter level. Thank goodness Cindy had been there to throw some order into it after Friday night; "Jonny" had really trashed their organization system (and Derek had spent most of yesterday at the hospital).

"Well, it doesn't look to me like we need to open a case," Ms. Novak said, glancing around the apartment once more.

"No..." Ms. Taylor muttered. "Are you going to be, er, supervising Robert often, Ms. Lane?"

Robert. Oh, the humanity.

"Well, I'm here today because the doctor, and Derek, weren't comfortable leaving him alone after the close call he had this weekend. They didn't foresee any problems, but better safe than sorry, right?"

"I know what you mean. Well, I don't expect you'll hear from us again. However, in the future you might want to work on picking up the place a little, just in case there's another call, and work on not disturbing the neighbors with your own private 'discussions'."

Cindy and Ms. Novak chuckled. People were thanked for their time. The case workers were standing in the doorway, shaking hands. Ms. Taylor was agreeing that Robbie seemed very self-sufficient. Cindy made a joke; they laughed. They were getting in their car. They were driving away.

Cindy closed the door, let out a deep breath, and smiled at Robbie.

"My word!" she sighed. "Our tax dollars at work, sending people around to disturb honest, normal families over a few anonymous complaints!"

Robbie focused on his breathing, covering his face with his hands. No case opened. No state interest. A cool, airy sensation breathed through him; it was all right now.

"I guess they're just doing their job," Cindy exclaimed, coming back to sit near Rob on the couch. "Still, it makes you nervous that the state has that kind of power. I'm glad there are case workers like Ms. Novak."

"Yeah…" Robbie wheezed.

She looked over at him. They both sat silent for a moment while the dishwasher rumbled on, unperturbed.

"I'm sure it helped that you weren't alone," she said. "I wonder if that's one of the reasons the doctor told you to have someone around."

"They can't do anything without a court order," Rob said. "They had to vet Derek before giving him custody, to make sure he could take care of me; but they couldn't yank me without a court order."

Cindy sighed and shrugged her shoulders. "I'm glad I was here."

"I…" He meant to say *I know*, but that sounded ungrateful. "I am, too," he mumbled sheepishly.

Cindy gazed at him a moment, and shot him a grin that crinkled up her eyes and made them sparkle. "Hey, come help me fold those clothes, huh? Then we'll find something fun to do."

"Like what?"

"Well…what do you do for fun?"

Rob's mind raced. He swallowed. "Ever played *Super Smash Brothers*?"

"Never. You'll cream me."

Rob laughed.

33. "Take Me To Your Leader"

Derek glanced around the dim-lit bar, musing on how many of the patrons he recognized from the mug-shot books. He wasn't here to finger someone for breaking parole, though. He had more specific business.

He began making his way toward a dark corner where a tough with matted black hair leaned against the wall. Billows of cigarette smoke swirled around his face, but Derek had still recognized him from the long scar on his right cheek. He must have gotten it young; it looked the same as it did in his last mug shot, from over five years ago. Petty theft. No violent acts that the law knew of — until now.

Derek strolled over casually, feeling the man's eyes trailing him as he crossed the room. Another puff of smoke streamed out of his mouth, and his eyes narrowed.

"Hi," Derek said…the best opener he could think of. "Jonny Santos?"

"I don't think so," the other muttered, glaring from under dark brows.

Derek straightened his back. *Okay…if that's the way you want it.* "You are," Derek answered. This was also one of the guys Robbie had picked out after last Friday night. "I'm Derek Hayes. We need to talk."

"I don't know you," Jonny growled, and straightened to move away.

"You know Brian Lane."

The gangster's head jerked up, and he coughed violently before taking a long pull at the cigarette.

"I knew him, too…by proxy. Let's talk about Lane."

"Stuff it," snapped Jonny, his wide eyes roving from Derek's belt to his face and back. "I don't know what you're talking about."

"Yes you do. I'm not a cop." Derek kept his hands in plain sight on his hips, and smiled. "You can frisk me if you really want, but I'm still not a cop. I'm interested in who killed Brian Lane, and you can help me."

"You're wasting your time," Jonny muttered, trying to back away. Derek thought his face might be growing paler, too. "I don't know any Brian Lane and I don't know what you're talkin' about."

"Yes you do…I know you weren't home that night, 'cause I talked with the lady at your house. I also talked with the kids who hang out across the street from that parking lot, and when I add that to what I learned from Brian, I think your case looks very grim."

"Lane's dead!" Jonny snarled.

"Right…murdered. By you. With heroin. Ringing any bells yet, Santos?"

Abruptly, Jonny sprang forward and shoved his shoulder into Derek's chest. Even as Derek spun around, he saw Jonny digging in his pants while plunging toward the door.

Derek leaped forward, pinning Jonny's arms to his sides. They both crashed to the ground, knocking over a chair. Derek struggled to stay on top, still groping for the object.

Finally, he caught Jonny's hand and twisted it behind his back, using his other arm to execute Hank's favorite lock.

After a few wild flails, Jonny quieted down. Derek rolled and dragged until they had both staggered to their feet, Derek still gripping one of Jonny's arms.

"Why don't you have a seat?" he asked, taking a moment to shove the gun under his own shirt.

He hazarded a glance at the rest of the bar. If the other patrons had turned to watch, they had since turned back to the poker game on the TV, apparently satisfied that the two in the corner had sorted their problem out themselves. The bartender shot a glare in their direction, as if warning them to keep their further interactions civil.

Derek glanced at a balding man in the corner. He was on parole for an assault charge and was a person of interest in a double murder. Might be best not to turn his back to the guy.

"You know you don't have a permit to carry this," Derek commented, maneuvering Jonny into a seat and sliding down across from him.

"Wha'd'you want?" Jonny growled, crossing his arms and slouching against the backrest. "I thought you said you weren't a cop."

"I'm not. But I'm interested in Brian Lane."

"So go to the police."

"It's not that simple." Derek shifted and leaned forward onto the table. For a moment, he stared into the dark, defiant eyes across from him, and drew a breath.

"You didn't do this on your own. I know somebody put you up to this, and I've got a pretty good idea who. Although I'm not a cop, I know some people; if you help me nail your boss they'll work on a deal for you."

Jonny sat blinking for several moments, and creased his forehead. Finally, he stirred, groping in his shirt pocket for a pack of cigarettes.

"Can't tell you," he mumbled.

"Yes, you can."

"No!" Jonny hissed back, pausing with a cigarette in his fingers, and darted his glance around the bar.

For a second, Derek regretted taking the seat that faced away from the door, but Jonny's eyes had no spark of recognition or alarm in them. He was just being wary. As he lifted the smoke to his mouth, Derek watched his hand shaking.

"You don't have many options here. Tell me, and–"

"Yeah, yeah, yeah..." Jonny pulled out a lighter, puffed for a second, and tapped the smoking implement against the tabletop. "You'll cut all sorts of deals. But the Boss...Get the Boss mad, and you're iced."

"Like Jimmy Cann?"

Jonny started coughing again. After a few minutes, Derek reached out and plucked the cigarette out of his hand.

"They still execute for murder in this state, you know," he murmured. "Especially first degree. They've got warrants out for you already. You really wanna take your chances against a jury?"

Derek could see Jonny swallow. The thug leaned back in his seat, scratching some sores on his forearm.

"Listen," Derek continued, leaning forward and holding the cigarette toward Jonny. "Brian was killed because he was a threat...because he'd learned too much. You killed Brian, on the boss's orders. You also are a threat, because you also know too much. It's only a matter of time, Santos. The boss doesn't care... he'll rub out anybody he feels like."

The gangster put his hand out gingerly and took the glowing butt from Derek. Derek kept his eyes fixed on the other's, dropping his voice ever so slightly.

"If you give us a break, *he'll* take the rap for this. And everything else he's done. Jimmy Cann. Lane. *He'll* pay for it."

Jonny's eyes kindled faintly, and he straightened in the chair.

"They'll know I talked," he breathed.

"Why? Do they know me? If not, who's to know?"

"They know these things."

"Not this time," Derek insisted. Only three people knew about Santos...Derek, Rob, and Hank. The other police officers knew that Rob had identified Jonny as one of his attackers, but they had no reason to connect the invasion of Derek's apartment with Brian's murder.

Jonny Santos sucked at his cigarette and glanced around the bar again.

"Look, I don't know who he is," he breathed. His forehead glistened, and he leaned toward Derek as his eyes scanned the room. "He's only kind of my boss. He talks to Marco a lot."

"Marco Jung."

Jonny gave a jerky little nod. "He's the top of the dealers. I get all my product from him, and gotta pay him my dues."

"Great."

Fine info for the Squad's distribution investigation, but Derek was interested in Brian. And in nailing Stillman.

"We never met him. Just get calls from him, and call in reports. Marco gave him my number."

"And he called you?"

"Yeah."

Jonny exhaled a great cloud of smoke, and swallowed again.

"Why'd he call you?"

The drug dealer squeezed his eyes shut for a moment, and shrugged. "I dunno. I never done nothing like this before. Wasting a guy – a fed – is something else."

Derek shifted in his seat, moving his fingers along the left side of his scalp. Jonny was no hit man. But he'd followed orders. So…why Jonny?

"Go on."

"I got the call—the night before. Told me what to do and what to say to him. Told me where he'd be waiting. It's weird, y'know? Shoot him up…and leave him?"

"And you drugged him first?"

"The boss said it'd be easier. Oh, and he'd said do the right arm. So I did."

A shiver went down Derek's spine at the cold simplicity of the execution order. The boss – Stillman – sure was meticulous.

It had to be Gerald Stillman. Brian hadn't contacted anyone else, and Jonny had been called directly by the "boss" for the killing. Unless Stillman hadn't kept his word to Brian about getting a meeting with Jonny – *and* had given away Brian's position to the "real" boss (as early as the night before it happened) – then Stillman was the real, actual Mr. Big.

Derek drew a deep breath, keeping his gaze fixed on Jonny's dark eyes.

"Did he pay you?"

"Yeah… Marco got me an envelope of cash a day or two later."

"Alright," Derek said, resting his elbows on the table. "What's this boss's phone number? If he's called you, you should have his phone number."

"Uh…" Jonny fumbled in his pocket. "I'm almost out of minutes…"

"Just look at it and tell me the number."

Jonny bit his cigarette and flipped the phone open. A few beeps later, he mumbled a number through his teeth.

Derek nodded slowly. He didn't know how far this would go in court, but at least he could confirm to himself that he was right. Having Stillman's gangster phone number might help Hank and Chief Freeman, too.

"He said not to call him," Jonny mumbled, toying with the cigarette. "He doesn't want anybody to call him."

"But you did, didn't you?"

The color drained from the thug's face as his wide eyes turned up towards Derek.

"Last Friday?" Derek prompted. "Probably around 6:50, or thereabouts. You did call him, didn't you?"

"That kid..." Jonny wheezed.

"My brother."

The cigarette lowered to the table. Jonny's eyes zipped from Derek's face, to his hands, to the bulge of Jonny's gun under Derek's shirt.

"Chill. You've got one murder on your hands, not two." Derek flexed his shoulders, his eyes narrowing. "Though you're very lucky."

Jonny's throat pulsed as he swallowed again. "The boss," he rasped, darting a shaking hand over his forehead. "The boss said to do that. We didn't think nobody was going to be there."

"He told you to do that?" Derek demanded in a low tone, digging his fingernails into his palm. Even Jonny Santos could tell Rob was just a kid. Would Stillman be able to prove he wasn't on the phone between 6:50 and 7 o'clock Friday night?

"I...I had some product on me," Jonny stammered, sliding as far back in his seat as he could go. "He said – give him all of it. His idea. Not ours. Marco said it don't matter anyway. Marco's the one who – held him down."

That matched what Robbie had said. Derek forced himself to ease back in his seat. He could prosecute Jonny for all it was worth – later. Not now. Now he had a DEA fink to catch — and Marco Jung, just for good measure.

He drew a breath and asked, "Where can I find Marco?"

There was a burst of chatter and laughs from the bar area. Derek shot a look over his shoulder; something exciting had happened in the poker game, or someone had said something funny.

When he looked back at Jonny, the drug dealer was fumbling with another cigarette. He pressed the glowing butt to the new end, his quaking fingers barely able to hold them.

"Can't," he panted through his teeth, stubbing the spent end against the table and scratching at some marks on the inside of his elbow. "He'd find me. He knows stuff, too. Can't..."

"Relax," Derek reached across and patted his arm. "The police will get in touch with you; probably within a few hours. After all, they can't get you in jail, can they?"

"They got ways," Jonny gasped, squeezing his eyes shut. "I'm sure they got ways."

"Look, just keep your head down for a bit. It won't be long."

Derek rose to his feet; he'd squeezed all he could out of the gangster. Unless he tried more, different threats or promises...and those were a little too risky. Jonny leaned against the seat back, his face shimmering with sweat. Maybe that's why the boss picked him...no violence record, and enough fear to keep his mouth shut. *Here's hoping Stillman doesn't find out he* has *talked.*

Derek hesitated a moment, and flipped a ten-dollar-bill onto the table before facing away. "I hope you don't mind me taking your gun, but you wouldn't want it on you when the police arrest you anyway. I can't promise anything, but I'm pretty sure your testimony will get you some points with the judge. Plus you'll have the satisfaction of bringing the head of the Assassin Squad down with you."

"If you get him," Jonny whispered.

"When. Don't worry; murder catches up with you."

Derek strode off while Jonny was still fingering the bill and staring at him. He avoided the bartender's glance and pushed the door open as casually as he could. His lack of tattoos had probably raised some of the pierced eyebrows there, but it didn't matter. Not unless they interrogated Santos before the police had a chance to get him into custody.

He kept his steps deliberately slow until he got around the block to the alley where Hank waited for him in a beat-up pick-up truck. He slid into the passenger seat, unable to keep from grinning.

"You look pumped," Hank commented as he started the engine and pulled out onto the road.

"You should've had me wired. He confessed to killing Brian *and* to drugging Robbie, both on the direct orders of the Big Boss. I've got the boss's number that he uses to talk to his gang officers, one of which is Marco Jung. And," Derek continued with a sigh, as he wrapped a handkerchief around his hand and pulled out Jonny's gun, "I got this. Uh…serial number's gone, but it might still have some cool prints on it – at least on the bullets."

"Well, I guess that confirms what we already knew…but I still don't see how it proves your theory about Stillman."

"The boss was willing to kill to get Brian's laptop; I figure because he didn't want us reading that email. The only people mentioned in the director's email are Santos and Stillman, and Santos was working on orders."

"You realize Dickerson won't back something with that little to go on. Especially against a DEA administrator."

"I'm working on it," Derek answered, dropping the gun into a plastic ziplock.

Hank gave a laugh that was part groan. "Look, I can go along with what you're saying, but a jury's going to ask more questions; especially since he's got that 'pillar of the community' image going for him. Just how does Santos's testimony help us pin this to Stillman?"

"Well, it is a little disappointing: Santos doesn't know who the boss is. However, it does tell us that Stillman wasn't on the level with what he told Brian. Santos wasn't called to go to a meeting; he was called to go to a murder. Besides, we might be able to have some fun with the phone number he gave me."

Hank grunted.

"You call the chief to tell him about Santos?" asked Derek.

"Yeah...they'll pick him up tonight for the job at your place. Don't you think that'll clue in Stillman that we're on to him?"

"He's bound to know Rob survived already." Derek settled back into the seat and crossed his arms. "The thing he doesn't know is that we cracked Brian's computer. That doesn't mean he's not worried, but I don't think he'll panic...not yet."

"Does he really think those emails are enough to convict him?"

"It's enough in my court," Derek muttered. "There's also the dossier Brian compiled, which is what got him killed originally."

Hank shook his head. "I just don't see Dickerson getting behind it, and Chief Freeman isn't going to ask for a warrant unless he thinks we can —"

Derek sat up. "Hold on. We've still got some tricks up our sleeve for convincing the chief." He smiled. "Like a confession."

"Way to go, Columbo. You just need him to confess. Stupendous."

"Exactly." Derek closed his eyes to a slit, watching the patches of street-light flick past across the windshield. A confession was exactly how they'd do it. All it'd take was a little cooperation from the chief of police.

34. "Killing My Old Man"

"Mr. Stillman? Derek Hayes."

"Ah, Mr. Hayes. How wonderful to hear from you. I was thinking about you the other day–"

"Very flattering. Listen, there's a very important matter I need to discuss with you, and I'm afraid we need to discuss it in person."

"Would you like to come to my office?"

"I'd prefer if we could meet in more of a neutral setting," Derek answered. "How about the office block by 29th and West St."

There was pause on the other end of the line. Derek flicked the phone cord back and forth.

"Oh?"

"Yes. See, I've been examining the data on Brian Lane's laptop, and there's some stuff I really think you'd be interested in seeing. Could I bring the laptop to show you?"

"Oh!"

Derek envisioned the director drooling into his mouthpiece.

"If you really think this information concerns the DEA, I would naturally appreciate your divulging it to us. When shall I see you?"

"I'm not available until after six on week days."

"All right…" Paper rustled on Stillman's end of the line – that or static. "It looks like I'm free next Friday, after six."

Derek nodded. "Next Friday, seven o'clock, suite 5B."

"Suite 5B. I look forward to seeing you."

"Thank you. Likewise."

You have no idea how. Derek set the receiver down, glancing at the police sergeant who'd been monitoring the call. The officer gave him a thumbs-up and pulled off his headphones.

Derek stood up and headed for the door, Sgt. Blake joining him.

"All right. The chief's signed off on the wire. Now all we have to do is sit tight for a week."

"Yeah…right."

Hank glanced at him and grinned. "You getting nervous all of a sudden?"

Derek smiled. "About this? No way. I keep remembering what Santos said about his orders from Stillman. That reptile needs to be caught."

"Then it *is* the lovely, charming, and intelligent Mrs. Cindy Lane."

Something caught in Derek's throat, and he coughed. "You got paperwork for me or something? I promised Robbie I'd be home on time."

"Oh, come on!" Hank protested, pausing in front of his office door. "You can't brush me off like that. She sure didn't give me a hug when I saw her safely to her house the other night."

Derek drew a breath and grunted. "I know. We're doing lunch tomorrow. It's just…I can't tell her about the sting. And she's going to want to know."

"Tell her it's a police thing."

"What if she goes all *You think I can't keep a secret* and *It's not my fault I ran into Mr. Stillman at the mall* and *It's my husband, for goodness' sake, you'd think you could tell* me, and…"

"So," Hank winked. "Then you'll think of something."

Derek pulled a face at him. "Boy, that's helpful."

"Seriously. You've got that connection with her; all you have to do is use your natural charm."

Derek groaned and rubbed his face. "Natural charm? Really…"

Hank grinned. "I'm waiting for you to get a ring."

Derek glared at him, but couldn't keep a smile from tugging at his face.

35. "I Can Be Friends With You"

Derek toyed with a mushroom on the end of his fork. "I...I really wanted to apologize."

Cindy lifted an eyebrow. "For...?"

"Last time. Making you worry like that."

"It's not your fault. How's Robbie?"

"Well enough that he went to Joey's birthday party," Derek answered. "At LaserQuest."

"That's a miracle."

"He's not doing the LaserQuest," Derek grinned. "But he's feeling good enough to get out and do stuff. We have a followup appointment with the doctor in a week or two to do a blood test, to make sure he's passed it out of his system."

Cindy shuddered. "I just can't imagine what sort of people would do something like that. Especially to a...well, a boy."

Derek clenched his jaw. From what Jonny Santos had told him, Stillman sure was a cold-blooded character. Thank goodness Robbie hadn't ended up one of his victims.

Hopefully, it wouldn't be long now. Less than a week, and that creep would be behind bars. Derek admitted to himself he was nervous. If the chief administrator of the DEA couldn't be trusted, who knew what contacts Stillman might have in the police department? Who might give him information – unwittingly or not?

Cindy turned toward him, her pony-tail swishing the collar of her tailored top. Sitting with her, wearing a tie to *Sam's Pizza* didn't feel like being over-dressed.

She frowned, stirring with her straw and staring him in the eye. "You're worried about something."

"I'm fine."

"Robbie?"

"Well..."

"I didn't think so." She put her head down to lean forward. "When's the trap?"

Derek blinked – then cleared his throat. "What trap?"

"You think I don't read the itemized expense sheets you give me? You rented an office space for one day. Why else would you need a third-party space for a single day?"

"There's this really cute secretary –"

Cindy reached out and slapped him – more of a soft tap on the cheek. "What secretary?"

"At the DEA office. She's got very distinguished grey hair and the demeanor of a female bird of prey."

Cindy laughed. Derek grinned.

The next moment, however, her eyebrows turned stern. "You're not making the same mistake as Brian, are you? The police will be there to back you up, right?"

"Look, what makes you think –"

"I called your place last night, and Robbie said you were at the police station to 'step it up'."

Derek swallowed. After all this time of refusing to talk to Cindy, now Robbie was ratting him out to her. "I see he can't keep secrets."

"I need *someone* on my side."

Derek smiled in spite of himself. "All right; of course the police are involved. But I really can't talk about it; I can't do anything to endanger the case we're building."

She dropped her eyes, picking at a slice of pizza. "Are you afraid I can't keep a secret, like the proverbial woman? Are you afraid you can't trust me?"

"Why would I think that?"

"Well..." Cindy reached back and pulled the hair-tie out of her hair, letting the dark waves brush down around her face. "I mentioned the laptop to Mr. Stillman when we met in the mall. That's probably why he sent the men to your house, and why Robbie was almost drugged to death, and why you've got a monster hospital bill, why the DCS showed up at your house, why..."

"Stop. None of that is your fault."

"I'm just saying –"

"Stop."

He was leaning forward, and smoothed some of Cindy's hair away from her face. She sniffed and rubbed her face, grabbing his hand and holding it.

"I'm sorry. I wish I knew how to help."

"The less you're involved, the less chance there is of Mr. Big viewing you as a threat."

She smiled. "I think it's a little late for that. And I want to help. I want to be there for you; I want you to trust me."

"That's not what this is about. You know I trust you, right?"

Cindy glanced up, then dropped her eyes, nodding. "I just...I can't afford to lose you."

Derek gave her hand a squeeze. She squeezed back.

"Then Brian and I will just have to wait for you together. In front of God's throne, I think we'll be able to get along."

Cindy sniffed.

"God's taken care of you so far. I know he'd take care of you and Robbie if anything happened to me." Derek smiled. "But don't worry. The hospital can't afford to lose a debtor like me, anyway."

She gave a chuckle and looked up, her eyes glinting through her dark lashes.

He winked at her, and she laughed again. He liked it when he made her laugh. He'd commit to a career of prat-falls and fake voices if it kept her laughing.

Cindy met his gaze for a long moment. With a sigh, she smoothed her hair back, winding the rubber band around a new pony tail.

Derek scooped the rest of his pizza slice into his mouth and sat staring at his plate. As he swallowed, he murmured, "Funny, I thought we weren't going to talk about the case today."

Cindy sighed. "I'm sorry. I got carried away."

Derek smiled. "I wonder what we'd talk about if there wasn't a case."

She shrugged. "I hope we get the chance to find out."

"We will. I'm counting on it."

For several moments, they sat in silence.

"How'd your lesson go last Sunday?" asked Derek.

"Great." Cindy smiled. "I was worried about one of the boys, that he wouldn't get into the play-acting, but he got to be the soldier who came to John the Baptist, and so he carried the sword around all morning, and was very self-controlled with it. It turned out to be a good picture of the lesson."

"You missed a heated discussion of works versus fruit," Derek told her.

She laughed. "Sounds like it was just as well. I don't think either of those people are going to convince each other."

"When are you back on the rotation?"

"Week after next. Then I do two weeks in a row, because Mrs. Goodwin will still be out from her surgery, and the Marshalls are going on vacation."

"Where to?"

"Camping."

"Like, deep in the woods camping, or electric-post-for-your-camper's-TV camping?"

Cindy laughed, and rolled her eyes. "I think actual tent-camping. Brian and I did a little camping, you know, when we were first married…"

Derek watched her eyes carefully. She stirred her soda for a moment, watching the bubbles swirl.

"I don't think he enjoyed it as much as I did," she said softly.

"Well, it's been years since I've had the chance to go camping," Derek smiled. He thought of Robbie, and his smile dropped.

"You should try it sometime; it's fun to get away from the bustle and lights, and see the stars and hear the bugs."

Derek chuckled. "I don't think the bugs are a very good selling point, but I hope I get the chance to go someday. Maybe with someone special."

Cindy cocked an eyebrow at him.

At the buzz of his cell phone, Derek jumped. He met Cindy's eye for her nod of permission, then slipped it out and checked the number.

It was a text from Robbie:

People starting to leave.

"Robbie?"

Derek nodded. "Sounds like the party's breaking up. Are you ready for a box?"

"I hope we can do this again," Cindy began, shuffling the pieces of pizza together. "Thanks for everything."

"Hang on, don't go anywhere yet," Derek said.

"Don't worry, I'm not going to stick you with the check–"

"No, no, I'm paying. I asked you. But I want to follow you home. Just in case, you know?"

She raised an eyebrow. "You think I'm worth being a target?"

"I'm not taking any chances."

Cindy shrugged and smiled. "All right; on one condition. Two conditions. You promise to not be an idiot when you do your meeting."

"Promise. And?"

"*I* pay for the pizza."

"Hey!"

36. "Whatcha Gonna Do When Your Number's Up?"

Derek let himself be five minutes late, to give Stillman plenty of time to scope out the room. As he let himself into the room, the director rose from his chair with a smile and a greeting. Derek chose the seat behind the desk and settled himself in it.

"Now, then, you said you had found something interesting on Agent Lane's computer?" the director prompted.

"Absolutely." Derek leaned back in his chair, letting one arm drape across the desk. That was the jacket sleeve that had the bug in it...here's to hoping Stillman didn't frisk him. "See, Brian was investigating the Assassin Squad. They seemed to get a free pass on everything, from their raw materials to the people they knock off for being in their way. When the Blackhearts started moving in on their territory, the DEA busted the Blackhearts' operation."

"Oh, really?" Mr. Stillman gave a tired nod. "Mr. Hayes, don't you think I'm aware of what the DEA has been doing?"

"Oh, absolutely, sir. So you must be aware that Brian and his teammates were making some arrests of Assassin Squad members. Unfortunately, the legal cases against those members have become a little unstable. They've got better defense lawyers than the average gangster can afford."

"It does seem that the Assassin Squad is becoming dangerously powerful," the director conceded. "But prosecution is the job of the police and the DA, not mine."

"The police and the Drug Enforcement Administration are working together to halt the spread of meth in the state," Derek answered, swinging his feet up to rest them on the table. "But you're right; the Squad is getting awfully powerful. Funny, how they always seem to be in the right place at the right time to avoid law enforcement. And then there's the case Brian and Crawford were working a year ago. They were setting up the Assassin Squad with some raw materials, waiting to catch them with the meth product and arrest them. Only, the Squadsters got tipped off and escaped, *with* the materials."

"Mr. Hayes, all this can be learned from DEA records. I don't see–"

"Yes, well, what *I* don't see," continued Derek, gesturing with one finger, "Is how Brian could gather all this data which clearly indicates a rat in the DEA who's tied to the Assassin Squad, but not realize that it had to be you!"

Stillman flinched, and sat for a moment, blinking and adjusting his glasses. Finally, he gave his own peculiar little laugh… the one that always sounded rehearsed, like a hokey movie track. "I can't fathom what you mean," he exclaimed, beginning to rise. "But I don't think I need to spend more time considering it."

"Oh, I think you should." Derek brought his feet back to the floor, reached inside his jacket, and pulled out the papers he'd brought. "Take a look at these. You've seen them before, of course."

The director's eyes flickered from the pages to the detective. Finally, he picked them up and flipped through them.

"They're email print-outs, as you can see," Derek explained, fiddling with the pen he had also found in his jacket. "From you to Brian, and from Brian to you. See, Brian sent his evidence about the DEA fink to you, unaware that you already knew all about yourself. You, in response, set him up to meet Jonny Santos, whom you instructed to kill him, in a very specific way."

"This is ridiculous," insisted Mr. Stillman, his eyes darting from Derek's face to the emails. "I had nothing to do with that."

"Your email address is right at the top there. You could claim that someone faked your email address before sending Brian that, but we could find the matching email on your computer. Even if you ran home tonight and deleted it."

"Just what makes you think I set Mr. Lane up for murder?" Stillman's voice quivered with a forced calm. He sank into his chair again, laying the papers deliberately on the table. "I knew Mr. Santos was a member of the Assassin Squad, and that he had valuable information that he could give to the DEA. Apparently, you believe that he killed Agent Lane rather than talk to him."

"By chloroforming him and then injecting him with meth and heroin. Not your typical gang hit. It is, however, very similar to what he did to my brother when you had him search my apartment for Brian's laptop. You've got a weird view of art, Mr. Stillman."

The director's mouth twitched into a smile, but he did not laugh. "I don't have to sit here and be maligned," he said. "I hope you're prepared for a defamation lawsuit, Mr. Hayes."

"I'm okay," Derek answered, rubbing his forehead. "I've still got the laptop. And not here."

Stillman paused. He cracked his knuckles and drew a breath. "I thought you wanted to share that information with me, as a director in the DEA. How is not bringing the laptop going to help that?" he asked.

"I'm sharing the information, just not the evidence. I'm not stupid enough to let you get your hands on that."

"Everything you're saying is ridiculous. A fifth columnist inside the DEA…?"

"Yep. And I know it's you," Derek answered, lifting his feet to the table again. "Not only did Brian die the day after receiving your email, but my apartment and Cindy Lane's house were both invaded shortly after she told you that we were getting close to opening Brian's email."

"Unfortunate coincidences, the reasons for which are still under investigation."

Derek rolled his eyes and pulled his phone out of his pocket. As Mr. Stillman watched, alternately squeezing his hands, Derek laid the phone on the table and began tapping in a number.

"I got this phone number from Jonny Santos the other day," Derek explained, hitting the call button. "He said it belonged to the boss who gave him orders."

A cellphone began to buzz. Stillman jumped, and made a grimace.

"Gee, sounds like your phone," Derek grinned, leaning his arm forward so Blake and the others could maybe hear it. "Feeling desperate yet?"

"That proves nothing," snapped Mr. Stillman. "You must have gotten my cell number from somewhere."

"Forgot to mention: Santos has testified that you're the one who told him to kill Brian and drug Robbie."

"He couldn't know!" A moment later, the director seemed to realize what he'd said. "This is all pointless," he exclaimed, folding his hands and forcing a smile to his face. "*If* I were, as you say, in control of a meth gang and dispensing my own justice as I saw fit, do you really think I would let my lackeys know my true identity? You have to learn to think like a gang leader. That's what I've been doing for years *in my position*; learning to think like the enemy to be better able to catch him."

"Thinking like the enemy is right," Derek muttered. "You forgot who was friend and who was foe."

"I don't have time for this," Stillman sighed, standing up once again. "I suggest you disengage from this investigation. You're clearly too emotionally involved to make rational decisions about it."

"My emotional involvement has nothing to do with it!" Derek rose to his feet, leaning forward on the table. "You had Jonny Santos kill Brian Lane, and I can prove it. But see, without the laptop, the police won't necessarily believe everything Jonny tells them."

The director frowned.

"See, they know he's the one who attacked my brother, since he's identified him. But they don't have any reason to tie him to Brian Lane. Yet."

"You're just grabbing at smoke," the director cried, spinning on his heel toward the door. "If you had any real proof, you'd go to the police!"

"Maybe. Would you, in my position?"

Stillman hesitated at the door. He turned back, eyeing Derek, and frowned. "What do you mean?"

"You live in a seven-figure house. I looked it up. I live in a one-bedroom apartment."

Mr. Stillman stepped slowly toward the desk. "Your point being?"

Derek shrugged and sat again. "What would you do in my position? Perform a civic service, and give the police everything I have?" He drew his finger back and forth across the table, pretending to watch his hand while watching Stillman under his eyebrows. "My brother's still alive, you know, but your boys did a number on my medical bills. And Robbie wasn't exactly cheap to start with."

The director eased back into his chair, the lines around his eyes and mouth starting to relax. "Is that what's getting at you, hm?"

"Among other things."

"Hgh. And what makes you think I can't arrest you for blackmailing as soon as I have the laptop?"

"Because I intend to be on a plane to New York."

Stillman straightened his back abruptly. "New York?" he coughed with a chuckle.

Derek nodded gravely. "What, you think I think I'm better than Brian Lane? It could be me lying wasted on the wrong side of town if I don't watch my step. I'm not dumb. Plus, the options for a private investigator down here are a little on the slim and dull side."

"I can imagine." Stillman rocked in his chair, his eyebrows furrowed, watching Derek's face. "Setting up in New York won't be cheap."

"Meth dealers pull in a lot."

Stillman glared, and cracked his knuckles. "So that's your price for the laptop? Two plane tickets to New York City, and a little extra?"

"Three tickets. And the hospital bills."

"Three?"

"Three." Derek leaned back in his chair, letting the director think whatever he wanted. If Hank could assume, so could Stillman — and he'd be expecting it. "Emotional involvement" indeed!

The director drew a deep breath. "You know, you're acting like I have no choice. Like I have to accept your terms."

"I don't see what other options you have. Unless you've got a thing for long prison stays."

Stillman rose and strolled a few feet away to stare at a blank wall. If Hank wanted good timing, this was pretty much it. Derek didn't know how much longer he could string the director along.

"You know…there comes a time in a man's life when he realizes how brief everything is. How small he is in relation to the world." Stillman turned and glanced at Derek. "And you are much smaller than you think you are."

"Are you saying I should do Hawaii?"

"I'm saying I don't have to do anything you say! I'm not just a man, I'm the coordinating agent for this whole subdistrict. I have authority from here to Minnesota and North Dakota; you have authority inside your own little head."

"You're guilty of murder and you know it," Derek replied, tapping his shoes together on top on the table. What were they waiting for...Stillman to offer to write it out longhand?

"I don't care what evidence you've got," the director snapped, crossing his arms. "My defense lawyer will clear me in 24 hours. *Your* defense lawyer will ask to be removed from the case...if he's smart."

"You talk big for someone who doesn't have Brian's laptop," Derek sighed, scratching his head and watching Stillman's hand movements like the professional he was.

"You're going to give me that laptop, and you're not going to get one red cent for it. You've got so much hanging over you, you'll beg me to forget you even exist."

"Oh, what could you possibly throw at me, assuming I'm smarter than Brian?" Derek smiled. "And assuming you've worn out the thugs-at-the-apartment-door trick."

"I could shut down your assets," Stillman growled, his face getting redder by the minute. "Freeze your bank account. Pull your license, arrest you for forgery and libel." He leaned forward over the table, his eyes glinting. "Yank your child custody. It's plain you're not at all a fit guardian. The boy belongs somewhere else."

"Over my dead body."

Stillman smiled. "Your call. But it'll happen. I'll destroy you."

"No, you won't," answered Derek, letting his eyes half-close and wondering what Hank thought he was doing.

"I have the authority. You think anyone would take your word over mine? You're an upstart private eye, who got kicked out of the police department."

Someone had done his homework, at least. Sort of.

"And on what are you basing your confidence?" Stillman demanded, making his knuckles snap like firecrackers. "What can you possibly do against me?"

"Plenty," Derek answered, bringing his feet down from the table and shifting in his seat. Just as well to have his feet under him if he needed to move fast — if Chief Freeman's shoelace came undone or something. "You try anything like that, and I'll make one five-minute drive. And you'll be toast. Brian-Lane kind of toast."

"What are you talking about?" snarled the director, leaning forward with his fists on the table. Derek watched the wrinkles around his eyes flex as he tried to keep his cool.

"I'll hand the computer over to Jonny Santos and Marco Jung," Derek continued in a low, distinct tone. "I'm sure they'll be more than thrilled to know who they've been taking orders from all this time. And you can bet their first thought won't be to call the district attorney's office."

Stillman's face went white. As he plunged his hand into his coat, Derek sprang to his feet.

"Don't move," growled the director, steadying the .45 with his other hand. Derek's blood rushed through his ears, as he tried to ignore the sheen along the barrel.

"All right, self-important fool," Mr. Stillman said. "We've played your game; now you're going to play mine. You're going to take me to the laptop."

"I–"

"That's enough," Stillman snapped, jabbing the firearm toward Derek's stomach. "If you want to crawl back to your one-bedroom apartment in one piece, you'll do as I say."

"I think you might not want to do that," Derek answered, tugging at his sleeve. "Thinking of you, here; I don't think you want to shoot me on tape." He pulled back his jacket, and the microphone flipped into sight.

The door swung open with a creak and a thump.

"Gerald Stillman, you're under arrest."

About time, Hank!

Director Stillman whipped his head around and stared at the police officers filing into the room, their weapons out and leveled at him. Slowly, he turned back and stared at Derek.

As Stillman laid his gun on the desk, Derek let out the breath he didn't know he'd been holding. The director smiled ever so slightly and inclined his head.

"I guess I'll see you in court, Mr. Hayes," he murmured, and followed the officer who took his arm.

Hank glanced at Derek, and shot him a thumbs-up. Derek ran a hand through his hair, closed his eyes, and heaved a sigh. *Check and mate.*

37. "Love Liberty Disco"

The church doors swung closed behind them as Derek and Robbie clattered across the narthex. They hadn't spoken on the ride over. Robbie didn't think there was much left to say.

Derek paused in the middle of the room and drew a deep breath.

"She's probably–" began Rob.

"I'll find her," Derek answered, and knelt down beside Robbie. "First I want to talk to you."

The back of Robbie's neck tingled. He thought they'd had their conversation; he wasn't sure he wanted to rehash things.

Derek reached into his pocket and pulled out something. As he held it out toward Rob, the metallic sheen of a business card case glinted. "I...It's a present for you."

Rob blinked and took it. Popping it open with his thumb, he slipped out one of the business cards. The bold black letters marched across the card.

Hayes and Hayes: Investigations

And underneath: *Rob Hayes*, followed by his email.

Robbie's hand started to shake.

"I was going to put something like *Cyber and Crime*; after the *Investigations* part," Derek was stammering. "Or, like, *Finding the Truth, on the Web or the Streets*, but everything I could think of sounded hokey."

Robbie opened his mouth, but nothing came out.

"You don't mind, do you? I mean, I wouldn't have cracked this thing without you. You're the one who–"

"Thanks," Rob rasped. He slid his card back into his case, and eased it closed. He stroked the smooth lid with his thumb. *Investigations*. He didn't have a license, but he could be a "specialist consultant," or something. He started grinning.

"Now you just need a venue to pass those out," chuckled Derek.

"Sweet."

"You really think so?"

Rob looked up and grinned at Derek. "I like it how it is. Short and to the point. It shows you don't waste time; that you're professional."

"That we're professional."

Rob dropped his eyes for moment, but nodded. "Wow. Thanks."

"I wouldn't be here if it wasn't for you." Derek glanced over his shoulder and pulled himself to his feet. "I mean that."

"Yeah."

Pastor Jones pushed open the door to the offices, holding a miniature Christmas tree. When he saw them, he smiled.

"Afternoon!" he exclaimed, setting it down on the tract table. "What a nice surprise. I didn't see you guys on the sign-up sheet…"

"Have you seen Cindy?" Derek asked, shoving one hand into his pocket.

"She was working on the tree in the sanctuary, last I saw," the pastor answered, gesturing at the glass paneled doors.

Derek hesitated a moment, and nodded. "Thanks."

He headed toward the doors to the sanctuary and paused, tugging aside the curtain that covered the glass. He nodded again. "Alright. Here I go."

Without even looking to see if Robbie had followed, he slipped inside.

As soon as the door fell closed behind him, Robbie smacked his forehead. Putting the business card case into his coat pocket, he'd felt the little box that Derek had given him for "safe keeping." Well, it was safe all right; but right now Derek would be wanting it.

Rob rolled up to the row of curtains; at least he could keep the rest of their plan. Leaning forward, he cautiously pulled aside the edge of the curtain to peek through the glass to the room beyond.

He felt Rev. Jones come up behind him, leaning his hands on Rob's shoulders to see in. Robbie didn't mind, though; he could still be "the first" to see Derek's dream come true.

He watched Derek walk down the aisle. Cindy put down the ornament she was holding and came toward him. Rob squeezed the front of his shirt with his free hand. He was pretty sure what Cindy would say, but Derek's nervousness had rubbed off on him. He'd always remember the way Derek looked after his last talk with Michelle…like a balloon shoved onto a pin or an ice cream sundae left out in the rain. But this would be different; he had confidence.

Derek was talking to Cindy. He couldn't hear the words, but he knew what he was saying. The pastor started rubbing his shoulder. He'd lived long enough that he didn't need to ask questions, either.

* * * *

Cindy picked up a string of Christmas lights and began unwinding them.

"So, are you here to volunteer, or did you have something else to do?"

"Um…I have something…I need to talk to you."

She looked up, forcing him to stare into her eyes. Her Christmas-tree green eyes. To match her sweater. It had Christmas trees embroidered in brown across the evergreen background. Did she have to look at him with those huge eyes? It was enough to make him forget part of who he was.

Make *him* forget. He, who could pick out their waitress at Denny's from five years ago, and could probably still identify her handwriting.

Yes, Cindy made him forget things...like the patterns of shattered glass on the road. He'd sat on the curb and stared at them through his knees while the nice stranger talked to 911 on his cell and the nice stranger's wife tried to give him some water to drink. Anything to keep him from trying to remove his family from the car. When he looked at Cindy, he even forgot details of Michelle's face.

"I'm waiting."

"I'm sorry; I...You do things to me. I lost my train of thought."

She smiled. "You said you had something to talk to me about."

"Oh, yes." He watched her deft hand movements as she worked out the tangles in the wire and flung it free up the aisle. "They've set a trial date for January," he stammered. "Stillman's lawyer tried to get it delayed further, but the judge blocked him."

"I knew that; Hank Blake told me earlier this week, and then you told me at Wednesday Bible study."

"Oh."

"Look, relax. I don't bite. What's bugging you?" Cindy put down the lights and took a step closer. "Is it something to do with Robbie?"

"No. I mean, not exactly. The doctor said he was fine, last visit."

She raised one hand. "So? Tell me."

Derek dropped his eyes for a moment. "I really feel like I've gotten to know Brian over the past year or so. He was quite a guy, and I almost feel like we could've gotten along together. Except..."

He stole a glance at Cindy. Her face showed nothing.

"Except I'd never want to take anything away from you. I know Brian loved you, and wanted to take care of you. And I know a part of him will never go away. And that's good. He was a worthy guy."

"But..."

"But, if you...I'll understand, no matter what you say. I don't want to hurt you. Please know that I want to take care of you and keep you happy, forever, even if that means I have to back off."

As he spoke, he began digging in his pockets for the ring—the best he could get for twelve easy payments. As he moved from his jeans to his coat, he suddenly wondered which finger she would wear it on, or if she would have to double up, or what...assuming she took it.

"You're a very gracious lady, but if I'm out of line, I want you to tell me."

Derek gave up rooting in his pockets. Cindy stepped forward and took his hands.

He remembered, now; he'd given the ring to Robbie, after they picked it out together yesterday afternoon. And like a dingbat, he'd forgotten to get it again just now. Oh well.

"I love you. I'm no Brian, but I do love you." He looked down at her hands in his, and saw that her left hand was empty.

As he stroked her knuckle with his thumb, she gave a little laugh. "I was thinking about Brian just a few days ago," she began, her voice not quite steady. "I know he's with Jesus now, but I'm still waiting. I remembered the passage that talks about how, in the resurrection, we won't be caught up in marrying or giving in marriage – we'll be like the angels, constantly worshipping God. I just felt like trying to cling to *what was* would be dishonoring to what God has planned for me next. I'm here for a purpose. God gave me

Brian for His own plan, and then He took Brian away. Blessed be the name of the Lord."

"Amen," murmured Derek.

She laughed again. "Which means what?" she prodded.

Derek caught his breath and exhaled before speaking. "Would you marry me?"

Cindy smiled, but something still lingered behind her eyes. She drew a breath, and asked, "What about Robbie?"

Derek's heart skipped a beat. "He has to stay with me. I mean…I promised him I'd keep him. Do you… I mean, would that be a problem?"

"No," she breathed. "But, I thought he might have a problem with – involving someone else in your household." She stepped forward and put her hands on his shoulders. Half-consciously, he put his arms around her. "You mean a lot to him. And I think he's afraid of losing you."

"We talked about it," Derek answered. "He said I needed to ask you. I promised him I would never give him up. He said – he'd be okay. He told me to ask you."

"Good. I want him to live with us." She smiled, making her eyes dance, and leaned into his chest. "I think he's a sweet kid. He's got some shyness to overcome…but I know what that's like."

Derek pressed her closer to him. "Us?"

Cindy looked at him. "Us." She reached up and planted a kiss on his cheek.

Us. As in, "Mr. and Mrs." As in, "not all alone". *Thank you, God. And Robbie.*

* * * *

Their arms linked together, Cindy and her actual, legitimate fiancé skipped up the aisle toward the narthex. Like a couple of college students, they had to tell Pastor Jones before they burst.

Then Robbie, and her parents. Then the rest of the church, and the rest of the world.

Cindy grinned as she rounded the door. Rev. Jones was just straightening guiltily, but Rob hadn't even bothered to drop the door-curtain.

"I see you, peeking-Toms," she cried. "I guess there's no point telling you the good news."

"Congratulations, all around!" exclaimed the reverend, seizing Derek's hand with both of his and giving it a vigorous shake. "You must admit, Cindy, that you made it a little obvious to the casual observer."

"Peeking through the glass doors is not casual," she scolded as he gave her a hug.

"It's my fault," Derek stammered. "I promised Robbie he'd be the first to know."

Cindy looked down at her future brother-in-law, and smiled. He looked a little flushed, but he met her eye steadily. It certainly looked like he'd made peace with her.

Rob made a self-conscious smile and slowly pulled a small blue box out of his coat pocket.

"Mr. Memory forgot something," he said.

"Yeah." Derek gave an awkward laugh. "I'll never live this down, will I."

Cindy laughed, dropping to her haunches to slip her arms around Rob. "It was in good hands," she murmured, and kissed his temple.

He gave a chuckle, and made his smile bigger. He was making eye contact, and not pulling away. Good. If this blended family was going to work, she'd need him on her side.

"Ellie, you'll never guess what just happened," Rev. Jones laughed as Mrs. Jones came out of the church office.

Ellie glanced from Cindy to Derek. Cindy could feel the flush lighting up her face. Derek was practically beaming.

"Don't tell me!" Ellie exclaimed, coming forward to embrace Cindy. "I'm so happy for you, dear! And for you, honey," she added, sparkling at Derek.

If Pastor Jones and his wife were celebrating with them, it must not be just her emotions playing with her. Cindy drew a breath to slow her racing heartbeat. Derek was a good man. He would take care of her.

"Here," Robbie insisted, holding out the ring box. "Take this."

As Derek took it from his brother, Mrs. Jones breathed, "Oh, I hadn't noticed you took off your rings."

Cindy nodded. "After all, I don't need to belong to the past. And Brian would understand."

She glanced up at Derek. If anyone had a messy past, it was him. But finally, he was breaking free of those tangled strands and moving on. Robbie was right, though; he needed someone to take care of him.

So did she. God would be with them wherever they went, but she was glad she didn't have to go forward alone. Their futures belonged to each other.

Derek reached out and held the hand she offered him for a moment, before slipping his ring onto it. The pastor and his wife broke out in applause. Robbie gave a suppressed laugh and clasped his hands together.

"Okay — group hug," Derek exclaimed, throwing one arm around Cindy and leaning over to grab Robbie into the embrace.

As Cindy clasped Rob's back, she smiled. She'd definitely noticed a difference these past few months. Robbie was running the church website, and Derek had been bringing him to Bible study every Wednesday night. He would be part of this – their marriage, and their home.

She met Rob's eyes and smiled again. "Now you'll be my brother, too," she whispered.

He reached his free arm around her to complete the hug, and grinned.

Author Bio

Kimia Wood's overactive elder-sibling instinct probably stems from the eleven younger siblings she had growing up (one homegrown, the rest borrowed).

In her free time, she likes to read, surf interesting blog posts that were linked in Twitter, and do any kind of handicraft involving yarn.

She currently lives somewhere in the American Midwest while waiting for a private investigator/police officer/computer genius to fall in love with her.

You can connect with her on Twitter (@KimiaTheAuthor) and Facebook, find her occasionally on Goodreads, or follow her latest thoughts on her blog (http://blog.kimiawood.com/).

SHARING IS CARING!

If you liked this book, please consider reviewing it online. Remember, other readers find worthy books through the thoughtful recommendations of people like you!

STAY CONNECTED!

Subscribe to the mailing list to follow Kimia's latest reading and writing exploits, and get a free copy of her exciting post-apocalyptic adventure *Soldier*:

http://blog.kimiawood.com/index.php/stay-connected/

Also By Kimia Wood

WHITE MESA CHRONICLES SERIES

Fifty years after the collapse of civilization, the gangs fight in the waste of the city for survival and resources, while a rising city-state tries to define its own version of "progress."

It's safer in White Mesa – the place that saw it coming. There, a God-centered worldview encourages personal responsibility and the value of human life…all human life…even the zombies.

Soldier (Book 1):

Fledgling militia officer Tommy Thaxton is used to scavenge missions in the ruined city. He's not used to being in charge of his team of young men…but he can handle it. They all can handle it. It's just a simple scavenge mission.

Until things go horribly wrong, and Tommy's team finds themselves facing a full-scale gang attack – something their superiors never anticipated.

Now, getting home on schedule is the least of Tommy's worries. Getting the entire team home alive is much more important.

http://blog.kimiawood.com/index.php/white-mesa-chronicles/

Zombie (Book 2):

They say every civilization is built on the backs of slaves... Tommy never thought it would look like this.

White Mesa operative Tommy Thaxton is used to dealing with the city gangs. But the New Republic is not a gang.

With a protected fence-line, plenty of food, and a welcoming atmosphere, the New Republic almost seems like a sister community to White Mesa...with a few crucial differences.

The zombies, for instance. They seem to be all over in the New Republic. And by the time Tommy finally finds out why, it might be too late...

http://blog.kimiawood.com/index.php/white-mesa-chronicles/

PREFER MEDIEVAL ADVENTURE?

A driven young man's quest for justice is transformed by a chance night-time encounter with his greatest rival.

A medieval adventure of family, secrets, and revenge by Kimia Wood.

http://myBook.to/SonsOfTheKing

Made in the USA
Monee, IL
10 August 2024

63600104R00148